THE
PERSEIDS

AND
OTHER STORIES

TOR BOOKS BY ROBERT CHARLES WILSON

DARWINIA
BIOS
THE PERSEIDS AND OTHER STORIES

THE
PERSEIDS

AND
OTHER STORIES

Robert Charles Wilson

A Tom Doherty Associates Book
New York

THE PERSEIDS AND OTHER STORIES

Copyright © 2000 by Robert Charles Wilson

This book is printed on acid-free paper.

Edited by Patrick Nielsen Hayden

A Tor Book
Published by Tom Doherty Associates, LLC
175 Fifth Avenue
New York, NY 10010

www.tor.com

Tor® is a registered trademark of Tom Doherty Associates, LLC.

Book Design by Jane Adele Regina

Library of Congress Cataloging-in-Publication Data

Wilson, Robert Charles.
    The Perseids and other stories / Robert Charles Wilson.
        p.   cm.
    Contents: The fields of Abraham—The Perseids—The inner inner city—The observer—Protocols of consumption—Ulysses sees the moon in the bedroom window—Plato's mirror—Divided by infinity—Pearl baby.
    ISBN 0-312-87374-3 (hc)
    ISBN 0-312-87524-X(pbk)
    1. Science fiction, Canadian. I. Title.
PR9199.3.W4987 P47 2000
813'.54—dc21   00-026704

First Hardcover Edition: August 2000
First Trade Paperback Edition: July 2001

Printed in the United States of America

0 9 8 7 6 5 4 3 2 1

COPYRIGHT ACKNOWLEDGMENTS

IT IS NOT A BAD THING TO HEAR VOICES . . . BUT YOU
MUSTN'T FOR A MINUTE IMAGINE THAT ALL IS WISE
THAT COMES TO YOU OUT OF THE NIGHT WORLD.

David Lindsay,
A Voyage to Arcturus

CONTENTS

THE
PERSEIDS

AND
OTHER STORIES

THE FIELDS OF ABRAHAM

1.

Jacob came into the small bookstore to get out of the brutal cold, and because he had an empty hour or two to fill up, and because (not least) he hoped Oscar Ziegler would give him another book.

The door snapped shut on snow and ice. The shop was heated by a modern basement coal furnace, the air perfumed with dust and paper and hot iron. Jacob, sixteen years old and numb inside his inadequate cloth coat, shivered with the particular chill of warming. He felt like an intruder in some exotic desert kingdom.

There were, as he had hoped, no other customers in the store. Oscar Ziegler sat alone behind the cash desk, snug in the heat. Ziegler's eyeglasses glinted over his fat cheeks when he smiled. "Jacob! You look miserable. Come in, come in, put your coat on the ladder to dry. Take a seat."

Ziegler, as usual, was hoping for a game of chess. Jacob, as usual, would oblige him. On the street, chess was a way to make money. Here, chess was the price of a book. Actually *buying* a book was out of the question. Every penny Jacob gleaned from his chess wagers and his language lessons served to feed and clothe and shelter himself and his sister Rachel. Books were frivolous. Although he loved them.

Jacob's father had been a scholar in Europe, a ragman in Canada until he died two years ago. From his father Jacob had learned Yiddish and English, French and Italian, German, even a little

Latin. Jacob had the ear for language, just as he had the head for chess. He taught English to new immigrants and their families for ten cents an hour. He played chess with the old men in the Ward for penny bets. In summer, the chess paid more than the language lessons. In winter, the lessons more than the chess.

He did not discriminate in either chess or language. He had tipped his king to impoverished Russian nobles; he had taught English to the pockmarked Ruthenian boy who lit the Shabbas torches.

The year that had begun (by the Christian calendar) just two weeks ago was 1911. Two prime numbers, Jacob observed, 19 and 11. Add them together, you got 30. The sum of two primes was always an even number—but even the mathematician Fermat had failed to produce a proof of that statement.

Numbers sometimes tormented him, just as demons tormented his sister.

Oscar Ziegler, who owned the bookshop and was its sole employee, lived in the rooms above the shop and was never seen in the street. He was in other ways equally inscrutable. His age, for instance. He was a short and burly man, gray-haired but not much wrinkled. He might have been forty, or sixty, or older. He wore an old-fashioned frock coat and ties that would have been grotesquely colorful if they hadn't faded to pastel. He seldom talked about himself or his past. His name sounded German to Jacob, but the very faint trace of a European accent in his voice was oddly liquid, almost Catalonian. He loved books and chess and opera, and would talk knowledgeably about Coleridge or Steinitz or Nellie Melba. But when had he ever ventured far enough from his heated cave to hear an opera? He had hired a woman to bring him groceries.

Jacob watched Ziegler set up the chessboard in a clear space on the desk. Jacob took the footstool for a chair. At sixteen, he had still not reached his full height. His shoulders barely reached the rim of the desk. Ziegler's creaking wooden accountant's chair became, from this perspective, as magisterial as a throne.

Ziegler put out his clenched fists with a pawn in each. Jacob touched a pale knuckle of Ziegler's left hand. Black.

The game was interesting at first. Ziegler worked through the book opening and Jacob arrayed his pieces in a crenellated defense that left him prepared to take advantage of any weakness in his opponent's position. Briefly, then, he was oblivious to his surroundings, letting the possibilities of the board focus his attention. It was like entering a trance—a *chess trance*, as Jacob thought of it. He watched Ziegler attempting to dig canals in the black defenses but at the same time exposing faults of his own, tiny channels of opportunity down which a single pawn might flow far enough to threaten the ivory king.

Past a certain point—in this case, a pawn sacrifice that put Ziegler's bishop at the rim of the board—the conclusion was foregone. Ziegler, however, chose to play to the end, smiling placidly as a Buddha at his own losses. Jacob returned a part of his attention to the prosaic reality of the bookshop. He felt drained, pleasantly tired. He wondered if this absolute absorption was how Rachel's trances felt, though hers were deeper and vastly more traumatic. Rachel sometimes stared into space for an hour or two at a time, her eyes tracking nothing at all. Sometimes she screamed.

"Did you read the book?" Ziegler asked, playing lazily now.

The last book Ziegler had given him was *The Stolen Bacillus and Other Incidents*, by H. G. Wells. A volume of strange stories. Jacob had indeed read the book, and enjoyed it immensely, although he had been forced to sell it for twenty-five cents to help make up the December rent. "Yes," he said.

"Did you find a particular favorite, Jacob?"

He told Ziegler his favorite story had been "The Remarkable Case of Davidson's Eyes," in which a man's vision was displaced halfway across the world, so that he could see the Antipodes Islands (or the deeps of the sea) as he stumbled blindly through urban London.

Ziegler smiled at that. "I think I prefer the title story, or 'The Moth.' But you're right, 'The Remarkable Case' is excellent. What did you like about it?"

"There was a line in the story. Davidson says, 'It seems to me that I see too much.' " It made him think of his sister and her bad spells.

When Rachel was in the grip of her madness she saw and spoke to things and persons no one else could see. There was something almost comforting in the idea that she might only be gazing into the deeps of a distant ocean, reacting with comprehensible fear to the creatures that lived there.

Inevitably, Ziegler's king succumbed to Jacob's siege. Almost too much time had passed. Rachel would be home from the factory. She didn't like to be alone. She wouldn't eat if Jacob wasn't there.

Ziegler thanked him for the game and said, "I owe you another book. You like Wells? I have another Wells. *The Time Machine and Other Stories*. Take it with you."

Jacob accepted the volume and tucked it under his shirt. He pulled his coat around himself and turned to the door, in which was set a rippled windowpane lacquered with ice. Outside, night had fallen.

"Thank you," he said.

"Come again," Ziegler said.

Jacob trudged through fresh falling snow along the narrow and torch-lit alleys of that part of the city called the Ward: north from the railway station, west of Yonge Street; east of University (unless you counted all the Macedonians around Eastern Avenue), south of College. Even in the cold, the Ward stank of privy pits and box closets. Shack flats over bare soil fronted the unpaved laneways. The snow had grown in dunes over broken stovepipes and heaps of rags.

The building he called home was hardly more than a shed. It was, by the standards of the Ward, not too bad. Small, narrow, dark, and impossible to heat, but better than the crowded boardinghouses on Elm Street.

He found his sister huddling by the woodstove. Rachel had lit more than a dozen candles and placed them randomly about the room. Bent under her shawl, she looked eighty. She was seventeen, a year older than Jacob himself.

"You're late," she said.

He heated a stew of vegetables and fish over the stove and served it in porcelain bowls. Rachel ate less than half of what he gave her. She was listless and silent. Jacob didn't mind the silence. He knew it wouldn't last. He used the opportunity to look at the book Ziegler had given him. *But some philosophical people have been asking why three dimensions particularly—why not another direction at right angles to the other three?—and have even tried to construct a Four-Dimensional geometry. . . .*

Later, she opened the door and walked to the latrine. When fifteen minutes passed and she hadn't returned, Jacob sighed and went to look for her. He found her squatting in the outhouse with her skirts raked up, snow settling on her thighs like lacework. She shivered, but her eyes were fixed with rapt attention on nothing at all. He covered her and walked her back inside.

"You're sick, Rachel," he said. "Settle down."

She lay on her mattress and buried herself in blankets. "No, I'm not sick."

"You're not yourself."

"I'm the Queen of the Moon, and you can go fuck yourself."

"Don't talk like that."

"I'll talk any way I like."

"I have to go out tonight," he said. "Will you be all right by yourself?"

"Of course I will."

So she said. But she was irritable, not a good sign, and she mumbled to herself under her breath, an even worse omen. He was afraid she would hurt herself or set fire to the building. But he couldn't warn her against those things because that would put ideas into her head, and then, God forbid, if something did happen, the fault would be his.

Rachel had been strange even before Mama and Papa died. Even as a small child: moody, often inarticulate, physically awkward. Papa had said there was a history of madness on his side of the family. Madness and genius: men who studied the Kaballah or wrote romantic poetry or killed themselves with pistols. Papa had been a scholar. Jacob was, in his way, a scholar too. Mama had been an ordinary woman, a doctor's daughter from Lodz. Rachel had inherited the madness.

Madness wasn't so colorful at close quarters. Jacob had seen his sister tear off her clothing and rake her skin with her fingernails until she bled. Everything Jacob had witnessed of madness was ugly, demeaning, and obscene.

His fear was that Rachel's deepening dementia would make it impossible for her to work, and what would they do then?

He tucked the blanket around his sister and hoped the warmth of it would coax her to sleep. Then he buttoned his cloth coat and walked through the falling snow to the rented room of Carlo Taglieri.

Taglieri always called Jacob "the Jew"—not in a brutal way, but persistently, as if challenging him.

Taglieri's curse was his harelip, his short leg, and his temper. He wasn't popular. People shunned him. He was thirty years old and unmarried. He lived in this dank room on Chandler Street, alone except for a bony black cat named Brivio.

"It's the Jew," Taglieri told Brivio as he opened the door. Taglieri spoke the Italian of Pisticci, his hometown. He wore a threadbare woolen sweater. "Come in, Jacob."

Like most of Jacob's students, Taglieri had attempted the English class at the Settlement House but had left in frustration. Taglieri was one of those people who translated everything in his head: if you said *cat* he would rummage through his mental ledgers until he found *gatto*. But by that time you might have said a dozen more words, of which he had registered none.

"English, please," Jacob said.

"Welcome," Taglieri told him.

Over the last several months Jacob had managed to impart to Taglieri a decent number of English verbs and nouns, which Taglieri had duly committed to memory. Currently he was strangling on tenses. Tonight Jacob worked through the labyrinth of *was* and *is* and *will be* and *has been*, hoping for some glimmer of understanding, but he sensed Taglieri stacking the verb forms like bricks, deaf to the music. The hour dragged.

"I was worked at the water mains," Taglieri said suddenly, his ruddy face gone somber and earnest.

"Work," Jacob corrected him. "You *work* at the water mains." Taglieri dug sewers for the city.

"I work at the the water mains five years—"

Jacob understood that Taglieri was attempting the imperfect tense. "You *have worked* at the water mains for five years."

"I have worked at the water mains five years and I want—wanted—want to asks—"

"Yes?"

"Your sister, your Rachel—"

Jacob said, in Italian, "Just tell me what it is you need to say."

"I'll give you money for her."

Jacob stood up, his heart beating harder, wanting to believe that this time he was the one who hadn't understood. "My sister is not a whore."

"I know, I know! Don't be insulted. Please, please, listen. All I want is companionship. I'm not a proud man, Jacob. You know how it is. The women don't like me, because of my lip, because of the way I walk."

Also, Jacob thought, because of the way Taglieri shouted obscenities at the children in the street, because of the way he smelled, because of the way he bullied anyone smaller than himself and simpered to anyone he feared. Taglieri had a respectable job. He might have married, in spite of everything, if he had cleaned himself up and attended mass once in a while and gone courting in a decent manner. But he wouldn't.

"I know about Rachel," Taglieri said. "She's not good at work, they say. She's a little crazy. She gets angry. Okay, I know all that. What I'm saying is, I can support her. I've worked for the city for five years now. I spend nothing except what it costs to keep this room and feed myself and Brivio."

Jacob said, "You're telling me you want to marry her?"

"Christ, no. I can't marry a Jew. Much less a crazy Jew. What would people think? She would be my housekeeper."

"Housekeeper."

"Yes."

"I have to go," Jacob said.

"I've hurt your feelings."

Jacob didn't know whether this was sincere or sarcastic. His Italian wasn't sufficiently nuanced. Anyway, with Taglieri, it was always an open question.

"Look," Taglieri said. He took a number of crumpled bills out of his hip pocket. "Five dollars. Everybody else is saving money so they can buy steamship tickets for their families back home. I don't have any family back home. I spend my money on what I want. Five dollars, Jacob. All she has to do is come over and clean the floor. Just one day! Then we'll see how we can get along, Rachel and I."

It was a lot of money.

"No, thank you, Signor Taglieri."

A great deal of money. Thus, obviously, not for the service of scrubbing a floor.

Taglieri added, in English, "Please don't say no."

Jacob closed the door behind him.

2.

The bookstore was closed on Sunday, but Jacob knocked and Ziegler opened the door for him and locked it quickly after.

Outside, the air was bitter and thin. In here, the heat and the smell of the old books made his eyes water. Ziegler's books were all secondhand. They had lost their glossy newness but gained something, Jacob thought, in the rich smell of tobacco and aging paper.

Ziegler set up the chessboard while Jacob confessed his problems with Rachel. He had confided in Ziegler before. Ziegler always listened patiently.

Jacob said, "I wish I could believe she was getting better. There are times when she's almost normal. Other times. . . ."

"She's not getting better," Ziegler said flatly. "She has a disease. In fifty years they'll call it 'schizophrenia' and admit that it's incurable. In a hundred—"

"How do you know that?"

He waved away the question. "Don't count on Rachel getting better, is what I'm saying."

"I can't support her by myself. Even if I could, I can't be with her all the time. If she gets worse she might hurt herself. I don't know how to protect her."

"You can't."

"She's my sister. She doesn't have anyone else."

Ziegler balanced the white queen in his hand, walking it between his fingers like a stage magician with a coin. "There are asylums. Or even this man, what's his name, Tarantula—"

"Taglieri. To be honest, I thought about it. A warm house and decent food, who knows? Maybe it would help her. But taking money for my sister. . . ." He didn't have words to express the vileness of it. And how could it matter if Rachel was warm and well-dressed, when the price was Taglieri forcing himself between her legs every night?

But didn't every married woman face the same troublesome bargain?

Ziegler said, "You know the story in the Bible, the story of Abraham and Isaac?"

"Of course."

"God instructs Abraham to offer his son as a sacrifice. Isaac makes it as far as the chopping block before God changes his mind."

Yes. Jacob had always imagined God a little appalled at Abraham's willingness to cooperate.

Ziegler said, "What's the moral of the story?"

"Faith."

"Hardly," Ziegler said. "Faith has nothing to do with it. Abraham never doubted the existence of God—how could he? The evidence was ample. His virtue wasn't faith, it was *fealty*. He was so simplemindedly loyal that he would commit even this awful, terrible act. He was the perfect foot soldier. The ideal pawn. Abraham's lesson: fealty is rewarded. Not morality. The fable makes morality *contingent*. Don't go around killing innocent people, that is, unless you're absolutely certain God wants you to. It's a lunatic's credo.

"Isaac, on the other hand, learns something much more interesting. He learns that neither God nor his own father can be trusted. Maybe it makes him a better man than Abraham. Suppose Isaac grows up and fathers a child of his own, and God approaches him and makes the same demand. One imagines Isaac saying, 'No. You can take him if you must, but I won't slaughter my son for you.' He's not the good and faithful servant his father was. But he is, perhaps, a more wholesome human being."

"What does this have to do with Rachel?"

"My point," Ziegler said, "is that sacrifice is a complicated business. If you give Rachel to this Taglieri, are you harming her or helping her? How can you be sure? And if you *don't* give her up—if you spend the rest of your enviable youth and all of your innate kindness protecting her from her own lunacy—have you put *yourself* on the altar?"

Jacob was startled. "There must be another choice."

Ziegler held out two clenched fists. Two hidden pawns. He smiled. "Choose."

As the game progressed Ziegler said, "I have to tell you something, Jacob. You're the best chess novice I've come across. Not terribly experienced and not subtle at all. But the way you *think* chess is genuinely remarkable."

"You play very well yourself."

"Thank you. I played Anderssen once, when he was a child."

"Adolph Anderssen, the German master? My father talked about him." Jacob frowned. "But Anderssen was an old man half a century ago."

Ziegler shrugged. "Some other Anderssen, then." The shopkeeper attempted an exchange of queens, which Jacob declined. The end was inevitable now. For once, Ziegler capitulated before the actual checkmate. He tapped his king with a thumbnail and sent it teetering against an impotent rook. Then he sat back in his chair and wrapped his hands over his belly. "You know, Jacob, there's another way to play this game."

"Another way to play chess?"

"A revision of the rules."

"I don't have time."

"Stay. Please. This won't take long."

The coal furnace roared and the bookshop's floorboards moaned with the heat. Jacob let himself be convinced to spend a little more time in the warmth. The game Ziegler proposed was something he called lateral chess: this involved an assumption that the chessboard was (in Ziegler's own strange words) "topographically looped"—that is, the final squares at the left edge of the board were connected immaterially to the first squares at the right. The rook, for instance, could take a pawn on the rank even with another piece interposed, simply by coming at it from the opposite direction.

Once Jacob grasped the idea, he enjoyed working out the possibilities. In effect, the new rule took away the center of the board. A conventionally dominant position looked suddenly very different: a knight or a bishop could dominate from the rim. Castling became moot.

And this time, Ziegler won the game. Jacob wanted to play again.

"If you like," Ziegler said mildly.

Jacob failed to take note of the dusky winter sky beyond the window. He had always enjoyed his chess trances but he found this kind of chess even more enthralling, if only for its novelty. He longed to abandon himself to it, one more time, one more game, win or lose. . . . "Good," Ziegler said approvingly as he set up the pieces once more, "but this time we wrap the board in *both* directions—rank and file, fore and aft. If one of my pieces reaches your first rank, it can keep going."

In effect, the looped board had become a sphere, a sphere represented on a plane, like a Mercator projection of the Earth. It would have meant instantaneous mutual checkmate if Ziegler had not added a set of first-pass rules. The consequences were subtle, at least until the endgame when the ranks had been thinned; then Ziegler took him with a knight fork Jacob had completely overlooked.

Spherical chess! He longed to play again.

But this time Ziegler wouldn't. "Look at the window, Jacob. The moon is up. You can feel the cold through the walls. Go home. Come see me again next week."

There was no new book this time. But that was all right. Spherical chess was a better gift. Anyway, Jacob hadn't finished *The Time Machine and Other Stories*.

Rachel had been alone for hours. She stared at him accusingly when he came through the door. She had let the fire in the stove die away to nothing. The shack was brutally cold. The water in the wash pots had grown brittle lids of ice.

3.

The February rent was due, and Jacob worked hard to make up the inevitable shortfall. He taught English to the Goldbergs, the Walersteins, the dimwitted Vincenzo sisters. He crept into Greek and Macedonian coffeehouses to accept bets on his chess prowess. He was punched once by a humiliated Galician dairy worker but escaped before he could be robbed. He developed a hole in his shoe.

Rachel had passed deeply into the orbit of her madness this winter. She was hostile and withdrawn, hardly eating, and Jacob had to remind himself of what she had been when they were younger: Rachel at the Brant Street School, her hair in red ribbons. For all her moodiness, she had seemed golden in those days. She would take Jacob on long walks to the docklands or to the fancy English shops. They had shared stories with each other. Rachel had been a great reader of fairy tales. She had read to him from *Struwelpeiter*, her favorite book.

In those days it had been possible to eke some kindness out of Rachel, before she closed herself to the world. He couldn't remember the last time she had said a kind word to him, though she sometimes admitted being frightened.

Was she dying? People don't always die all at once, Ziegler had told him. Sometimes they die a little at a time. That makes it hard.

Thursday of that week she came home at noon. Jacob saw her in the window as he was passing on his way to the Settlement House, and that was distressing, because she should have been at the factory. Now, of all times, they couldn't afford the loss of her pay.

"Cobb sent me home," Rachel confessed when he hurried inside. She knotted her hands behind her back, and her voice was like ground glass in butter.

"Why? What for?"

She mumbled something about "the roof," that she had heard "bees on the factory roof."

"Bees?" Jacob said, feeling sick.

"They start fires," Rachel said calmly. "They steal women."

She tried to warn Mr. Cobb but he wouldn't listen. Jacob could imagine the scene altogether too easily. Of course there were no bees on the steep peaked roof of Cobb's attic factory. Only Rachel's demons.

"Cobb fired you?"

Rachel shrugged and nodded.

Jacob turned away from her to hide his fear. He had known this would come. But it had come too soon. He wasn't ready.

When he fixed dinner that night he put Rachel's bowl in front of her without bothering to make sure she ate. She said, "You have a hateful face." And later, "You think you can control me, but you can't."

No, he thought, I can't, but that wouldn't stop him taking care of her, enduring her insults, cleaning her messes. She was his sister. He owed her a certain loyalty. No matter the cost. No matter how often she cursed him or how much he might resent it.

He woke after midnight, shivering. The door was open and the wind pushed it wider, blowing snow against the hissing stove.

Rachel's mattress was empty. Jacob pulled on his boots and ran out into the darkness.

He found her a hundred yards down the alley, humming tunelessly and drawing loops and crooked figure-eights in fresh snow with the tip of a broken umbrella. Her fingers were white with the cold. She didn't resist when he steered her back to the shack. She cursed him, but softly, almost affectionately.

"Fuck you, Jacob." The snow lay on her dark, wild hair like a crown. "Fuck you. Fuck you."

The question, Jacob told Ziegler, was not whether she would be happy with Taglieri—he doubted Rachel would ever be happy again in any meaningful way—but whether Taglieri would be willing to take care of her when he understood just how profound Rachel's madness had become.

"Of course he won't," the shopkeeper said. "As you well know."

Jacob supposed that was true. "But she could clean his floor. As a temporary job, I mean."

"I suspect your Taglieri won't settle for that. It's not what he has in mind."

"After a day with Rachel, would he still want to take her? I mean," Jacob blushed, "as a woman?"

"Almost certainly not. So you can accept his five dollars, if that's what you're leading up to, and disillusion the poor man. Really, this is none of my business. Let's play chess."

Chess was an unforgivable waste of time, but Jacob wanted to enter a trance, wanted the selfish pleasure of being away from himself, even briefly, and he couldn't do that in the coffeehouses. The deeper Rachel sank into her madness the more Jacob yearned to enter his own private space of mind, as if there were a necessary balance, some equilibrium of sanity.

How to describe the trance to someone who hadn't experienced it? First there was the willed focus of attention, when the chessboard grew to fill the whole of his vision. Then came the evolution of the game itself, a fluid shape in which chessmen moved almost of their own will, like microbes in a drop of water.

And, finally, an absolute immersion, as deep and embracing as the Nile.

"Did you read 'The Time Machine,' Jacob?" Ziegler asked.

Jacob nodded, studying the board.

"Intriguing, isn't it? The idea of a higher dimension? Like wrapping the chessboard, in a way. It's a question of perspective, really. Of what the mind is accustomed to."

Jacob said he supposed so.

"You have the talent for it," Ziegler said obscurely.

"Your move," Jacob told him.

And the fugue began. He was distantly aware of Ziegler saying, "One has to admire the bloodlessness of the conquest, given the ruthlessness of the game. A chess piece literally displaces its victim. Such as this pawn of yours. The vanquished piece leaves the plane of the board entirely. But it does not, in a higher sense, cease to exist."

Then the light changed, and Jacob felt as if he was falling in his chair and the bookstore falling along with him, but it wasn't frightening at all; it was as natural as falling asleep.

"Only the rare person," Ziegler said from an incalculable distance, "can rise above the chessboard."

Jacob didn't emerge from the trance but seemed to wake up inside it.

Ziegler had gone to the door of the shop, where warm yellow light flooded through window glass no longer etched with frost.

"Come and see," Ziegler beckoned him.

Jacob stood up, dazed and doubtful, thinking, *The game*—

But the game didn't matter. This *was* the game.

He went to the door as Ziegler opened it. He thought of the H. G. Wells story "The Door in the Wall," which had read only yesterday. The story of an elusive, impossible door; a door, Wells had called it, "into peace, into delight, into a beauty beyond dreaming."

There was a garden beyond Oscar Ziegler's door. No, not a garden. A sort of forest. But very strange. A warm, wintergreen-scented breeze flooded the shop. A box of summery yellow light spilled over the worn floorboards.

Jacob decided this was a dream, if a very strange one, and that he wouldn't question it, dreams being what they were.

The explanation Ziegler offered him was worse than no explanation at all.

"It's not a place," the shopkeeper said, "more like the sum of all places, the heir of all times . . . the afterlife, if you like."

"Heaven?" Jacob asked.

"Ah, *Heaven*." Ziegler smiled, the strange light warm on his ruddy face. "Suppose there *is* a Heaven, Jacob. But imagine a Heaven without a God. Heaven as a natural phenomenon. No reward, no punishment, and no moral order. Only an ecology . . . what you might call a jungle."

Jacob stepped out wonderingly into the golden light.

There were no obvious hills in this Heaven; no valleys, unless they were hidden by the forest. A point of vivid light, not quite the familiar sun, stood motionless in an empty blue sky.

Jacob couldn't see a horizon but he imagined the plain continuing uninterrupted forever, or turning back on itself insensibly, like Ziegler's imaginary chessboard.

He took another step and saw that the things he had mistaken for trees weren't trees at all. Like trees, they radiated in branches to terminal clusters of new growth. But the boles were of some substance as smooth and translucent as amber. Yellow amber, Jacob thought, and here and there crimson or emerald green veined with ruby lines. They bore, not leaves, but bunches of conical or rodlike tendrils. So many of these had fallen that the forest floor (if he could call it that) was a mass of decaying crystals, soft mica melting into earth. Things that resembled jeweled scarabs scuttled through the fallen growth.

Each tree, Ziegler told him, was a world, independent and alive, and from another perspective Jacob's world would look just the same. Ziegler's voice hummed like a bee in his ear. "There are greater and lesser worlds, Jacob, nested inside one another like Russian dolls. But everything is organic, in the end. Everything lives, eats, hunts, dies. That's what the universe *is*."

"Why have you brought me here?"

"You brought yourself. You have that extremely unusual ability. You're one of the rare ones."

"*Why?*" Jacob repeated, unsure what he meant by the question. His own voice sounded distant and peculiar in the thin air. (Was it air at all? Was he in fact breathing? Was he asleep, dead, drunk on *kif* or absinthe?)

"You were drawn here," Ziegler said.

There was life in the forest. Above the trees Jacob saw hovering swarms of brightly colored insects. They flashed in the sunlight like massed diamonds. The drone of them was the forest's only constant sound, now loud, now faint.

Then something moved in the shadow of the crystalline trees very close to him, some object vaporous but purposeful. When it drew nearer he saw that it had a gauzy but human form, and for the first time Jacob was genuinely frightened. He turned back to the door of the bookshop.

The door and its frame—but only the door, and no other part of the building—hovered inches above the ground like an impossible piece of stage dressing.

He stumbled into its enclosed volume of dry heat as Oscar Ziegler took his arm.

Ziegler took his arm, and Jacob woke to the chessboard, the book-lined walls, the crackling of pellet snow against the window.

"Did you see—?" Jacob began, but Ziegler only shrugged and touched his fingers to his lips.

"It's late, young Jacob," the shopkeeper said.

The chessboard was in disarray, as if he had fallen across it. Fallen asleep, he supposed. He tried to shake the dream from his mind. He was embarrassed by the vividness of it, embarrassed that he had almost admitted to Ziegler how real it had felt.

For lack of anything sensible to say he asked the shopkeeper, "Did you really play against Anderssen?"

"Anderssen, Morphy, Steinitz, the Man in the Moon. Time to go."

Jacob was nervous about the door, but when he opened it there was nothing outside more threatening than the wind of a winter night.

4.

"Rachel. Listen to me. Do you want a job?"

His sister had pulled her mattress next to the woodstove. She was wrapped in blankets, all the blankets in the house, it looked like, including Mama's tattered old Gypsy quilt. "Rachel, are you paying attention?"

The whites of her eyes were clear, the pupils crisp dark nuclei. "Yes."

"Do you want a new job? Just for a day?"

She frowned. "What job?"

"Wash floors for Taglieri. Clean up, cook him a meal. Just for a day."

Just for a day.

"That's all?" Rachel asked.

"That's all. But you know Taglieri. If he tries to take advantage of you, you come home. If he tries to hurt you, you come home. Do you understand, Rachel?"

She nodded passively.

"Jacob," she said. "I'm sorry I lost the factory job."

"It's not your fault."

"I'm sorry," she said, "about—about—" And waved her hand. Everything.

"Do you feel better tonight?"

"I feel all right."

"Tomorrow we'll go to Taglieri's. If you feel well enough, I mean. I'll go with you."

"Tomorrow's Sunday."

"That's right."

"He has a cat."

"Yes. Brivio. Try to sleep, Rachel."

Jacob crept away. He felt flooded with shame.

But if Taglieri touched her the wrong way, Jacob would kill him. The thought helped assuage his guilt. He lay in bed, hoping he could make Taglieri understand the terms of the bargain.

His mind was racing and he couldn't sleep. When he closed his eyes he thought of the overdue rent, or Rachel and the Italian, or the crystalline forest beyond Oscar Ziegler's door.

Better to think of chess. He played chess in his mind, working out an opening Ziegler had showed him, but he couldn't stop thinking of the "wrapped" board and the subtle grammar of its topology, of "The Time Machine" and "The Door in the Wall," of what a chess game might look like as a four-dimensional object. He spiraled at last down these odd alleys into sleep.

The indistinct shape moving in the refracted shade of the trees came closer to him. (*You were drawn here*, Ziegler had said.)

Bolder now that he was here alone, Jacob let the thing approach him. From a distance it had looked as insubstantial as a winter breath. Closer, it took on a hazy substance, a human form.

It looked like Rachel.

Its face was like Rachel's—a reflection of Rachel in a mirror of fog—but smooth, young, not at all careworn. The apparition was naked but moved with the simple shamelessness of a child. Jacob felt the creature's gentle interest in him. He smiled, and the sister-thing returned his smile. It moved its mouth as if to speak, but Jacob heard no sound. He let the apparition walk around him, inspecting him, and the impression he took from its motion was a mixture of uneasiness and great patience.

The buzzing of the faraway insects surrounded him like a child's gentle murmur. Jacob felt no ill will from the ghost and he let it linger. He thought of Rachel as she had been before her madness—as spritely as this shadow of her.

The memory comforted him even when the dream faded and he woke.

———

The Italian counted out five dollars as Rachel stood with her head bowed in the shadows outside Taglieri's cheap room.

"You don't touch her," Jacob whispered into Taglieri's gnarled ear. "Do you understand?"

"Of course," Taglieri said. "I'm not an animal." He put his huge hands on Rachel's shoulders. She flinched away. Taglieri held on. "Come in, Rachel. Let me look at you."

Oscar Ziegler beamed with pleasure as Jacob entered the store. He reached for the chessboard, but Jacob said, "No. First we talk."

He took off his coat.

The dream about Rachel had unsettled him. Jacob told Ziegler bluntly about his chess trances, his hallucination at the store, his doubts about his own sanity. Ziegler astonished him by saying, "But *of course* you were there! I told you, Jacob, you're one of the rare ones. Did you really imagine it was a hallucination?"

Jacob had to sit down. "But if it *wasn't*—"

"Yes, yes. Spare me your incredulity. I should have thought it would be more astonishing if you had discovered the world *didn't* have a back-of or an inside. Don't be small-minded."

He felt dizzy. "You said it was the afterlife."

"Among other things, yes."

"But it's a forest."

"There are as many afterlives as there are caverns in the earth, and each one is a unique ecology, godless and strange. As above, so below."

Jacob ignored the unfamiliar word, *ecology*. "I dreamed Rachel was there."

"So she is, and you found your way to her very efficiently."

"But she's still alive."

"I explained this, Jacob. People don't always die all at once. Sometimes they die little by little, inch by inch. The part of Rachel that lives in the forest is the part of her that was eaten by her madness." Ziegler added, "Neither part of her is whole, at the moment."

And Jacob struggled with this idea, that Rachel had been dying by fractions for much of her life, that the better part of her was already lost in the chaotic and indefinite paradise Ziegler had shown him.

It would have been inconceivable if he hadn't experienced it himself. He said, "I want to go back."

"Nothing could be simpler."

5.

At first Jacob couldn't concentrate on the game, knowing what he knew and anticipating what was to come. But the shopkeeper pressed a sharp attack and Jacob was forced to defend his vulnerable queen.

When he looked up from the board, the door was open. Golden light drew him out of his chair.

He felt infinitely more certain of himself than he had the last time he had crossed that threshhold. He knew what he wanted. He wanted to see Rachel: the perfected Rachel who lived among the ruby and golden trees, the Rachel of his childhood.

He followed Ziegler through the door.

He wasn't conscious of the moment when the shopkeeper slipped away from him, no doubt bound on some occult business of his own. Ziegler knew more than he was saying, obviously. More than he was willing to tell Jacob. Ziegler might have been anything . . . but it was Jacob who had opened the door.

He stood near the isolated entranceway, briefly worried that he might lose himself in the trackless iridescence. Insects swarmed high overhead, droning like bees in a summer garden. He willed Rachel to come to him, and now she did, emerging from the darkly glittering shadows and smiling at him. She seemed far more solid than she had before. The sunlight, if this pointillistic radiance could be called sunlight, fell on rather than through her. The last time he had seen her she was mute; today, to Jacob's astonishment, she spoke.

"Jacob," she said. "It's a pretty day."

He groped for words. "Aren't all the days pretty here?"

"There's only one day." She grinned. "We can have a picnic."

The absurdity of it charmed him. She might have been ten-year-old Rachel blithely summoning him to the park. She was not really the Rachel he knew, Jacob reminded himself. This was the simple part of her, really a child, the child she had lost inside herself. But that was all right. He had missed the child in Rachel. "All right, a picnic," he said. "But we don't have any food."

"We don't need any."

He reached for her hand, but his fingers closed on nothing. She was still not a whole, substantial thing. Rachel shrugged at his disappointment and led him with a look.

The jeweled scarabs on the forest floor scuttled away from her feet.

He was content, at least for a time, to let questions wait. Rachel led him to a clearing where the chaos of the forest floor gave way to a sort of mosaic of living tiles, hexagonal and octagonal, slate-gray and ochre. It was heartbreaking to watch her kneel on that yielding and lichenous surface pouring imaginary tea into imaginary cups.

He knelt beside her. "Rachel?"

"Yes, Jacob?"

"What do you remember?"

"A lot. More than I used to."

"Do you remember Mama and Papa?"

"Of course."

"Are they here?"

She shook her head.

"Are you alone?"

"Yes."

"Except for me," Jacob said.

"Except for you."

"And Mr. Ziegler."

She frowned. "Sometimes."

"Anyone else?"

"Just shadows."

"Aren't you lonely?"

"I've only been here a day," Rachel said.

It was a flexible day, Jacob presumed, like the seven days of creation, which somehow encompassed the Age of Fish and the Age of Reptiles. "Aren't you cold at night?"

"There isn't any night."

Disconcerting, this childish obtuseness, almost an unwillingness to *understand* his questions; but Jacob reminded himself that she was only part of a human being. The better part, surely, but still only part.

If Rachel died, would Rachel be whole again?

"Don't you miss home, Rachel?"

"I don't miss anything at all." She regarded him quizzically. "How did *you* get here?"

"Chess," Jacob said automatically.

"Oh." As if it made sense.

And they passed more time in silence. There was no sign of Ziegler, no sound or motion but the swarming of the rainbow-bright insects above the forest canopy. At length he told Rachel, "You know I can't stay." Time had passed on Earth. The other Rachel, the wounded and angry Rachel, might need him—might have fled Taglieri's room or even fought with him.

"Play with me before you go," Rachel demanded regally.

Jacob nodded and raised an imaginary cup of tea to his lips. "It's very good," he said.

She smiled.

She began to talk more freely then.

She reminisced about the Brant Street School and the Settlement House, about the docklands and the shops. She talked about Mama and Papa. Jacob immersed himself in her chatter, knowing that this was why he had come, not to visit Rachel but to revisit her innocence. Despite the strangeness of the surroundings—the shining trees, the pinpoint sun that never left the summer-blue sky—he was unwilling to force an end to the visit.

After a time they stood and walked. She took him to the brink of a gently rolling hill, and he saw the forest running unbroken to an impossibly far horizon white with radiant light. Every world a growing thing, Ziegler had said. As many afterlives as caverns in the earth. As above, so below.

A tree had fallen here, a broken universe as opaque as ebony or black pearl. They rested against it where the scarabs had not yet begun to eat. Rachel's eyes glowed and she seemed more physically present than ever. "I'm sorry, Jacob," she said.

"For what? There's nothing to be sorry about."

"I'm sorry for all the times I hurt you. Called you names, humiliated you."

He reached for her hand. "You remember that, too?"

Her eyes clouded. "I think . . . I remember everything now."

Jacob touched her hand, and this time there was palpable substance to it. Her hand was cold but he was able to wrap his own fingers around hers.

But that was wrong.

She was immaterial, half-present, because (Ziegler had insisted) she was dying by inches, and what died of her on Earth came here.

What died of her on Earth . . .

So cold, her hand.

He dropped it and backed away.

"Don't be frightened," the Rachel-thing said. "I don't blame you for what Taglieri did."

Then he saw the dark flowering of bruises on her flawless face, the bruises on her neck blue and finger-shaped.

"Rachel!"

"I'm sorry if this frightens you. It's just the way things work. Go home now, Jacob. Try not to grieve."

He would have said more, but the gaily colored insects came diving out of the sky as if they had scented her, a shrieking torrent of them.

They were immense, the size of dray horses. Their bodies were of faceted crystal and their eyes of polished bone. They grasped Rachel in their dangling black arms and carried her aloft as Jacob watched with a scream frozen in his throat.

He ran, it seemed, forever, through an endless humming noon, until he found the hovering door into Ziegler's arid bookshop.

As soon as he stepped across the threshhold everything felt wrong—his body, the weight of himself, the pressure of his feet against the floor.

He had, like Alice, grown precariously large and thick. The ceiling was too close, his arms were too heavy. His heart beat in his chest with a breathless, faltering rhythm.

For a long moment he failed to recognize the boy who stood by the chessboard.

It was the face he had seen in every mirror he had every confronted. It was himself. But the expression of gloating triumph was purely Oscar Ziegler's.

"Don't look so dumbfounded," the boy-man said. "The topology is simple enough. Like chess, Jacob! Remember? The attacking piece displaces its victim. The vanquished piece leaves the plane of the board entirely. But it does not, in a higher sense, cease to exist."

"My sister," Jacob wheezed from clotted lungs.

"To capture the pawn, threaten the queen."

"Taglieri murdered her."

The boy shrugged.

"You've made me old."

"Why not? You would only have wasted your youth on her."

"Goddamn you," Jacob said.

"There's no damnation, Jacob. No Heaven but the forest and no God but the hive."

The boy-thing opened the door and ran out into winter light.

The sky was blue. The city smelled fetid and alive. Frigid air crackled in his nose, but sunlight warmed the skin of his face. He flexed his arms. Blood flowed in his veins as bracingly as cold creek water.

It was the world of Steinitz and Anderssen, the world of Puccinni and Verdi and Nellie Melba. The world where night followed day. He had missed it. He ran into its embrace.

6.

It maddened him at first, but in time Jacob grew accustomed to the bookstore.

Its perimeters fit this aging body he had acquired. He explored the rooms upstairs, the cluttered basement, enummerating the contents of his cell, his new possessions. He took his time. He had time enough, he supposed.

The woman who brought him groceries called him Mr. Ziegler. He grew used to that, too.

He was polite to customers, both regulars and strangers, because they bore messages: stories, fashions, the smells of spring and summer, from a world he could only glimpse as they opened the door. He had tried to reenter that world, but there was only this single door and beyond it—for Jacob, at least—always the crystalline forest, the hovering swarms of insects.

He locked Ziegler's chessboard in a closet. He tried not to think about it. It was one of those things Jacob couldn't allow himself to dwell on, like the loss of Rachel, or the fate of Taglieri or of the body Ziegler had stolen. Questions better left unanswered. He passed the empty time by reading books, of which there were many, and his only fear was that somewhere in this mass of literature he might discover the secret Oscar Ziegler had withheld from him—that he would see the disposition of all the chess pieces of the universe, and then the door to the world would open and some bright-faced young man would enter, and Jacob would smile and ask him to stay for a game, and play cleverly, and feint against the doomed queen, and lift a lost pawn from the board as if it were nothing more than a piece of carven wood.

THE PERSEIDS

The divorce was finalized in the spring; I was alone that summer.

I took an apartment over a roti shop on Bathurst Street in Toronto. My landlords were a pair of ebullient Jamaican immigrants, husband and wife, who charged a reasonable rent and periodically offered to sell me grams of resinous, potent ganja. The shop closed at nine, but most summer nights the couple joined friends on a patio off the alley behind the store, and the sound of music and patois, cadences smooth as river pebbles, would drift up through my kitchen window. The apartment was a living room facing the street, a bedroom and kitchen at the rear; wooden floors and plaster ceilings with rusting metal caps where the gas fixtures had been removed. There was not much natural light, and the smell of goat curry from the kitchen downstairs was sometimes overwhelming. But taken all in all, it suited my means and needs.

I worked days at a secondhand book shop called Finders, sorting and shelving stock, operating the antiquated cash register, and brewing cups of yerba maté for the owner, an ancient myopic aesthete who subsisted on whatever dribble of profit he squeezed from the business. I was his only employee. It was not the work I had ever imagined myself doing, but such is the fortune of a blithe thirty-something who stumbles into the recession with a B.A. and negligible computer skills. I had inherited a little money from my parents, dead five years ago in a collision with a lumber truck on Vancouver Island; I hoarded the principal and supplemented my income with the interest.

I was alone and nearly friendless and my free time seemed to stretch to the horizon, as daunting and inviting as a desert high- way. One day in the bookshop I opened a copy of *Confessions of an English Opium-Eater* to the passage where de Quincey talks about his isolation from his fellow students at Manchester Gram- mar School: "for, whilst liking the society of some amongst them, I also had a deadly liking (perhaps a morbid liking) for solitude." Me, too, Thomas, I thought. Is it that the Devil finds work for idle hands, or that idle hands seek out the Devil's work? But I don't think the Devil had anything to do with it. (Other invisible entities, perhaps.) Alone, de Quincy discovered opium. I discov- ered Robin Slattery, and the stars.

We met prosaically enough: she sold me a telescope.

Amateur astronomy had been my teenage passion. When I lived with my parents on their country property north of Port Moody I had fallen in love with the night sky. City people don't understand. The city sky is as gray and blank as slate, faintly luminous, like a smoldering trash fire. The few celestial bodies that glisten through the pollution are about as inspiring as beached fish. But travel far enough from the city and you can still see the sky the way our ancestors saw it, as a chasm beyond the end of the world in which the stars move as implacably and un- approachably as the souls of the ancient dead.

I found Robin working the show floor at a retail shop called Scopes & Lenses in the suburban flatlands north of the city. If you're like me, you often have a powerful reaction to people even before you speak to them: like or dislike, trust or fear. Robin was in the *like* column as soon as she spotted me and smiled. Her smile seemed genuine, though there was no earthly reason it should be: we were strangers, after all; I was a customer; we had these roles to play. She wore her hair short. Long, retro paisley skirt and two earrings in each ear. Sort of an art-school look. Her face was narrow, elfin, Mediterranean-dark. I guessed she was about twenty-five.

Of course the only thing to talk about was telescopes. I wanted to buy one, a good one, something substantial, not a toy. I lived frugally, but every couple of years I would squeeze a little money out of my investments and buy myself an expensive present. Last year, my van. This year, I had decided, a telescope. (The divorce had been expensive, but that was a necessity, not a luxury.)

There was plenty to talk about. 'Scopes had changed since I was teenager. Bewilderingly. It was all Dobsonians, CCD imagers, object-acquisition software. . . . I took a handful of literature and told her I'd think about it. She smiled and said, "But you're serious, right? I mean, some people come in and look around and then do mail-order from the States. . . ." And then laughed at her own presumption, as if it were a joke, between us.

I said, "You'll get your commission. Promise."

"Oh, God, I wasn't *angling* . . . but here's my card . . . I'm in the store most afternoons."

That was how I learned her name.

Next week I put a 10-inch Meade Starfinder on my VISA card. I was back two days later for accessory eyepieces and a camera adapter. That was when I asked her out for coffee.

She didn't even blink. "Store closes in ten minutes," she said, "but I have to do some paperwork and make a deposit. I could meet you in an hour or so."

"Fine. I'll buy dinner."

"No, let me buy. You already paid for it. The commission— remember?"

She was like that.

Sometime during our dinner conversation she told me she had never looked through a telescope.

"You have to be kidding."

"Really!"

"But you know more about these things than I do, and I've looked through a lot of lenses."

She poked her fork at a plate of goat cheese torta as if wondering how much to say. "Well, I know telescopes. I don't know much astronomy. See, my father was into telescopes. He took photographs, thirty-five-millimeter long exposures, deep-sky stuff. I looked at the pictures; the pictures were great. But never, you know, through the eyepiece."

"Why not?" I imagined a jealous parent guarding his investment from curious fingers.

But Robin frowned as if I had asked a difficult question. "It's hard to explain. I just didn't want to. Refused to, really. Mmm . . . have you ever been alone somewhere on a windy night, maybe a dark night in winter? And you kind of get spooked? And you want to look out a window and see how bad the snow is but you get this idea in your head that if you open the curtain something truly horrible is going to be out there staring right back at you? And you know it's childish, but you still don't open the curtain. Just can't bring yourself to do it. You know that feeling?"

I said I'd had similar experiences.

"I think it's a primate thing," Robin meditated. "Stay close to the fire or the leopard'll get you. Anyway, that's the way I feel about telescopes. Irrational, I know. But there it is. Here we are on this cozy planet, and out there are all kinds of things—vast, blazing suns and frigid planets and the dust of dead stars and whole galaxies dying. I always had this feeling that if you looked too close something might look back. Like, don't open the curtain. Don't look through the 'scope. Because something might look back."

Almost certainly someone or something was looking back. The arithmetic is plain: a hundred billion stars in the galaxy alone, many times that number of planets, and even if life is uncommon and intelligence an evolutionary trick shot, odds are that when you gaze at the stars, somewhere in that horizonless infinity another eye is turned back at you.

But that wasn't what Robin meant.

I knew what she meant. Set against the scale of even a single galaxy, a human life is brief and human beings less than microscopic. Small things survive because, taken singly, they're inconsequential. They escape notice. The ant is invisible in the shadow of a spruce bud or a cloverleaf. Insects survive because, by and large, we only kill what we can see. The insect prayer: *Don't see me!*

Now consider those wide roads between the stars, where the only wind is a few dry grains of hydrogen and the dust of exploded suns. What if something walked there? Something unseen, invisible, immaterial—vaster than planets?

I think that's what Robin felt: her own frailty against the abysses of distance and time. *Don't look. Don't see me. Don't look.*

It was a friend of Robin's, a man who had been her lover, who first explained to me the concept of "domains."

By mid-September Robin and I were a couple. It was a relationship we walked into blindly, hypnotized by the sheer unlikeliness of it. I was ten years older, divorced, drifting like a swamped canoe toward the rapids of midlife; she was a tattooed Gen-Xer (the Worm Oroborous circling her left ankle in blue repose) for whom the death of Kurt Cobain had been a meaningful event. I think we aroused each other's exogamous instincts. We liked to marvel at the chasm between us, that deep and defining gulf: Winona Ryder vs. Humbert Humbert.

She threw a party to introduce me to her friends. The prospect was daunting but I knew this was one of those hurdles every relationship has to jump or kick the traces. So I came early and helped her clean and cook. Her apartment was the top of a subdivided house in Parkdale off Queen Street. Not the fashionable end of Queen Street; the hooker and junkie turf east of Roncesvalles Avenue. Rent was cheap. She had decorated the rambling attic space with religious bric-à-brac from Goodwill thrift shops and the East Indian dollar store around the corner: ankhs, crosses, bleeding hearts, gaudy Hindu iconography. "Cultural stew," she said. "Artifacts from the new domain. You can ask Roger about that."

I thought: *Roger?*

Her friends arrived by ones and twos. Lots of students, a few musicians, the creatively unemployed. Many of them thought black was a party color. I wondered when the tonsure and the goatee had come back into style. Felt set apart in jeans and sweat-shirt, the wardrobe-for-all-occasions of another generation. But the people (beneath these appurtenances: people) were mostly friendly. Robin put on a CD of bhangra music and brought out a tall blue plastic water pipe, which circulated with that con-spiratorial grace the cannabis culture inherits from its ancestors in Kennedy-era prehistory. This, at least, I recognized. Like Kennedy (they say), unlike Bill Clinton, I inhaled. But only a little. I wanted a clear head to get through the evening.

Robin covered a trestle table with bowls of kasha, rice cooked in miso (her own invention), a curry of beef, curry of eggplant, curry of chicken; chutneys from Kensington Market, loaves of sourdough and French bread and chapatis. Cheap red wine. There was a collective murmur of appreciation and Robin gave me more credit than I deserved—all I had done was stir the pots.

For an hour after dinner I was cornered by a U. of T. poli-sci student from Ethiopia who wanted me to understand how Mao had been betrayed by the revisionists who inherited his empire. He was, of course, the son of a well-to-do bureaucrat, and bru-tally earnest. I played vague until he gave up on me. Then, cut loose, I trawled through the room picking up fragments of con-versation, names dropped: Alice in Chains, Kate Moss, Michael-angelo Signorile. Robin took me by the elbow. "I'm making tea. Talk to Roger!"

Roger was tall and pale, with a shock of bleached hair threat-ening to obscure the vision in his right eye. He had the emaciated frame of a heroin addict, but it was willful, an aesthetic state-ment, and he dressed expensively.

Roger. "Domains." Fortunately I didn't have to ask; he was already explaining it to a pair of globe-eyed identical twins.

"It's McCluhanesque," one twin said; the other: "No, ecolog-ical . . ."

Roger smiled, a little condescendingly, I thought, but I was already wondering what he meant to Robin, or Robin to him. He put out his hand: "You must be Michael. Robin told me about you."

But not me about Roger. At least not much. I said, "She mentioned something about 'domains'—"

"Well, Robin just likes to hear me bullshit."

"No!" (The twins.) "Roger is *original*."

It didn't take much coaxing. I can't reproduce his voice—cool, fluid, slightly nasal—but what he said, basically, was this:

Life, the biological phenomenon, colonizes domains and turns them into ecologies. In the domain of the ocean, the first ecologies evolved. The dry surface of the continents was a dead domain until the first plants (lichens or molds, I suppose) took root. The air was an empty domain until the evolution of the wing.

But domain theory, Roger said, wasn't just a matter of biology versus geology. A living system could itself become a domain. In fact, once the geological domains were fully colonized, living systems became the last terrestrial domain and a kind of intensive recomplication followed: treetops, colonizing the air, were colonized in turn by insects, by birds; animal life by bacteria, viruses, parasites, each new array creating its own new domain, and so ad infinitum.

What made Roger's notion original was that he believed human beings had—for the first time in millennia—begun to colonize a wholly new domain, which he called the gnososphere: the domain of culture, art, religion, language. Because we were the first aboard, the gnososphere felt more like geology than ecology: a body of artifacts, lifeless as bricks. But that appearance was already beginning to change. We had seen in the last decade the first glimmerings of competition, specifically from the kind of computer program called "artificial life," entities that live and evolve entirely in the logarithms of computers, the high alps of the gnososphere. Not competing for *our* ground, obviously, but that time might come (consider computer "viruses"), and—who knows?—the gnososphere might eventually evolve its own independent entities. Maybe already had. When the gnososphere was "made of" campfire stories and cave paintings it was clearly not complex enough to support life. But the gnososphere at the end of the twentieth century had grown vast and intricate, a landscape both cerebral and electronic, born at the juncture of technology and human population, in which crude self-replicating structures (Nazism, say; Communism) had already proven their ability to grow, feed, reproduce, and die. Ideologies were like primitive DNA floating in a nutrient soup of radio waves, television images, words. Who could say what a more highly evolved creature—with protein coat, nucleus, mitochondria; with eyes and genitals—might be like? We might not be able to experience it at all, since no single human being could be its host; it would live through our collectivity, as immense as it was unknowable.

"Amazing," the twins said, when Roger finished. "*Awesome.*"

And suddenly Robin was beside me, handing out tea, taking my arm in a proprietary gesture meant, I hoped, for Roger, who smiled tolerantly. "He *is* amazing, isn't he? Or else completely insane."

"Not for me to say," Roger obliged. (The twins laughed.)

"Roger used to be a Fine Arts T.A. at the University," Robin said, "until he dropped out. Now he builds things."

"Sculpture?" I asked.

"*Things.* Maybe he'll show you sometime."

Roger nodded, but I doubted he'd extend the invitation. We were circling each other like wary animals. I read him as bright, smug, and subtly hostile. He obviously felt a powerful need to impress an audience. Probably he had once greatly impressed Robin—she confirmed this later—and I imagined him abandoning her because, as audience, she had grown a little cynical. The twins (young, female) clearly delighted him. Just as clearly, I didn't.

But we were polite. We talked a little more. He knew the bookstore where I worked. "Been there often," he said. And it was easy to imagine him posed against the philosophy shelves, long fingers opening Kierkegaard, the critical frown fixed in place. After a while I left him to the twins, who waved me good-bye: "Nice meeting you!" "*Really!*"

When I was younger I read a lot of science fiction. Through my interest in astronomy I came to sf, and through both I happened across an astronomer's puzzle, a cosmological version of Pascal's

Wager called the Fermi Paradox. It goes like this: If life can spread through the galaxy, then, logically, it already has. Our neighbors should be here. Should have been here for millennia. So where are they?

I discussed it, while the party ran down, with the only guest older than I was, a graying science fiction writer who had been hitting the pipe with a certain bleak determination. "The Oort cloud," he declared, "that's where they are. I mean, why bother with planets? For dedicated space technologies—and I assume they would send machines, not something as short-lived and finicky as a biological organism—a planet's not a really attractive place. Planets are heavy, corrosive, too hot for superconductors. Interesting places, maybe, because planets are where cultures grow, and why slog across all those light years unless you're looking for something as complex and unpredictable as a sentient culture? But you don't, for God's sake, fill up their sky with spaceships. You stick around the Oort cloud, where it's nice and cold and there are cometary bodies to draw resources from. You hang out, you listen. If you want to talk, you pick your own time."

The Oort cloud is that nebulous ring around the solar system, well beyond the orbit of Pluto, composed of small bodies of dust and water ice. Gravitational perturbation periodically knocks a few of these bodies into elliptical orbits; traversing the inner solar system, they become comets. Our annual meteor showers—the Perseids, the Geminids, the Quadrantids—are the remnants of ancient, fractured comets. Oort cloud visitors, old beyond memory.

But in light of Roger's thesis I wondered if the question was too narrowly posed, the science fiction writer's answer too pat. Maybe our neighbours had already arrived, not in silver ships but in metaphysics, informing the very construction and representation of our lives. The cave paintings at Lascaux, Chartres Cathedral, the Fox Broadcasting System: not their physicality (and they become less physical as our technology advances) but their intangible *grammar*—maybe this is the evidence they left us, a ruined archeology of cognition, invisible because pervasive, inescapable: they are both here, in other words, and not here; they are us and not-us.

When the last guest was gone, the last dish stacked, Robin pulled off her shirt and walked through the apartment, coolly unself-conscious, turning off lights.

The heat of the party lingered. She opened the bedroom window to let in a breeze from the lakeshore. It was past two in the morning and the city was relatively quiet. I paid attention to the sounds she made, the rustle as she stepped out of her skirt, the easing of springs in the thrift-shop bed. She wore a ring through each nipple, delicate turquoise rings that gave back glimmers of ambient light. I remembered how unfamiliar her piercings had seemed the first time I encountered them with my tongue, the polished circles, their chilly, perfect geometry set against the warmer and more complex terrain of breast and aureole.

We made love in that distracted after-a-party way, while the room was still alive with the musk of the crowd, feeling like ex-hibitionists (I think she felt that way too) even though we were alone.

It was afterward, in a round of sleepy pillow talk, that she told me Roger had been her lover. I put a finger gently through one of her rings and she said Roger had piercings, too: one nipple and under the scrotum, penetrating the area between the testicles and the anus. Some men had the head of the penis pierced (a "Prince Albert") but Roger hadn't gone for that.

I was jealous. Jealous, I suppose, of this extra dimension of intimacy from which I was excluded. I had no wounds to show her.

She said, "You never talk about your divorce."

"It's not much fun to talk about."

"You left Carolyn, or she left you?"

"It's not that simple. But, ultimately, I guess she left me."

"Lots of fighting?"

"No fighting."

"What, then?"

I thought about it. "Continental drift."

"What was her problem?"

"I'm not so sure it was her problem."

"She must have had a reason, though—or thought she did."

"She said I was never there." Robin waited patiently. I went on, "Even when I was with her, I was never *there*—or so she claimed. I'm not sure I know what she meant. I suppose, that I wasn't completely engaged. That I was apart. Held back. With her, with her friends, with her family—with anybody."

"Do you think that's true?"

It was a question I'd asked myself too often.

Sure, in a sense it was true. I'm one of those people who are often called loners. Crowds don't have much allure for me. I don't confide easily and I don't have many friends.

That much I would admit to. The idea (which had come to obsess Carolyn during our divorce) that I was congenitally, hopelessly *set apart*, a kind of pariah dog, incapable of real intimacy . . . that was a whole 'nother thing.

We talked it around. Robin was solemn in the dark, propped on one elbow. Through the window, past the halo of her hair, I could see the setting moon. Far away down the dark street someone laughed.

Robin, who had studied a little anthropology, liked to see things in evolutionary terms. "You have a night watch personality," she decided, closing her eyes.

"Night watch?"

"Mm-hm. Primates . . . you know . . . protohominids . . . it's where all our personality styles come from. We're social animals, basically, but the group is more versatile if you have maybe a couple of hyperthymic types for cheerleaders, some dysthymics to sit home and mumble, and the one guy—let's say, *you*—who edges away from the crowd, who sits up when everybody else is asleep, who basically keeps the watches of the night. The one who sees the lions coming. Good night vision and lousy social skills. Every tribe should have one."

"Is that what I am?"

"It's reassuring, actually." She patted my ass and said, "Keep watch for me, okay?"

I kept the watch a few minutes more.

———

In the morning, on the way to lunch, we visited one of those East Indian/West Indian shops, the kind with the impossibly gaudy portraits of Shiva and Ganesh in chrome-flash plastic frames, a cooler full of ginger beer and coconut pop, shelves of sandalwood incense and patchouli oil and bottles of magic potions (Robin pointed them out): St. John Conqueror Root, Ghost Away, Luck Finder, with labels claiming the contents were an Excellent Floor Polish, which I suppose made them legal to sell. Robin was delighted: "Flotsam from the gnososphere," she laughed, and it was easy to imagine one of Roger's gnostic creatures made manifest in this shop—for that matter, in this city, this English-speaking, Cantonese-speaking, Urdu-speaking, Farsi-speaking city—a slouching, ethereal beast of which one cell might be Ganesh the Elephant-headed Boy and another Madonna, the Cone-breasted Woman.

A city, for obvious reasons, is a lousy place to do astronomy. I worked the 'scope from the back deck of my apartment, shielded from streetlights, and Robin gave me a selection of broadband lens filters to cut the urban scatter. But I was interested in deep-sky observing and I knew I wasn't getting everything I'd paid for.

In October I arranged to truck the 'scope up north for a weekend. Robin reserved us a cabin at a private campground near Algonquin Park. It was way past tourist season, but Robin knew the woman who owned the property; we would have the place virtually to ourselves and we could cancel, no problem, if the weather didn't look right.

But the weather cooperated. It was the end of the month—coincidentally, the weekend of the Orionid meteor shower—and we were in the middle of a clean high-pressure cell that stretched from Alberta to Labrador. The air was brisk but cloudless, transparent as creek water. We arrived at the campsite Friday afternoon and I spent a couple of hours setting up the 'scope, calibrating it, and running an extension cord out to the automatic guider. I attached a thirty-five-millimeter SLR camera loaded with hypersensitized Tech Pan film, and I did all this despite the accompaniment of the owner's five barking Yorkshire Terrier pups. The ground under my feet was glacier-scarred Laurentian Shield rock; the meadow I set up in was broad and flat; highway lights were pale and distant. Perfect. By the time I finished setting up, it was dusk. Robin had started a fire in the pit outside our cabin and was roasting chicken and bell peppers. The cabin overlooked a marshy lake thick with duckweed; the air was cool and moist and I fretted about ground mist.

But the night was clear. After dinner Robin smoked marijuana in a tiny carved soapstone pipe (I didn't) and then we went out to the meadow, bundled in winter jackets.

I worked the 'scope. Robin wouldn't look through the eyepiece — her old phobia—but took a great, grinning pleasure in the Orionids, exclaiming at each brief etching of the cave-dark, star-scattered sky. Her laughter was almost giddy.

After a time, though, she complained of the cold, and I sent her back to the cabin (we had borrowed a space heater from the owner) and told her to get some sleep. I was cold, too, but intoxicated by the sky. It was my first attempt at deep-sky photography and surprisingly successful: when the photos were developed later that week I had a clean, hard shot of M100 in Coma Berenices, a spiral galaxy in full disk, arms sweeping toward the bright center; a city of stars beyond counting, alive, perhaps, with civilizations, so impossibly distant that the photons hoarded by the lens of the telescope were already millions of years old.

When I finally came to bed Robin was asleep under two quilted blankets. She stirred at my pressure on the mattress and turned to me, opened her eyes briefly, then folded her cinnamon-scented warmth against my chest, and I lay awake smelling the hot coils of the space heater and the faint pungency of the marijuana she had smoked and the pine-resinous air that had swept in behind me, these night odors mysteriously familiar, intimate as memory.

We made love in the morning, lazy and a little tired, and I thought there was something new in the way she looked at me, a certain calculating distance, but I wasn't sure; it might have been the slant of light through the dusty window. In the afternoon we hiked out to a wild blueberry patch she knew about, but the season was over; frost had shriveled the last of the berries. (The Yorkshire Terriers were at our heels, there and back.)

That night was much the same as the first except that Robin decided to stay back at the cabin reading an Anne Rice novel. I remembered that her father was an amateur astronomer and wondered if the parallel wasn't a little unsettling for her, a symbolic incest. I photographed M33 in Triangulum, another elliptical galaxy, its arms luminous with stars, and in the morning we packed up the telescope and began the long drive south.

She was moodier than usual. In the cabin of the van, huddled by the passenger door with her knees against her chest, she said, "We never talk about relationship things."

"Relationship things?"

"For instance, monogamy."

That hung in the air for a while.

Then she said, "Do you believe in it?"

I said it didn't really matter whether I "believed in" it; it just seemed to be something I did. I had never been unfaithful to Carolyn, unless you counted Robin; I had never been unfaithful to Robin.

But she was twenty-five years old and hadn't taken the measure of these things. "I think it's a sexual preference," she said. "Some people are, some people aren't."

I said—carefully neutral—"Where do you stand?"

"I don't know." She gazed out the window at October farms, brown fields, wind-canted barns. "I haven't decided."

We left it at that.

She threw a Halloween party, costumes optional—I wore street clothes, but most of her crowd welcomed the opportunity to dress up. Strange hair and body paint, mainly. Roger (I had learned his last name: Roger Russo) showed up wearing a feathered headdress, green dye, kohl circles around his eyes. He said he was Sacha Runa, the jungle spirit of the Peruvian *ayahuas-*

queros. Robin said he had been investigating the idea of shamanic spirit creatures as the first entities cohabiting the gnososphere: she thought the costume was perfect for him. She hugged him carefully and pecked his green-dyed cheek, merely friendly, but he glanced reflexively at me and quickly away, as if to confirm that I had seen her touch him.

I had one of my photographs of the galaxy M33 enlarged and framed; I gave it to Robin as a gift.

She hung it in her bedroom. I remember—it might have been November, maybe as late as the Leonids, mid-month—a night when she stared at it while we made love: she on her knees on the bed, head upturned, raw-cut hair darkly stubbled on her scalp, and me behind her, gripping her thin, almost fragile hips, knowing she was looking at the stars.

Three optical illusions:

(1) Retinal floaters. Those delicate, crystalline motes, like rainbow-colored diatoms, that swim through the field of vision.

Some nights, when I've been too long at the scope, I see them drifting up from the horizon, a terrestrial commerce with the sky.

(2) In 1877, Giovanni Schiaparelli mapped what he believed were the canals of Mars. Mars has no canals; it is an airless desert. But for decades the educated world believed in a decadent Martian civilization, doomed to extinction when its water evaporated to the frigid poles.

It was Schiaparelli who first suggested that meteor showers represent the remains of ancient, shattered comets.

(3) Computer-generated three-dimensional pictures—they were everywhere that summer, a fad. You know the kind? The picture looks like so much visual hash, until you focus your eyes well beyond it; then the image lofts out, a hidden bas-relief: ether sculpture.

Robin believed TV worked the same way. "If you turn to a blank channel," she told me (December: first snow outside the window), "you can see pictures in the static. Three-dee. And they move."

What kind of pictures?

"Strange." She was clearly uncomfortable talking about it. "Kind of like animals. Or bugs. Lots of arms. The eyes are very . . . strange." She gave me a shy look. "Am I crazy?"

"No." Everyone has a soft spot or two. "You look at these pictures often?"

"Hardly ever. Frankly, it's kind of scary. But it's also. . . ."

"What?"

"*Tempting.*"

I don't own a television set. One summer Carolyn and I had taken a trip to Mexico and we had seen the famous murals at Teotihuacán. Disembodied eyes everywhere: plants with eyes for flowers, flowers exuding eyes, eyes floating through the convolute images like lost balloons. Whenever people talk about television, I'm reminded of Teotihuacán.

Like Robin, I was afraid to look through certain lenses for fear of what might be looking back.

That winter, I learned more about Roger Russo.

He was wealthy. At least, his family was wealthy. The family owned Russo Precision Parts, an electronics distributor with a near-monopoly of the Canadian manufacturing market. Roger's older brother was the corporate heir-designate; Roger himself, I gather, was considered "creative" (i.e, unemployable) and allowed a generous annual remittance to do with as he pleased.

Early in January (the Quadrantids, but they were disappointing that year) Robin took me to Roger's place. He lived in a house off Queen West—leased it from a cousin—a three-story brick Edwardian bastion in a Chinese neighborhood where the houses on each side had been painted cherry red. We trekked from the streetcar through fresh ankle-high snow; the snow was still falling, cold and granular. Robin had made the date: we were supposed to have lunch, the three of us. I think she liked bringing Roger and me together, liked those faint proprietary sparks that passed between us; I think it flattered her. Myself, I didn't enjoy it. I doubted Roger took much pleasure in it, either.

He answered the door wearing nothing but jogging pants. His

solitary silver nipple ring dangled on his hairless chest; it reminded me (sorry) of a pull-tab on a soft drink can. He shooed
us in and latched the door. Inside, the air was warm and moist.

The house was a shrine to his eccentricity: books everywhere,
not only shelved but stacked in corners, an assortment too random to categorize, but I spotted early editions of William James
(*Psychology*, the complete work) and Carl Jung; a ponderous
hardcover *Phenomenology of the Mind*, Heidegger's *Being and
Time*, none of them books I had ever read or ever intended to
read. We adjourned to a big wood-and-tile kitchen and made
conversation while Roger chopped kohlrabi at a butcher-block
counter. He had seen *Natural Born Killers* at a review theater
and was impressed by it: "It's completely post-post—a decon-
struction of *itself*—very image-intensive and, you know, florid,
like early church iconography. . . ."

The talk went on like this. High-toned media gossip, basically.
After lunch, I excused myself and hunted down the bathroom.

On the way back I paused at the kitchen door when I heard
Roger mention my name.

"Michael's not much of a watcher, is he?"

Robin: "Well, he is, actually—a certain kind of watcher."

"Oh—the astronomy. . . ."

"Yes."

"That photograph you showed me."

"Yes, right."

That photograph, I thought. *The one on her bedroom wall.*

Later, in the winter-afternoon lull that softens outdoor sounds
and amplifies the rumble of the furnace, Robin asked Roger to
show me around the house. "The upstairs," she said, and to me:
"It's so weird!"

"Thanks," Roger said.

"You know what I mean! Don't pretend to be insulted. Weird
is your middle name."

I followed Roger's pale back up the narrow stairway, creaking
risers lined with faded red carpet. Then, suddenly, we were in
another world: a cavernous space—walls must have been

knocked out—crowded with electronic kibble. Video screens, raw circuit boards, ribbon wire snaking through the clutter like eels through a gloomy reef. He threw a wall switch, and it all came to life.

"A dozen cathode-ray tubes," Roger said, "mostly yard-sale and electronic-jobber trash." Some were black-and-white, some crenellated with noise bars. "Each one cycles through every channel you can get from satellite. I wired in my own decoder for the scrambled channels. The cycles are staggered, so mostly you get chaos, but every so often they fall into sync and for a split second the same image is all around you. I meant to install another dish, feed in another hundred channels, but the mixer would have been . . . complex. Anyway, I lost interest."

"Not to sound like a Philistine," I said, "but what is it—a work of art?"

Roger smiled loftily. "In a way. Actually, it was meant to be a ghost trap."

"Ghost trap?"

"In the Hegelian sense. The *weltgeist*."

"Summoned from the gnososphere," Robin added.

I asked about the music. The music had commenced when he threw the switch: a strange nasal melody, sometimes hummed, sometimes chanted, thick as incense. The words, when I could make them out, were foreign and punctuated with thick glottal stops. There were insect sounds in the background; I supposed it was a field recording, the kind of anthropological oddity a company called Nonesuch used to release on vinyl, years ago.

"It's called an *icaro*," Roger said. "A supernatural melody. Certain Peruvian Indians drink *ayahuasca* and produce these songs, *icaros*. They learn them from the spirit world."

Ayahuasca is a hallucinogenic potion made from a mixture of *Banisteriopsis caapi* vines and the leaves of *Psychotria viridis*, both rain-forest plants. (I spent a day at the Robarts looking it up.) Apparently it can be made from a variety of more common plant sources, and *ayahuasca* churches like the *União do Vegetal* have popularized its use in the urban centers of Brazil.

"And the third floor," Robin said, waving at the stairs dimly visible across the room, "that's amazing, too. Roger built an addition over what used to be the roof of the building. There's a greenhouse, an actual greenhouse! You can't see it from the street because the facade hides it, but it's huge. And there's a big open-air deck. Show him, Roger."

Roger shook his head: "I don't think it's necessary."

We were about to leave the room when three of the video screens suddenly radiated the same image: waterfall and ferns in soft focus, and a pale woman in a white skirt standing beside a Datsun that matched her blue-green eyes. It snagged Roger's attention. He stopped in his tracks.

"*Rainha da Floresta*," he murmured, looking from Robin to me and back again, his face obscure in the flickering light. "The lunar aspect."

The winter sky performed its long procession. One clear night in February, hungry for starlight, I zipped myself into my parka and drove a little distance west of the city—not with the telescope but with a pair of 10×50 Zeiss binoculars. Hardly Mount Palomar, but not far removed from the simple optics Galileo ground for himself some few centuries ago.

I parked off an access road along the ridge top of Rattlesnake Point, with a clear view to the frozen rim of Lake Ontario. Sirius hung above the dark water, a little obscured by rising mist. Capella was high overhead, and to the west I was able to distinguish the faint oval of the Andromeda galaxy, two-million-odd light-years away. East, the sky was vague with city glare and etched by the running lights of airliners orbiting Pearson International.

Alone in the van, breathing steam and balancing the binoculars on the rim of a half-open window, I found myself thinking about the Fermi Paradox. They ought to be here . . . where are they?

The science fiction writer at Robin's party had said they wouldn't come in person. Organic life is too brief and too fragile for the eons-long journeys between stars. They would send machines. Maybe self-replicating machines. Maybe sentient machines.

But, I thought, why machines at all? If the thing that travels most efficiently between stars is light (and all its avatars: X-rays, radio waves), then why not send *light itself*? Light *modulated*, of course; light alive with information. Light as medium. Sentient light.

Light as domain, perhaps put in place by organic civilizations, but inherited by—something else.

And if human beings are truly latecomers to the galaxy, then the network must already be ancient, a web of modulated signals stitching together the stars. A domain in which things—entities—creatures perhaps as diffuse and large as the galaxy itself, creatures made solely of information—live and compete and maybe even hunt.

An ecology of starlight, or better: a jungle of starlight.

The next day I called Robin's sf-writer friend and tried out the idea on him. He said, "Well, it's interesting. . . ."

"But is it possible?"

"Sure it's possible. Anything's possible. Possible is my line of work. But you have to keep in mind the difference between a possibility and a likelihood." He hesitated. "Are you thinking of becoming a writer, or just a career paranoid?"

I laughed. "Neither one." Though the laughter was a little forced.

"Well, then, since we're only playing, here's another notion for you. Living things—species capable of evolving—don't just live. They eat." (*Hunt*, I thought.) "They die. And most important of all: they reproduce."

You've probably heard of the hunting wasp. The hunting wasp paralyzes insects (the tarantula is a popular choice) and uses the still-living bodies to incubate and feed its young.

It's everybody's favorite Hymenoptera horror story. You can't help imagining how the tarantula must feel, immobilized but for its frantic heartbeat, the wasp larvae beginning to stir inside it . . . stir, and feed.

But maybe the tarantula isn't only paralyzed. Maybe it's entranced. Maybe wasp venom is a kind of insect ambrosia—*soma, amrta, kykeon.* Maybe the tarantula sees God, feels God turning in hungry spirals deep inside it.

I think that would be worse—don't you?

Was I in love with Robin Slattery? I think this narrative doesn't make that absolutely clear—too many second thoughts since—but yes, I was in love with Robin. In love with the way she looked at me (that mix of deference and pity), the way she moved, her strange blend of erudition and ignorance (the only Shakespeare she had read was *The Tempest*, but she had read it five times and attended a performance at Stratford), her skinny legs, her pyrotechnic fashion sense (one day black Goth, next day tartan mini-skirt and knee socks).

I paid her the close attention of a lover, and because I did I knew by spring (the Eta Aquarids . . . early May) that things had changed.

She spent a night at my place, something she had been doing less often lately. We went into the bedroom with the sound of soca tapes pulsing like a heartbeat from the shop downstairs. I had covered one wall with astronomical photographs, stuck to the plaster with pushpins. She looked at the wall and said, "This is why men shouldn't be allowed to live alone—they do things like this."

"Is that a proposition?" I was feeling, I guess, reckless.

"No," she said, looking worried, "I only meant. . . ."

"I know."

"I mean, it's not exactly *Good Housekeeping.*"

"Right."

We went to bed troubled. We made love, but tentatively, and later, when she had turned on her side and her breathing was night-quiet, I left the bed and walked naked to the kitchen.

I didn't need to turn on lights. The moon cast a gray radiance through the rippled glass of the kitchen window. I only wanted to sit a while in the cool of an empty room.

But I guess Robin hadn't been sleeping after all, because she came to the kitchen wrapped in my bath robe, standing in the silver light like a quizzical, barefoot monk.

"Keeping the night watch," I said.

She leaned against a wall. "It's lonely, isn't it?"

I just looked at her. Wished I could see her eyes.

"Lonely," she said, "out there on the African plains."

I wondered if her intuition was right, if there was a gene, a defective sequence of DNA, that marked me and set me apart from everyone else. The image of the watchman-hominid was a powerful one. I pictured that theoretical ancestor of mine. Our hominid ancestors were small, vulnerable, as much animal as human. The tribe sleeps. The watchman doesn't. I imagine him awake in the long exile of the night, rump against a rock in a sea of wild grasses, shivering when the wind blows, watching the horizon for danger. The horizon and the sky.

What does he see?

The stars in their silent migrations. The annual meteor showers. A comet, perhaps, falling sunward from the far reefs of the solar system.

What does he feel?

Yes: lonely.

And often afraid.

In the morning, Robin said, "As a relationship, I don't think we're working. There's this *distance* . . . I mean, it's lonely for me, too . . ."

But she didn't really want to talk about and it and I didn't really want to press her. The dynamic was clear enough.

She was kinder than Carolyn had been, and for that I was grateful.

I won't chronicle the history of our breakup. You know how this goes. Phone calls less often, fewer visits; then times when the messages I left on her machine went unreturned, and a penultimate moment of drawing-room comedy when Roger picked up her phone and kindly summoned her from the shower for me. (I pictured her in a towel, hair dripping while she made her vague apologies—and Roger watching.)

No hostility, just drift; and finally silence.

Another spring, another summer—the Eta Aquarids, the Delta Aquarids, at last the Perseids in the sweltering heat of a humid, cicada-buzzing August, two and half months since the last time we talked.

I was on the back deck of my apartment when the phone rang. It was still too hot to sleep, but by some miracle the air was clear and dry, and I kept the night watch in a lawn chair with my binoculars beside me. I heard the ring but ignored it—most of my phone calls lately had been sales pitches or marketing surveys, and the sky, even in the city (if you knew how to look), was alive with meteors, the best display in years. I thought about rock fragments old as the solar system, incinerated in the high atmosphere. The ash, I supposed, must eventually sift down through the air; we must breathe it, in some part; molecules of ancient carbon lodging in the soft tissue of the lung.

Two hours after midnight I went inside, brushed my teeth, thought about bed—then played the message on my answering machine.

It was from Robin.

"Mike? Are you there? If you can hear me, pick up . . . come on, pick up! [Pause.] Well, okay. I guess it's not really important. Shit! It's only that . . . there's something I'm not sure about. I just wanted to talk about it with someone. With you. [Pause.] You were always so *solid*. It thought it would be good to hear your voice again. Not tonight, huh? I guess not. Hey, don't worry about me. I'll be okay. But if you—"

The machine cut her off.

I tried calling back, but nobody answered the phone.

I knew her well enough to hear the anxiety in her voice. And she wouldn't have called me unless she was in some kind of trouble.

Robin, I thought, what lens or window did you look through? And what looked back?

I drove through the empty city to Parkdale, where there was no traffic but cabs and a few bad-tempered hookers; parked and pounded on Robin's door until her downstairs neighbors complained. She wasn't home, she'd gone out earlier, and I should fuck off and die.

I drove to Roger's.

The tall brick house was full of light.

When I knocked, the twins answered. They had shaved their heads since the last time I saw them. The effect was to make them even less distinguishable. Both were naked, their skin glistening with a light sheen of sweat and something else: spatters of green paint. Drops of it hung in their wiry, short pubic hair.

They blinked at me a moment before recognition set in. I couldn't recall their names (I thought of them as Alpha and Beta)—but they remembered mine.

"Michael!"

"Robin's friend!"

"What are you doing here?"

I told them I wanted to talk to Robin.

"She's real busy right now—"

"I'd like to come in."

They looked at each other as if in mute consultation. Then (one a fraction of a second after the other) they smiled and nodded.

Every downstairs light had been turned on, but the rooms I could see from the foyer were empty. One of Roger's *icaros* was playing somewhere; the chanting coiled through the air like a tightening spring. I heard other voices, faintly, elsewhere in the house, upstairs.

Alpha and Beta looked alarmed when I headed for the stairs. "Maybe you shouldn't go up there, Michael." "You weren't *invited*."

I ignored them and took the steps two at a time. The twins hurried up behind me.

Roger's ghost trap was switched on, its video screens flashing faster than the last time I had seen it. No image lingered long enough to resolve, but the flickering light was more than random; I felt presences in it, the kind of motion that alerts the peripheral vision. The *icaro* was louder and more insinuating in this warehouse-like space, a sound that invaded the body through the pores.

But the room was empty.

The twins regarded me, smiling blandly, pupils big as half-dollars. "Of course, all this isn't *necessary*—"

"You don't have to *summon* something that's already *inside you*—"

"But it's *out there*, too—"

"In the images—"

"In the *gnososphere* . . ."

"Everywhere. . . ."

The third floor: more stairs at the opposite end of the room. I moved that way with the maddening sensation that time itself had slowed, that I was embedded in some invisible, congealed substance that made every footstep a labor. The twins were right behind me, still performing their mad Baedeker.

"The greenhouse!" (Alpha.)

"Yes, you should see it." (Beta.)

The stairs led to a door; the door opened into a jungle humidity lit by ranks of fluorescent bars. Plants were everywhere; I had to blink before I could make sense of it.

"*Psychotria viridis*," Alpha said.

"And other plants—"

"Common grasses—"

"*Desmanthus illinoensis*—"

"*Phalaris arundinacea*—"

It was as Robin had described it, a greenhouse built over an expansion of the house, concealed from the street by an attic riser. The ceiling and the far walls were of glass, dripping with moisture. The air was thick and hard to breathe.

"Plants that contain DMT." (The twins, still babbling.)

"It's a drug—"

"And a neurotransmitter."

"N, N-dimethyltryptamine. . . ."

"It's what dreams are made of, Michael."

"Dreams and imagination."

"Culture."

"Religion!"

"It's the *opening*—"

I said, "Is she drugged? For Christ's sake, where is she?"

But the twins didn't answer.

I saw motion through the glass. The deck extended beyond the greenhouse, but there was no obvious door. I stumbled down a corridor of slim-leaved potted plants and put my hands against the dripping glass.

People out there.

"She's the *Rainha da Floresta*—"

"And Roger is *Santo Daime!*"

"All the archetypes, really. . . ."

"Male and female, sun and moon. . . ."

I swiped away the condensation with my sleeve. A group of maybe a dozen people had gathered on the wooden decking outside, night wind tugging at their hair. I recognized faces from Robin's parties, dimly illuminated by the emerald glow of the greenhouse. They formed a semicircle with Robin at the center of it—Robin and Roger.

She wore a white T-shirt but was naked below the waist. Roger was entirely naked and covered with glistening green dye. They held each other at arm's length, as if performing some elaborate dance, but they were motionless, eyes fixed on one another.

Sometime earlier the embrace must have been more intimate. His paint was smeared on Robin's shirt and thighs.

She was thinner than I remembered, almost anorexic.

Alpha said, "It's sort of a wedding—"

"An *alchemical* wedding."

"And sort of a birth."

There had to be a door. I kicked over a brick and board platform, spilling plants and bonemeal as I followed the wall. The door, when I found it, was glass in a metal frame, and there was a padlock across the clasp.

I rattled it, banged my palm against it. Where my hand had been I could see through the smear of humidity. A few heads turned at the noise, including, I recognized, the science fiction writer I had talked to long ago. But there was no curiosity in his gaze, only a desultory puzzlement. Roger and Robin remained locked in their peculiar trance, touching but apart, as if making room between them for . . . what?

No, something *had* changed: now their eyes were closed. Robin was breathing in short, stertorous gasps that made me think of a woman in labor. (*A birth*, the twins had said.)

I looked for something to break the glass—a brick, a pot.

Alpha stepped forward, shaking her head. "Too late for that, Michael."

And I knew—with a flood of grief that seemed to well up from some neglected, swollen wound—that she was right.

I turned back to the wall. This time, to watch.

Past understanding, there is only observation. All I know is what I saw. What I saw, with the glass between myself and Robin. With my cheek against the dripping glass.

Something came out of her.

Something came out of her.

Something came out of her and Roger, like ectoplasm; but especially from their eyes, flowing like hot blue smoke.

I thought their heads were on fire.

Then the smoke condensed between them, took on a solid form suspended weightless in the space between their bodies.

The shape it took was complex, barbed, hard-edged, luminous, with the infolded symmetries of a star coral and the thousand facets of a geode. Suddenly translucent, it seemed made of frozen light. Strange as it was, it looked almost obscenely organic. I thought of a seed, the dense nucleus of something potentially enormous: a foetal god.

I don't know how long it hovered between their two tensed bodies. I was distantly aware of my own breathing. Of the hot moisture of my skin against the greenhouse glass. The *icaro* had stopped. I thought the world itself had fallen silent.

Then the thing that had appeared between them, the bright impossibility they had given birth to, began to rise, at first almost imperceptibly, then accelerating until it was suddenly gone, transiting the sky at, I guessed, the speed of light.

Commerce with the stars.

Then Robin collapsed.

I kicked at the door until the clasp gave way; then there were hands on me, restraining me, and I closed my eyes and let them carry me away.

She was alive.

I had seen her led down the stairs, groggy and emaciated but moving under her own volition. She needed sleep, the twins said. That was all.

They brought me to a room and left me alone with my friend the science fiction writer.

He poured a drink.

"Do you know," he asked, "can you even begin to grasp what you saw here tonight?"

I shook my head.

"But you've thought about it," he said. "We talked. You've drawn some conclusions. And, as a matter of fact, in this territory, we're all ignorant. In the gnososphere, Michael, intuition counts for more than knowledge. My intuition is that what you've seen here won't be at all uncommon in the next few years. It may become a daily event—a part, maybe even the central part, of the human experience."

I stared at him.

He said, "Your best move, and I mean this quite sincerely, would be to just get over it and get on with your life."

"Or else?"

"No, 'or else.' No threats. It doesn't matter what you do. One human being . . . we amount to nothing, you know. Maybe we dive into the future, like Roger, or we hang back, dig in our heels, but it doesn't matter. It really doesn't. In the end you'll do what you want."

"I want to leave."

"Then leave. I don't have an explanation to offer. Only a few ideas of my own, if you care to hear them."

I stayed a while longer.

The Orionids, the Leonids: the stars go on falling with their se-
rene implacability, but I confess, it's hard to look at them now.
Bitter and hard.

Consider, he said, living things as large as the galaxy itself. Consider their slow ecology, their evolution across spans of time in
which history counts for much less than a heartbeat.

Consider spores that lie dormant, perhaps for millennia, in the
planetary clouds of newborn stars. Spores carried by cometary
impact into the fresh biosphere (the *domain*) of a life-bearing
world.

Consider our own evolution, human evolution, as one stage in
a reproductive process in which human culture itself is the
flower: literally, a flower, gaudy and fertile, from which fresh seed
is generated and broadcast.

"Robin is a flower," he said, "but there's nothing special about
that. Roger hastened the process with his drugs and parapher-
nalia and symbolic magic. So he could be among the first. The
avant-garde. But the time is coming for all of us, Michael, and
soon we won't need props. The thing that's haunted us as a species, the thing we painted on our cave walls and carved into our
pillars and cornices and worshipped on our bloody altars and
movie screens, it's almost here. We'll all be flowers, I think, before long."

But even a flower can be sterile—set apart, functionally alone, a
genetic fluke.

But in another sense the flower is our culture itself, and I can't
help wondering what happens to that flower after it broadcasts
its seed. Maybe it wilts. Maybe it dies.

Maybe that's already happening. Have you looked at a newspaper lately?

Or maybe, like every other process in the slow ecology of the
stars, it'll take a few centuries more.

I cashed in my investments and bought a house in rural British Columbia. Fled the city for reasons I preferred not to consider.

The night sky is dark here, the stars as close as the rooftop and the tall pines—but I seldom look at the sky.

When I do, I focus my telescope on the moon. It seems to me that sparks of light are gathering and moving in the Reiner Gamma area of Oceanus Procellarum. Faintly, almost furtively. Look for yourself. But there's been nothing in the journals about it. So it might be an optical illusion. Or my imagination.

The imagination is also a place where things live.

I'm alone.

It gets cold here in winter.

Robin called once. She said she'd tracked down my new number, that she wanted to talk. She had broken up with Roger. Whatever had happened that night in the city, she said, it was finished now. Life goes on.

Life goes on.

She said she got lonely these days, and maybe she understood how it was for me, out there looking at the sky while everyone else sleeps.

(And maybe the watchman sees something coming, Robin, something large and terrible and indistinct in the darkness, but he knows he can't stop it and he can't wake anyone up. . . .)

She said we weren't finished. She said she wanted to see me. She had a little money, she said, and she wanted to fly out. Please, she said. Please, Michael. Please.

God help me, I hung up the phone.

THE INNER INNER CITY

"Invent a religion," John Carver said, and for the first time I really took notice of him.

It wasn't the invitation. All of us in the group had been asked to do stranger things. It was the way he said it. I had pegged Carver as one of those affluent post-grads perfectly content to while away a decade in a focusless quest for a Ph.D., one of the krill of the academic ocean. He would float until he was swallowed . . . by the final onus of a degree, by an ambitious woman, by his own aimlessness. In the meantime he was charming enough company.

But he posed his challenge with an insouciance and an air of mischief that took me by surprise. He perched on the arm of the leather recliner and looked straight at me, though there were fifteen of us crowded into the living room. He wore casually expensive clothes, tailored jeans and a pastel sweatshirt, the sort of items whose brand names I felt I was expected to recognize, though I never did. His face was lean and handsome. Not blandly handsome—aggressively handsome. He looked, not like a rapist, but like the sort of actor who would be cast as one in an afternoon drama.

Deirdre Frank peered at him through the multiplying lenses of her enormous eyeglasses. "What kind of religion? *Any* kind of religion?"

"A new religious doctrine," Carver said, "or dogma, article of faith, heresy, occultism, cosmology. Original in its elements. Submissions marked on a ten-point sliding scale, we all mark each other, and in the event of a tie I cast the deciding vote." All this was as usual. "Are we game?"

Someone had to go first. In this case it was Michelle, my wife. She opened the carved-basswood jewelery box we kept for the occasion and slipped a hundred-dollar bill inside. "I'm in," she said. "But it's a toughie, John."

In the end we all anted up, even Chuck Byrnie, the tweedy atheist from the U. of T. chemistry department, though he grumbled before committing himself. "Somewhat unfair. More in Deirdre's line than mine."

Most of us were faculty. Deirdre was our chief exception. She had no credentials but an arts degree, class of '68, and a long perambulation through Toronto's evolving fringe cultures: Yorkville, Rochdale, Harbord Street, Queen Street. She owned the Golden Bough Gem and Crystal Shoppe, where Michelle worked part-time. She was perhaps the paradigm of the aging hippie, gray-tressed and overweight, usually draped in a batiqued caftan or some other wildly inappropriate ethnic garb. But she wasn't stupid and she wasn't afraid to match egos with the rest of us. "Stop whining, Chuck. Even the physicists are mystics nowadays."

"You've read Mary Baker Eddy. You have an advantage."

"Oh? And where would you guys be without Roger Bacon? Admit it—all you science types are closet alchemists."

Fifteen hundred dollars in the kitty. Michelle locked the box in our safe, where it waited for a winner. Gatherings were held weekly, but the contest was quarterly. We had three months to play Christ, Buddha, Zoroaster. Winner take all.

The challenge sparked an evening's conversation, which was the purpose of it. What was religion, exactly, and where did you start? A new paganism or a new Christian heresy? Did UFOs count? ESP?

From these seeds would spring our ideas, and after tonight we wouldn't mention the subject again until the results were presented in November. It was our fifth year. The contest had started with a friendly wager between Michelle and a self-styled performance artist named Heather, something about whether Whitman was a better poet than Emerson. I had ended up refereeing the debate. Our Friday night social circle rendered final judgment, and we all enjoyed it so much (except Heather, who vanished soon thereafter) that we made it an institution, with rules: a Challenge, a Challenger, a hundred-dollar ante, judgment by tribunal. Challenges had ranged from the whimsical (rewrite your favorite fairy tale in the style of William Faulkner) to the grinding (explain the theory of relativity using words of one syllable, points for clarity and brevity). Our best pots had topped two thousand dollars.

Carver's challenge was . . . interesting, and I wondered what had prompted it. To my knowledge he had never shown much interest in religion or the occult. I remembered him from my course on the Romantics, blithely amused but hardly fascinated. Something Byronesque about him, I thought, but without the doomed intensity; say, Byron on Zoloft. Tonight he was animated and engaging, and I wondered what else I had missed about him.

Sometime past midnight I stepped out onto the balcony for a breath of air. We had lived in this apartment for ten years, Michelle and I. Central but a little north, seventeen stories up, southern exposure. The city scrolled away from us like a vast and intricate diagram, as indecipherable as the language of the Hittites. Lights dim as stars cut into the black vastness of Lake Ontario, all quivering in the rising remains of the heat of the day. Here was a religion, I thought. Here was my religion. My secret book, my Talmud.

I had known this about myself for a long time, my addiction to the obscure beauty of the city. For most of my life I had consoled myself in its contradictions, its austerities and its baroque recomplications. Here was the short answer to Carver's challenge. I would make a city religion. An urban occultism. Divination by cartography. Call it paracartography.

Carver came through the sliding door as if I had summoned him. His presence broke the mood, but I was excited enough to describe my notion to him. He smiled one of his odd and distant smiles. "Sounds promising. A sort of map . . ."

"A sacred map," I said.

"Sacred. Exactly. Very clever, Jeremy. In fact, I—"

He would have said more, but Michelle barged onto the balcony to regale him with some idea of her own. She had been reading too many of Deirdre's New Age tracts, or simply drinking too much; she was flushed and semicoherent, tugging Carver's sleeve as she talked, something about posttemporal deities, model worlds, gods from the end of time.

The party wound down around two. We gently hastened hence our last guest an hour later and went to bed without washing the dishes. Michelle was less feverish but still feeling the alcohol; she was impatient about making love. Drinking makes her eager, but I don't drink and have always found her occasional drunkenness an antiaphrodisiac; her breath smelled like a chem lab and she looked at me as if she wasn't quite sure who had tumbled into bed with her.

But she was still fundamentally beautiful, still the brash and intelligent woman I had married a dozen years ago, and if our climaxes that night drew us deeper into ourselves and farther from each other . . . well, here's a mystery I have never understood: ecstasy hates company.

One more thing I remember from that time. (And memory is the point of writing this.) We woke to breakfast among the ruins. Actually we took breakfast about eleven, on the balcony, because the weather had turned lovely and cool, and the sun came slantwise between the bars of the railing and warmed our feet. Michelle mimed a hangover but said she actually felt okay, just a little rueful. Wide sheepish grin. We turned our faces to the breeze and sipped orange juice. We didn't talk about the contest, except this:

"Carver's interesting," she said. "Funny, I never really noticed him before."

"You noticed him last night."

"Well, that's the point. He used to be so quiet."

Did he? He struck me as evasive, mercurial—the whole idea

of John Carver had become slippery. I wondered aloud who had brought him to the group.

Michelle looked at me curiously. "*You* did, genius. Last year sometime."

Was that possible? Carver had audited one of my classes— that was the first I saw of him—but afterward?

"A couple of meetings at Hart House," Michelle supplied. "He read your Coleridge book. Then you brought him to a Friday night and introduced him around. You said he was bright but a little withdrawn, sort of a lost puppy."

Funny thing to forget.

I let the challenge slide for a month or so. By daylight, it lost some of its charm. Labor Day passed, and I was obliged to untangle the annual knotted shoestring of schedules and lectures, the endless autumn minutiae. In what began as a half-gesture toward the contest, I took up walking again.

Not that I had ever completely abandoned it. By "walking" I mean long, late walks—walks without destination, often after midnight, sometimes until dawn. Compulsive as much as therapeutic. I lived in one of the few cities in North America where such urban wandering was less than mortally dangerous, and I had learned the places to avoid—the after-hours clubs, the hustlers' alleys, the needle parks.

All this, of course, constitutes suspicious behavior. Cops are apt to stop you and read your I.D. into their dashboard databanks. Young male steroid abusers from the suburbs on a gaybashing soiree might turn their attention your way. Some years ago a belligerent drunk had broken my jaw, for reasons known only to himself.

I think even Michelle wondered about these expeditions at first. I wouldn't have been the first dutiful husband with a secret career in the midnight toilet stalls. But that wasn't it. The only solace I wanted or needed was the solace of an empty street. It clears the mind and comforts the soul.

At least, it used to.

Walking took my mind off my work and turned it back toward

Carver's challenge. I was neither religious nor dogmatically atheistic—I had years ago shelved all those issues in a category marked "Unanswerable Questions," after which what more was there to say? I had been raised in a benign Anglicanism and had shed it without trauma. But I wasn't empty of the religious impulse. It's no secret that my fascination with the Romantic poets was equally a fascination with their opiated gnosticism, their sense of an *aeternitas* haunting every crag and glen.

What is perhaps strange is that the city gave me the same sensation. We contrast the urban and the natural, but that's a contemporary myth. We're animals, after all; our cities are organic products, fully as "natural" (whatever that word really means) as a termite hill or a rabbit warren. But how much more interesting: how much more complex, dressed in the intricacies and exfoliations of human culture, simple patterns iterated into infinite variation. And full of secrets, secrets beyond counting.

I think I had always known this. When I was seven years old and allowed to stay up to see *The Naked City* (intrigued even then by the title), the best part wasn't the melodrama but the opening credits, the ABC announcer's "There are a million stories in the Naked City," which I understood as a great and terrible truth.

So my religion of the city would have to unite the two domains, the gnostic and the urban. Paracartography implied the making of maps, city maps, a map of this city, but not an ordinary map; a map of the city's secret terrains, the city as perceived by a divine madman, streets rendered as ecstasies or purgatories; a map legible only at night, in the dark.

Too complex and senseless a piece of work, even with fifteen hundred dollars at stake, but I couldn't dismiss it, and wondered if some hint of the idea might be enough to take the pot.

I thought about it as I walked—one night a week, sometimes two, rarely three. I bought a pocket notebook in case of inspiration. I carried paracartography with me like a favorite paperback novel, always at the back of my mind waiting for a free hour or a tedious subway ride or, best of all, an evening's walk.

But the walks were still their own reward. Even after almost

a quarter century of periodic exploration there were still neigh-
borhoods and terrains that took me absolutely by surprise, and
surprise was the purpose and reward of the exercise: to come
around a corner and find some black and shadowed warehouse,
some abandoned railway siding, an angle of moonlight on a crumbling coal silo.

What I rediscovered that autumn was my ability to get lost.
Toronto is a forgiving city, essentially a gridwork of streets as
formal and uninspiring as its banks. Walk in any direction long
enough, you'll find a landmark or a familiar bus route. As a rule.
But the invention of paracartography exercised such trancelike
power that I was liable to walk without any sense of time or
direction and find myself, hours later, in a wholly new neighborhood, as if my feet had followed a map of their own.

Which was precisely what I wanted. Automatic pathfinding,
like automatic writing. How better to begin a paracartographic
survey?

The only trouble was that I began to look a little ragged at
work. Friends inquired about my health. I didn't feel the sleep
deprivation but I began to use drops to disguise the inevitable
red-eye. My best friends worried more than I thought appropriate.

One afternoon early in October I phoned Michelle to tell her
I'd be late, took transit to the Dundas subway station, transferred
to a streetcar and rode it east until I felt like getting off. Heady,
that first moment of freedom. The air was crisp, the sun was
about to set on the other side of the Don River Valley. I remember
a cheap meal, curry and fried bread at a Pakistani diner while I
watched the traffic through a steam-drenched window. Then out
again into the fresh night. I walked west, where the sky was still
faintly blue.

I remember the first evening star over the Armory; I remember
amber streetlights reflected in the barred and dusty windows of
Church Street pawnshops; I remember the sound of my own footsteps on empty sidewalks. . . .

But memory falters (more often now), and apart from a general sensation of cold and uncertainty, the next thing I remember

is finding myself in full daylight, about a half block from Deirdre's gem shop.

According to my watch it was after ten, a sunny Saturday morning. There was no place I had to be. But Michelle might be worried. I stopped by the shop to use the phone.

Deirdre was at the back, hanging dream-catchers from the pegboard ceiling. Kathy, her other part-timer, lounged behind the counter looking impatient. "Morning, Dr. Singer," she trilled.

Deirdre looked down from her stepladder. "Hey, Jeremy. Geez, look at you. Been eroding the shoe leather again?"

"It shows?"

"Sort of a Bataan Death March look . . ."

"Tactful as ever. Mind if I call Michelle?"

"My guest."

Michelle was relieved to hear from me, said she hadn't been worried but would I be home for lunch? I told her I would and put the phone back under the counter.

"Don't sneak off," Deirdre said. "Kathy can mind the store a while. Buy me coffee."

I said I could spare half an hour.

She stopped at a hardware store across the street and bought a box of houseplant fertilizer. "For the ladies?" I asked.

"The ladies."

Deirdre's "ladies" were the female marijuana plants she grew in her basement. If Deirdre trusted you, she'd tell you about her garden. I had seen it once, a fragrant emerald oasis tucked into the cupboard under the stairs and illuminated with a football-sized halide bulb. She grew cannabis for her own use and to my knowledge never sold any, though Deirdre was so customarily level-headed and so seldom publicly stoned that I wondered what exactly she used it *for*. She was a pothead but not a social pothead; she kept her intoxications to herself.

We bought coffee at a Starbucks and took a window table. Deirdre gulped her her double latte and frowned at me. "You really do look like shit, Jeremy. And you don't smell much better."

Half-moons of sweat under my arms. I was aware of my own stink, the low-tide smell of too much exercise on a cold night. My thighs ached and my feet were throbbing. I admitted I might have overdone it a little.

"So where'd you go?"

"Started out across the Don, ended up here."

"That's not an all-night walk."

"I took the scenic route."

"And saw—?"

I realized I didn't have an answer. An image flitted past my mind's eye, of a gray street, gray flagstone storefronts, shuttered second-story windows, but the memory was sepia-toned, faded, fading. "Shadows on a cavern wall," I said.

"What?"

"Plato."

"You're so fucked up sometimes." She paused. "Listen, Jeremy, is everything okay between you and Michelle?"

"Me and Michelle? Why do you ask?"

"That's an evasion. Why do I ask? I ask because I'm a nosy old lady who can't mind her own business. Also because I'm your friend."

"Has she said something?"

"No. Nothing at all. It's just—"

"Just what?"

She drummed her fingers on the table. "If I say it's a hunch, that doesn't cut much ice, huh?"

"If it's a hunch, Deirdre, I'd say thanks for thinking of us, but your hunch is wrong. We're fine."

"There's something that happens to married people. They lose track of each other. Everything's routine, you know, dinner and TV and bed, but meanwhile they're sailing separate boats, spiritually I mean. Until one of 'em wakes up alone, going, 'What the fuck?' "

"Thank you, Dr. Ruth."

"Well, okay." The last half of her coffee chased the first. "So are you writing another book?"

"What?"

"That little notepad sticking out of your pocket. And your pen's starting to leak, there, Jeremy."

I grabbed the ballpoint out of my pocket, but the shirt was going to be a casualty. As for the notebook, I began to tell Deirdre how I kept it around for inspiration regarding the Challenge, but it was empty so fan . . . except it *wasn't* empty.

"Good part of a book right there," Deirdre said, watching me flip through the pages.

Every page was filled. The handwriting was tiny and cramped, but it looked like my own.

Only one problem. I couldn't read a word.

Here the question becomes: Why didn't I see a doctor?

It wouldn't have helped, of course, but I didn't know that then. And I had read enough pop-medical books to realize that the combination of periodic fugues and graphomania spelled big trouble, at least potentially.

Nor was I afraid of doctors. In my forty-one years I had made it through an appendectomy, a kidney stone, and two impacted wisdom teeth. No big deal.

Of course a brain tumor would have been a big deal, but the idea of talking to a doctor didn't even occur to me; it was beyond the pale, unnecessary, absurd. What had happened was not a medical but a metaphysical mystery. I think it half delighted me.

And half terrified me. But the terror was metaphysical too. If this discontinuity was not imaginary then it must be external, which implied that I had crossed a real boundary, that I had stepped at least a little distance into the land beyond the mirror.

In short, I didn't think about it rationally.

But I did think about it. Come November, I thought about it almost constantly.

The details of a descent into obsession are familiar enough. I came to believe in my own psychological invulnerability even as friends began to ask delicately whether I might not want to "see someone." I let my work slide. Missed lectures. I told myself I was achieving a valuable insight into the Romantic sensibility, and I suppose that was true; Novalis's hero eternally hunting his blue flower could hardly have been more single-minded.

Single-mindedly, I began to assemble my map.

I won't tell you how I did it. In any case there was no single method, only materials and intuition. I will say that I obtained the largest and most comprehensive survey map of the city I could find and then began to distort and overlay it according to my own perceptions, certain that each new deposit of ink and color, each Mylar transparency, was not obscuring the city but revealing it— the occult, the hidden city.

I kept the work private, but we all did in a Challenge; even Michelle and I were competing for that fifteen hundred dollars (though the money was the least of my considerations). She didn't mention temporal deities to me. And although she knew something had gone awry—for one thing, our sex life suffered— she said very little. Humoring me, I thought. The good and faithful wife. But she didn't have to speak; I read a volume of recrimination in her frowns and silences, and there were moments when I hated her for it.

"You realize," Deirdre said, "he's fucking us over."

November had come in on the last breath of autumn, sunny and warm. Deirdre had shown up early for our Friday night, the night we judged the Challenge. Michelle was busy in the kitchen. I sat with Deirdre on the balcony, the fragile heat of the day evaporating fast.

Deirdre wore XL denim bib overalls and a baseball cap turned sideways. She took a joint from the grimy deeps of her purse and held it up. "Mind?"

"Not at all."

"Want to share?"

"No, thanks."

She hunted for a lighter. "We don't even know who he is or where he comes from."

She was talking about John Carver. "He's been shy about his past, true."

"He's not shy about anything, Jeremy. Haven't you figured that out? If there's something he hasn't told us, it's 'cause he doesn't want us to know.".

"That's a little harsh."

"Watch him tonight. He's the center of attention. We huddle at his feet like he's Socrates or something, and people forget it wasn't always like that. Better yet, keep your eyes off Carver and look at the crowd. It's like hypnotism, what he does. He radiates this power, this very deliberate sexual thing, and it pins people. I mean, they don't blink!"

"He's charismatic."

"I guess so. Up to a point. I don't get it, myself. And he does not welcome criticism, our Mr. Carver."

"He doesn't?"

She lit the joint and exhaled a wisp of piney smoke. "Try it and see."

If I had been less concerned with my map I might have paid Deirdre closer attention. But I was nervous. Now that the map was about to become public it began to seem doomed, chimerical, stupid. I considered forfeiting the prize money and keeping my obsession to myself.

More guests arrived. The group was slightly diminished lately. A few regulars had dropped out. There were seven of us present when we took up the Challenge.

Each participant was allowed ten minutes in which to convince the others he or she deserved the prize. Showmanship counted. The contest was graded point-wise and we were scrupulously fair; it benefited no one to deliberately mark down the competition—and we were honorable people, even with fifteen hundred dollars at stake.

I forget who went first. Some ideas were novel, some half-hearted. Ellie Cochrane, one of Chuck Byrnie's students, proposed a sort of techno-divination, reading the future in blank-channel TV noise. Ted Fishbeinder, an Arts Department teaching assistant, did a funny riff on "esthetic precognition," in which, for instance, the Surrealist movement represented a "psychic plagiarism" of contemporary rock videos.

Then it was Michelle's turn.

She used more than her allotted time, but nobody said a word. We were astonished. Myself most of all. Michelle wasn't much of a public speaker, and her part in previous Challenges had always been low-key. But this Challenge was different.

She spoke with a steady, articulate passion, and her eyes were fixed on Carver throughout.

Suppose, she said—and this is the best recollection I can muster—suppose that sentient creatures become their own God. That is, suppose God is human intellect at the end of time, a kind of teleological white hole in which consciousness engulfs the universe that created it. And suppose, furthermore, that the flow of time is not unidirectional. Information may be extracted from the past, or the past re-created in the body of God. Might not our freshly created supreme being (or beings) reach back into human history and commit miracles?

But take it another step, Michelle said: Suppose the teleological gods want to re-create history in miniature, to rerun each consecutive moment of universal history as a sort of goldfish bowl at the end of the universe.

Would we know, if *we* were such a simulation? Probably not . . . but there might be clues, Michelle said, and she enumerated a few. (Physics, she said, asks us to believe in a discontinuous quantum-level universe that actually makes more sense if interpreted as information—a "digital" universe, hence infinitely simulatable . . . or already a simulation!)

And there was much more, speculation on teleological entities, the multiple nature of God, wars in Heaven—but memory fails.

I do remember John Carver returning her stare, the silent communication that seemed to pass between them. Mentor and student, I thought. Maybe he'd helped her with this.

When she finished, we all took a deep breath. Chuck Byrnie murmured, "We seem to have a winner." There was scattered applause.

It was a tough act to follow. I let Michelle dash to the kitchen before I screwed up my courage and brought out the map—poor feeble thing it now seemed. A round of drinks, then the crowd gathered. I stumbled through an explanation of paracartography that sounded incoherent even to me, and then I displayed the map, by this time a thickly layered palimpsest of acetate and rainbow-colored acrylic paints and cryptic keys legible only to myself. Nobody reacted visibly to it, but for me the map was a silent reassurance, pleasant to stand next to, like a fire on a cold night. Maybe no one else sensed its power, but I did. I felt the promise of its unfollowed and hidden avenues, the scrolls of spiritual code concealed in its deeps.

The map, I thought, would speak for itself.

Eventually Chuck Byrnie averted his eyes from it. "Enterprising," he said. "More art than map. Still, it's quite wonderful, Jeremy. You should be proud. But why is it empty at the center?"

"Eh?" The question took me by surprise.

"I mean to say, why is it blank in the middle? I can see how it bears a certain relationship to the city, and those arteries or veins, there, might be streets . . . but it seems odd, to have left such a hole in the middle."

No one objected. Everybody seemed to think this was a reasonable question.

I stared at the map. Squinted at the map. But try as I might, I couldn't see "a hole in the middle." The map was continuous, a single seamless thing.

I felt suddenly queasy. He waited for an answer, frowning.

"Terra incognita," I said breathlessly. "Here there be tygers, Chuck."

"I see."

I didn't.

Deirdre was the last contestant, and we were all a little tired. Midnight passed. Michelle had brought out the basswood box, and it rested on the coffee table waiting for a winner, but it had ceased to be the centerpiece of the evening.

Chuck Byrnie yawned.

Deirdre wouldn't win the prize, and I think we all knew it. But this wasn't only pro forma. Watch Carver, she had said. And I did: I watched Carver watch Deirdre. He watched her fiercely.

No one else seemed to notice (and I know the obvious is often invisible), but the expression on his face looked like hatred, hatred pure as distilled vitriol. For a moment I had the terrifying feeling that an animal was loose in the room. Something subtle and vicious and quick.

Deirdre said, "I think we should reconsider the history of divine intervention."

She looked frail, I thought, for all her twenty or thirty excess pounds, her apparent solidity. Her eyes were bright, nervous. She looked like prey.

Every culture, she said, has a folk tradition of alien visitations. Think of Pan, the *sidhe*, Conan Doyle's fairies, Terence McKenna's "machine elves," or any of the thousands of North American men and women who fervently and passionately believe they've been abducted by almond-eyed space creatures.

It isn't a pretty history, Deirdre said. Look at it dispassionately. Much as we might want to believe in benign or enlightened spirits, what do these creatures do? Kidnap people, rape women, mutilate cattle, substitute changelings for human infants, cast lives into disarray. They mislead and they torture.

If these creatures are not wholly imaginary, Deirdre said, then we should regard them as dangerous. Also sadistic, petty, lascivious, and very powerful. However seductive they might sometimes seem, they're clearly hostile and ought to be resisted in any way possible.

Carver said, "That seems a little glib. What do you suppose these creatures want from us? What's in it for them, Deirdre?"

"I can't imagine. Maybe they're Michelle's 'temporal deities'— half-gods, with the kind of mentality that delights in picking wings off flies. There's a sexual component in most of these stories. Sex and cruelty."

"They sound more human than divine."

"I think we're a playground for them. They inhabit a much larger world. We're an anthill, as far as they're concerned."

"But why the hatred?"

"Even an ant can bite."

"Time's up," Chuck Byrnie said.

"Thank you, Deirdre," John Carver said. "Very insightful. Let's tally the votes."

There's a city inside the city—the city at the center of the map.

I couldn't see the hole in the map because for me there was no hole: the gap closed when I looked at it, or else the most important part of the map was invisible to anyone but myself.

And that made sense. What I had failed to understand was that paracartography must necessarily be a private matter. My map isn't your map. The ideal paracartographical map charts not a territory but a mind, or at least it merges the two: the inner inner city.

Michelle took the prize. She seemed less pleased with the money than with John Carver's obvious approval.

Deirdre took me aside as the evening ended. "Jeremy."

"Mm?"

"Are you blind or just stupid?"

"Do I get another choice?"

"I'm serious." She sighed. "There's something in you, Jeremy, something a little lost and obsessive, and he found that—he dug it out of you like digging a stone out of the ground. He used it, and he's still using it. It amuses him to watch us screw around with these scary ideas like little kids playing with blasting caps."

"Deirdre, I don't need a lecture."

"What you need is a wake-up call. Ah, hell, Jeremy. . . . This is not the kind of news I love to deliver, but it's obvious she's sleeping with him. Please think about it."

I stared at her. Then I said, "Time to leave, Deirdre."

"It matters to me what happens to you guys."

"Just go."

Michelle went wordlessly to bed.

I couldn't sleep.

I sat on the balcony under a duvet, watching the city. At half-past three, the peak (or valley) of the night, I thought I saw the city itself in all its luminous grids begin subtly to shift, to move without moving, to part and make a passage where none had been.

I closed my aching eyes and went inside. The map was waiting for me.

My department head suggested a sabbatical. She also suggested I consult a mental health specialist.

I took the time off, gratefully. It was convenient to be able to sleep during the day.

There is a city inside the city, but the road there is tortuous and strange.

I glimpsed that city for the first time in December, late on a cold night.

I was tired. I'd come a long way. The lost city was not, at first sight, distinctly different. It possessed, if anything, a haunting familiarity, and only gradually did I wake to its strangeness and charm.

I found myself on an empty street of two-or three-story brick buildings. The buildings looked at least sixty or seventy years old, though the capstones had no dates. The brick was gray and ancient, the upper-story windows shuttered and dark. Remnants of Depression era advertising clung to the walls like scabs.

The storefronts weren't barred. Cracks laced the window glass. The goods dimly visible behind the panes were generic, neglected, carelessly heaped together: pyramids of patent leather shoes or racks of paperback books in various languages. The businesses were marginal, tobacco shops or junk shops or shops that sold back-issue magazines or canned food without labels. Their tattered awnings rattled in the wind.

It sounds dreary, but it wasn't, at least not in my eyes; it was a small magic, this inexplicable neighborhood glazed with December moonlight, chill and perfect as a black pearl. It should not have existed. Didn't exist. I couldn't place it in any customary part of the city nor could I discern any obvious landmarks (the CN Tower, the bank buildings). Streets parted and met again like the meanders of a slow river, and the horizon was perpetually hidden.

The only light brighter than the winter moon came from an all-hours coffee shop at a corner bereft of street signs. The air inside was moist but still cold. Two men in dowdy overcoats sat huddled over a faded Formica tabletop. Behind the cash counter, a middle-aged woman in a hairnet looked at me blankly.

"Coffee," I said, and she poured a cup, and I took it. It didn't occur to me to pay, and she didn't ask.

Things work differently at the heart of the heart of the city.

And yet it was familiar. It ached with memory. I'd been here before, sometime outside the reasonable discourse of history.

I took my notebook from my jacket pocket. Maybe this was where I had invented my ideoglyphs, or where the invisible city had generated them, somehow, itself. I flipped open the notepad and was only mildly surprised to find the words suddenly, crisply legible. This did not astonish me—I was past that—but I read the contents with close attention.

Every page was a love letter. Concise, nostalgic, sad, sincere, my own. And every page was addressed to Michelle.

Finding my way home was difficult. The hidden city encloses itself. There are no parallel lines in the hidden city. Streets cross themselves at false intersections. There are, I think, many identical streets, the peeling Edwardian town houses and bare maples layered like fossil shale. I don't know how long it took to find my way back, nor could I say just where the border lay or when I passed it, but by dawn I found myself on a pedestrian bridge where the railway tracks run south from Dundas, among the warehouses and empty coal-dust factories of the city as it should be.

I checked my pocket, but the notebook was gone.

Most of the universe is invisible—invisible in the sense of unseen, unexperienced. The deserts of Mars, the barrens of Mercury, the surfaces of a million unnamed planets, places where time passes, where a rock might tumble from a cliffside or a glacier calve into a lifeless sea, invisibly. Did you walk to work today, or take a walk after dinner? Everyday things are rendered or remain invisible: the mailbox you passed (where is it exactly?), the crack in the sidewalk, the sign in the window, this morning's breakfast.

I think I didn't see Michelle. I think I hadn't seen her for a long time.

Have I described her? I want to. I can't. What memory loses is invisible; it evaporates into the desert of the unseen universe.

I'm writing this for her. For you.

Michelle wasn't home when I looked for her. That might have been normal or it might not. I had lost track of the days of the week. I went to look for her at Deirdre's store.

Winter now, skies like blue lead, a brisk and painful wind. The wind ran in fitful rivers down Bay Street and lifted scrap newspapers high above gold-mirrored windows.

The store was closed, but I saw Deirdre moving in the dim space inside. She unlocked the door when I tapped.

"You look—" she said.

"Like shit. I know. You don't look too good yourself, Deirdre."

She looked, in fact, frightened and sleepless.

"I think he's after me, Jeremy."

"Who, Carver?"

"Of course Carver."

She pulled me inside and closed the door. Wind rattled the glass. The herbal reek of the store was overpowering.

Deirdre unfolded a director's chair for me, and we sat in the prism light of her window crystals. "I followed him," she said.

"You did what?"

"Does that surprise you? Of course I followed him. I thought it was about time we knew something about John Carver, since he seems to know more than enough about us. Did he ever tell you where he lives?"

"He must have."

"You remember what he said?"

"No. . . ."

"No one remembers. Or else it didn't occur to them to ask. Don't you find that a little odd?"

"Maybe a little."

"Turns out he lives in the Beaches, out near the water-treatment plant. Here, I'll write down the address."

"That's not necessary."

"The fuck it's not necessary. Information about John Carver has this interesting way of disappearing."

"I came here to ask you about Michelle."

"I know."

She scrawled the address on the back of a register receipt. "And Jeremy, one more thing."

"What?"

"Be careful of him. He's not human."

Don't be ridiculous, I began to say, but the words stuck. In the realm of what was possible and what was not, I had lost all compass. "Do you really believe that?"

"I've spent a lot of time reading the strange books, Jeremy, and talking to the strange people. It's hard to believe in hidden information in the information age, but there are still some mysteries that haven't made the Internet. Trust me on this."

"What should I do?"

She looked away, ashamed of her impotence. "I don't know."

Long story short: I went home; Michelle hadn't shown up, nor did she come home that night.

I didn't sleep. I watched TV, and when that was finished I watched the minute hand sweep the face of Michelle's bedroom clock. Michelle didn't believe in digital clocks—hated them. The only digital clock in the apartment was the one on my wrist. She believed time ran in circles.

I fell asleep at dawn and woke to find daylight already fading, snow on the windowsill, snow falling in sheets and ribbons over the city. No Michelle.

I tried phoning Deirdre. There was no answer at the store or at her home number.

Then I remembered the address she had scrawled for me— John Carver's address.

I was in my jacket and headed for the door when the phone rang.

"Jeremy?"

Deirdre, and she sounded breathless. "Where are you?"

"Doesn't matter. Jeremy, don't try to get hold of me after this."

"Why not?"

"They busted my garden! Raided the store, too—on principle, I guess."

"The police?"

"It wasn't the fucking Girl Guides!"

"You're in custody?"

"Hell no. I was having lunch with Chuck Byrnie when it happened. Kathy managed to warn me off." She paused. "I guess I'm a wanted criminal. I don't know what they do to you for growing grass anymore. Jail or a fine or what. But they trashed my house, Jeremy, and my place of business, and I can't afford legal fees." She sounded near tears.

"You can stay here," I said.

"No, I can't. The thing is, only half a dozen people knew about the garden. Somebody must have tipped the police."

"I swear I never—"

"Not *you*, asshole!"

"Carver?"

"I never told him about the plants. Somebody else must have."

The wind scoured grains of snow against the balcony door, a sandpaper sound.

"You're saying Michelle—"

"I'm not pissed at Michelle. It comes down to John Carver, and that's why I called. He means business, and he isn't pleased with me. Or you."

"You can't be sure of that."

"I can't be sure of anything. I think he's been manipulating us from the word go."

"Deirdre—"

"My advice? Throw that fucking map away. And good luck, Jeremy."

"How can I reach you?"

"You can't. But thanks."

———

Time passes differently in the secret city.

Day follows night, sunlight sweeps the sundial streets, seasons pass, but the past eats itself and the future is the present, only less so. We pace the sidewalks, we few citizens of this underpopulated city, empty of appetite, wordless, but how many others are keeping secret diaries? Or keeping the same diary endlessly rewritten, stories worn smooth with the telling.

I took a last look at the map. The map was mounted on a pressboard frame leaning against the wall of my study.

The map was sleek, seductive, and inexpressibly beautiful, but I didn't need it anymore. It had never been more than a tool. I didn't need the map because I contained it—I *was* the map, in some sense; and it would be dangerous, I thought, to leave so potent a self-portrait where strangers might find it.

So I destroyed it. I carved it into pieces, like a penitent debtor destroying a credit card, and then I pushed the pieces down the garbage chute.

Then I went to look for Michelle.

What Michelle hadn't said, what Michelle hadn't guessed and Deirdre hadn't figured out, was that a temporal deity, even a minor and malevolent one, must own *all* the maps, all the ordinary and the hidden maps, all the blueprints and bibles and Baedekers of all the places there are or might be or have ever been.

I took the Queen car east. The scrap of paper on which Deirdre had written Carver's address was in my pocket, more out than in, really, since I felt compelled to check it and check it again as the streetcar stuttered past the racetrack, the waterworks. The numbers were elusive.

The address was well off the transit routes. What I found when I approached on foot was an ordinary Beaches neighborhood, snow-silent and still. The houses were fashionable restored freeholds above the frozen lakeshore, a few lights still burning in second-and third-story bedroom windows. Carver's was no different. I wondered whether he owned it or rented it, whether money had ever been a problem for him. I doubted it.

And now what: Should I knock on the door and demand to see Michelle? What if she wasn't there? What if Deirdre and I had drawn all the wrong conclusions? I stood in the snow feeling useless and foolish.

Then—I presume not coincidentally—Carver's door opened, and I stepped behind a snowbound hedge as he came smiling into the night with Michelle on his arm.

She wore her navy winter coat with the collar turned up. She looked cold and bewildered, both very young and very old. Carver wore jeans and a flannel shirt, and the snow seemed not to touch him.

I blinked, and they were at the end of the block.

I called Michelle's name. She didn't look back—only inclined her head as if an errant thought had troubled her.

There was nothing to do but follow them.

He turned corners I had never seen before. Narrow alleys, a corridor of trees in an empty park, a wood-paved ravine walk dense with swirling snow.

I ran, they strolled, but the gap between us widened until Michelle was a distant figure, vague among the snow-spirals, and Carver—

John Carver, I believe, began to grow translucent, not-quite-invisible, became a gap in the falling snow that might have been a human shape or something taller, more agile, sleek, potent, pleased.

At last he turned and looked directly at me. I felt but couldn't see his smile. His eyes, even at this distance, were distinctly yellow.

He folded his arm around Michelle as if claiming a trophy and turned a corner I have never been able to find.

I suppose it had been a sort of contest all along.

That was the last I saw of her.

The invisible city seals its exits. Enter once and walk away. Enter twice and the way back to the world is more elusive.

Enter a third time—

———

I walked for hours—it might have been days—but every road turned back to those elliptical streets and jigsaw alleys.

Only a few of us live in the secret city, and we seldom speak. Things work differently here. It is, I think, a sort of mirror world, an empty and imperfect shell of a city, sparsely colonized.

Its shabbily furnished upper rooms are mainly empty. I live in one now. I sleep on its crude spring mattress and I gaze through its grime-crusted windows and I breathe its dry and dust-heavy air. I eat what I find in unattended stores. Canned food without labels. The stock is periodically replenished. I don't know how.

Something in the hidden city inhibits curiosity, and memory. . . .

Memory fades into the air like morning fog.

I write to remember. I write in these lined tablets of cheap pulp paper manufactured in Taiwan or Indonesia, places incomprehensibly far away.

I think I'm not the only one. I think there are others scribing their thin and thinning memoirs, diary entries that grow more stark with every passing day, letters to lovers whose names we have forgotten.

Spring now. The wind is cold, wet, cutting.

I do not despair of finding a way home. Just yesterday I thought I saw Deirdre in the street, looking for me, perhaps; but if she's found the hidden city, she needs to be warned.

I called her name, but she vanished.

If you find this, will you warn her?

And if you know Michelle, if you see Michelle, please give her these pages.

I mail the pages from my window. I mail them on the wind. As yesterday. As the day before. On a good day the wind carries the yellow leaves of paper up above the stone capitals and pebbled roofs, above the tarpaper and the wind vanes and the chimneys of the city, and I hope and believe that for the wind there are no borders. The wind, I think, is wholly invisible and utterly free.

THE OBSERVER

I've never told anyone this story. I wouldn't be telling it now, I suppose, except that—they're back.

They're back, after almost fifty years, and although I don't know what that means, I suspect it means I ought to find a voice. Find an audience.

They won't confirm or deny, of course. They are, as ever, enigmatic. They do not speak. They only watch.

I was fourteen years old when my father decided to send me to spend the summer of 1953 with my uncle, Carter Lansing, an astronomer at the then-new and marvelous Mt. Palomar Observatory in California.

The visit was billed as therapy, which I suppose is why Carter agreed to suffer the company of a nervous teenage girl for two consecutive months. The prospect, for me, was both exhilarating and intimidating.

Exhilarating because—well, it must be hard to imagine what plush iconography was contained in that word, "California," at the dawn of the 1950s. I was a Toronto girl in the age of Toronto the Good; I had passed a childhood in chilly cinderblock schools where the King's (and lately the young Queen's) portrait gazed stonily from every wall, in the age of Orange parades and war privation and the solemn politics of nation-building. I knew the names of Wilfred Laurier and Louis Riel. My idea of a beach was the gray pebbled lakeshore at Sunnyside. Oatmeal breakfasts and snowsuits: *that* Toronto.

California, I understood, was somewhere between New York City and Xanadu. I had seen its picture, in *Life* or at the movies. Blue Kodak seashores, breezy palmettos, Spanish missions with terra-cotta tiles; William Randolph Hearst bathing with movie stars in Venetian mosaic pools.

It was intimidating for much the same reason. I had trouble imagining my awkward and pasty-white body tucked into its one-piece bathing suit and salmon-pink rubber cap for a frolic on the sands of Malibu. Surely everyone would laugh?

And intimidating because of my uncle Carter, the family celebrity. The smart brother, my father called him. Carter had attended MIT on a scholarship. Carter had been tutored by the famous, had excelled, had been groomed for his ascension into the elite of the astronomical community. His picture had been in *Time* magazine, smiling, handsome, the opposite of the neurasthenic cartoon "scientist," a young and vital genius. He knew Igor Stravinsky; he knew the Huxleys.

Whereas my father managed a branch-plant greeting card business entombed in a Leaside industrial park.

So there was the daunting possibility that Carter had agreed to take me as an act of noblesse oblige: some restorative Altadina air for a crazy Canadian niece. For the girl who sees monsters. The girl who floats through walls.

He met me at the airport, unmistakable in his leather flying jacket and sunglasses. We said hello, and that was about all we said during the long ride that followed, apart from a brief session of how-are-you, how's-the-family. I was dazed by the overnight flight but fascinated by the passing landscape. California was much browner than I expected, much drier and dustier, more provisional, like something under construction. The earthmovers and oil wells outnumbered the palms.

At least until we climbed into the hills where Carter lived. Here the houses were painted in pastel colors, the lawns immaculate and gleaming. Automatic sprinklers gushed rainbows into the vertical sunshine. Dwarf palms shaded cool, arched doorways. We parked at last, and Carter carried my luggage into his house, which was clean-smelling and carpeted and quiet as some ancient arboretum.

"This is your room," he said, dropping my suitcases. It was a small room, spare, the bed merely functional, but a palace as far as I was concerned. The window looked out on the garden; the heads of bird-of-paradise poked over the sill, Picasso birds with a dab of sap for an eye. The air smelled warm and somehow safe, somehow forgiving.

I asked, "Does the window lock?"

Carter's smile faded abruptly. "It locks," he said, "but you might want to leave it open a crack these summer nights. There's jasmine in the garden. Smells good."

"But it locks—the window *does* lock."

He sighed. "Yes, Sandra, it locks."

I thought at first they couldn't find me, that I had evaded them.

"Them." *They* or *them*—I had no other words. We didn't talk about "the grays" in those days, as we do now, when every encounter is shoehorned into the typology of the standard abduction scenario. I had no name for them, for the same reason children in those times referred to their genitals as "thing" or "down there." Code words for the unspeakable.

Because events happened to me that were impossible, and because I described these events in great detail, I had been taken to doctors, who called me "nervous and imaginative" and wrote referrals. So I'd learned the painful equation. Talk + diagnosis = punishment. I was tired of my mother taking the blame. (My mother died when I was ten years old, and I was supposed to resent her for dying, but I didn't; I only missed her.) I was tired of my father's obstinate, stony disbelief, his dutiful mustering of a sympathy he clearly didn't feel.

And I was tired of the nights, the fear. Let California wash all that away, I thought. Smother it with eucalyptus musk and bury it in cypress shade. Take me a few degrees closer to the warm equator. Show me some southern stars. Let me look into the sky at night and not be afraid.

Days passed. I was alone more often than not, but never

lonely. The sunshine was blissfully exhausting. And sleep was sweet, at least for a while.

"I'm having some friends over," my uncle announced.

Late July. We had fallen into a fixed routine that suited us both, Carter and I. We ate dinner each night at eight, an impeccable meal prepared by Evangeline, Carter's housekeeper. Tonight was no exception. In the last weeks I had seen more of Evangeline than of my uncle. Evangeline was a large black woman with a personal dignity as imposing as her waistline. I thought she liked me more than she liked Carter, but Evangeline's true feelings were hard to divine.

She put a bowl of peas on the table, gave me an inscrutable look, turned back to the kitchen. Carter wore his making-conversation-with-Sandra expression, as if he wanted credit for his fabulous patience.

"That sounds nice," I ventured.

"The thing is, Sandra, it's more or less an adults-only affair."

I wasn't especially disappointed. I had figured out how it was with Carter Lansing. He didn't dislike me, but he had no common ground with a teenage girl. Nor did he care to develop any. When I was forced to beg a ride to the drugstore to buy sanitary pads, he had turned chalk-white and treated me like an invalid.

(Years later I would learn that my uncle was gay and that my visit had doubtless put a crimp in his social life, and that everyone knew this fact about him save myself. Had I known, I might have understood. Or perhaps not: I was in some ways exactly as conventional as he expected me to be.)

A gathering of Carter's adult friends. How tedious, I thought. "I'll lock myself in my room. Listen to the radio."

"No need to lock yourself in anywhere, Sandra. I'm just afraid you'll be bored. It's a pretty stuffy group, actually."

"I'm sure you're right."

He was completely wrong.

In the morning I wrote in my pocket diary:

Another night. No sign of THEM. Am I FREE AT LAST?

Don't be misled. I *admired* my uncle. I envied his work.

I had read about the observatory on Mt. Palomar; I knew more about it than I admitted to Carter. (Sensing that this aloof god would not appreciate my worship.)

The Hale Observatory was new, the freshest and finest outpost on the frontier of human knowledge. It housed the first 200-inch telescope, the Big Eye, a monument to contemporary technology. Designed and built at Cal Tech, it had been wheeled up the mountain—insured for six hundred thousand dollars by Lloyds of London—in 1947, just six years ago, and it was formally dedicated to George Ellery Hale in 1948. At the dedication ceremony, a Cal Tech trustee had read *"Benedicite, Omnia Opera Domini"* from the Book of Common Prayer, and it must have seemed appropriate: the telescope would look deeper into the heavens than anything before it, some five hundred million light-years deeper.

And at the helm of that telescope (encased, most nights, high up the barrel of the device like a dove in a dovecote, in heated clothing) was Edwin Hubble, the aging astronomer who had scaled the expansion of the universe, who had peered into the most ancient history of the sky.

I met Edwin Hubble at my uncle's party.

Palomar drew celebrities, and there were celebrities at the house that night, though I didn't recognize them. I spent most of the evening in the kitchen with Evangeline, helping her spread sturgeon roe over crackers for the guests. We held our noses and shared our amazement that intelligent adults would eat such trash. And while Evangeline served the guests, I peered at the action through the crack of the kitchen door.

She caught me looking.

"That's a funny bunch," she said when the door was safely closed and we were alone again. "That half-blind Englishmen with the big glasses and pretty little mouth, that's Mr. Huxley. A book writer."

Aldous Huxley! I said I knew the name. Secretly, I was thrilled—authors!—but I let Evangeline think I was unimpressed. (Perhaps she wasn't altogether fooled.)

"The mannish-looking woman is his wife. That old man with the foreign accent? Name of Stravinsky. Writes music. The little bitty lady in the easy chair? Anita Loos. And the gray-haired gentleman, that's Mr. Edwin Hubble himself. Just back from England."

I knew about Hubble, too.

I had done the kind of reading my teachers called "precocious." This was the Hubble who was charting the universe, calculating the volume of infinity; the Hubble of the red shift, the expanding-universe Hubble.

He didn't look at all like a scientist. He looked like an aging athlete—which he also happened to be. (He played basketball and football in school and won letters. He still liked to fish and hike, though he had suffered a debilitating heart attack in 1949.) He smoked a plain black pipe, which rode in his solid jaw like a prosthetic device, and he looked as stern and unforgiving as a high school vice-principal.

I opened the kitchen door wider.

Evangeline's eyes widened with it. "Best not go in there, honey."

"It'll be okay, Evangeline."

I appeared in the midst of this mixed-drink-driven crowd like, I suppose, the unwelcome ghost of vulgar America, in my Capri pants, my gull-wing glasses, my hideous braces. Conversation stopped.

Carter rushed to introduce me, but I saw the indignation in his eyes. "This is Sandra," he said, "my niece. She's staying with me for the summer. If you're looking for food, Sandra, there's plenty in the kitchen."

"Nonsense," announced a strong, high-pitched voice. Here was Anita Loos, author of *Gentlemen Prefer Blondes*, posed in an easy chair like a cynical munchkin. "Sandra—it *is* Sandra, isn't it?—don't let Carter chase you away so soon. My God, a niece. Of all things."

I thanked Miss Loos but walked directly to Hubble, who was at the window gazing down into the Hollywood lights, pipe in hand.

"Dr. Hubble," I said.

He turned and looked at me, glanced unhappily at Carter, then offered his huge hand.

I took it eagerly. "You discovered the expanding universe," I said.

"Well, not quite."

"But you know more about it than anyone else."

"Did your uncle tell you that?"

"No."

"No? Are you interested in astronomy?"

"Kind of."

Wrong answer. He nodded dismissively and turned away. The window opened on a constellation of city lights. Los Angeles, a city Huxley had once called "the great Metrollopis of the West."

"The universe is expanding," I said, "but there's no center. Wherever you are, that's the center. Here or a million light-years away, wherever there's an observer, he's at the center of the universe."

Hubble turned back. I had his attention again. He frowned at me. "Yes?"

"Is that right?"

"More or less."

"Well, I don't understand. Everything I've read talks about an observer. The observer is at the center of the universe. But what's an *observer*, exactly? Why is an *observer* at the center of the universe?"

He exhaled a great blue cloud of smoke into the jasmine-scented air.

"Bring a chair," he said. "Let's talk."

We talked, solemnly, intently, until Hubble's wife, Grace, came to drag him back to the party. Carter looked daggers at me from across the room.

But then Hubble turned back and said the words that left me breathless:

"You must visit Palomar," he said. "You must see the telescope."

That night they came again.

The party was over. The house was silent and quite dark. I woke and was motionless, not only paralyzed but suspended—it seemed to me—between the tickings of the clock. The sense of helplessness, of vulnerability, was absolute. Moonlight shone through the window, and I remember dust motes hovering in that pearly light like weightless diamonds.

They were all around me—maybe a dozen of them, gathered around the bed.

Huge, their eyes. Black, and unblinking, and sad.

A great part of the terror resides in those eyes. Powerful, these creatures, to come through walls, to move so silently, to immobilize their victims, float them perhaps into shining spaces, probe their bodies with the casual indifference of a woman rummaging in her purse for a lost key. . . .

But their eyes are so sad!

To all the obvious questions—what are they, what do they want, why me?—there was no answer but that ferocious and hungry nostalgia, the sadness of their eyes.

By daylight I might wonder: Are they sad for themselves? Or are they, somehow, sorry for *me*? But at night the questions are wordless, moot. That night in California they took me nowhere, only gazed at me, their huge heads bobbing, their eyes, all pupil, sad and frank as a child's eyes.

I could only lie motionless in bed and draw weak, stertorous breaths. I was afraid they would take me away with them, to the place that clouds memory, to the palace of unbearable light.

But they only peered at me until suddenly they were gone, and I could draw my breath at last and scream, scream until Carter burst into the room, scream until he put his hand against my cheek and said in wide-eyed wonder, "Sandra! My God! Sandra!"

In modern quantum physics, as well as in astronomy, there is an entity called "the observer." Seldom defined, "the observer" hovers over the textbooks like a restless ghost. An electron is a particle or a wave, depending on "the observer." "The observer" collapses the wave function. "The observer" turns future into past, makes history of possibility.

But what's an observer? It was the question I had posed to Hubble, the question that still nags, even now, so many years later. What is an observer? Where do observers come from?

A week later Carter drove me to Palomar, up the breathless heights of the mountain.

Hubble had made the arrangements. Carter's own feelings about the visit were mixed. He didn't have enough seniority at the Hale to bring in a tourist—an adolescent girl, of all things—and he was still afraid I would embarrass him or, worse, annoy Edwin Hubble himself. At the same time, I had already attracted positive attention: not a bad thing.

He had been treating me with a little more respect since the party, though my occasional night terrors continued to frighten him.

(Join the club, I thought.)

We drove up the steepening slope along black asphalt switchbacks, even stopped for lunch at the Palomar Gardens, a restaurant halfway to the Hale Observatory. It was owned, I later learned, by George Adamski, an amateur astronomer and publicity-seeker who would later author a flock of books about "flying saucers" and his implausible adventures therein. Watch the skies.

"He doesn't like children, you know," Carter said, talking about Hubble over cheeseburgers at the Gardens. "Keeps to himself. Likes to fly-fish, for Christ's sake. You know he was hit by lightning?"

"Really?"

"He was out in the woods somewhere, probably with his boots in the water and a fishing rod over his head. They say his heart nearly stopped. Some say he hasn't been the same since."

I think this was meant to intimidate me, but it only succeeded in making Hubble seem more vulnerable, more like myself. Maybe I'd been struck by lightning too; maybe that's what was wrong with me.

We drove on to the observatory. The staff treated me like visiting royalty, gave me the tour. Palomar was about as romantic as an industrial plant, with the exception of the telescope itself, a heroic act of engineering, a five-hundred-ton machine floating on a skin of pressurized oil. The horseshoe mount was so immense it had been shipped to California from Westinghouse by way of the Panama Canal. The mirror, hidden in a steel iris like the bud of a night-blooming flower, had been the subject of bomb threats—it had been trucked up the mountain under police guard, to protect it from lunatics who believed the sky would open and rain fiery vengeance if stripped of all its secrets.

I looked a long time at the elevator that lifted an astronomer up to the observation perch, imagined Hubble disappearing into the throat of this grand and terrifying creation.

Of Hubble himself there was no sign, until I was escorted to a long trestle table in a concrete chamber where the staff took meals. He was there, alone, all furrowed brows, sketching on a paper napkin. I learned later that his presence was something of a novelty. The altitude was supposed to be bad for his heart. He hadn't been up the mountain for months, and his first telescope run in nearly a year was scheduled for September.

I sat down and drank Coke from a chilled bottle while he showed me what he'd drawn: a single dense much-penciled O at the center of the paper.

"O for Observer," he said.

"And the napkin is the universe?"

"The observable universe. Here at the edge, farthest from the observer, the red shift becomes infinite." He peppered the napkin with dots. "These are stars. But here is the observer's dilemma, Miss Lansing. He occupies the center of the observable universe, which is bounded by its own primordial past." He tapped the napkin. "From the observer's point of view, what part of the universe is the oldest?"

The speed of light is finite. Most of the stars the observer sees are younger than his own sun, younger still the more distant they are. A star ten thousand light-years distant is ten thousand years closer to the beginning of the universe, ten thousand years less old than the observer's own space. So I tapped the dot in the middle.

"Precisely! Here at the edge is the youngest universe, perhaps the universe moments after its birth. The past. While here at the very center is . . . the present. So where on this map, Miss Lansing, do we find the future?"

I shrugged.

"Not shown," he said. "Very good. And yet, time passes. The universe expands. It *emanates*. The future, not yet existent, emerges from this point, this absolute spaceless point. . . ."

"From the observer?"

"From the observer as a spaceless point in his own subjective universe."

"From me?"

"From any observer."

I thought about it. "From my eyes? From my brain?"

He smiled quizzically and shrugged.

I was dazed by the idea of time radiating from my skull like the lightning bolts from the RKO radio tower at the beginning of certain movies. The future was deep inside me. But I could only see the past: my eyes looked out, not in.

I thought about it while Hubble ate his lunch, taking delicate spoonfuls of soup.

"Does the universe expand," I asked, "or does the observer shrink?"

He smiled again. "The statements are commutable. It amounts to the same thing."

We shrink into the future, collapse into it. Nowadays people talk about black holes, singularities. The observer collapses into his own singularity, shrinking away from the universe at large.

I said, "If there was such a thing as a time machine—"

"If there was such a thing as a time machine, you would be able to pop out of your own skull and look at yourself."

I didn't want to imagine it. Too frightening.

"You're a very bright girl," the famous astronomer told me.

"Thank you."

"A very astute observer."

He lit his pipe. I blushed.

The night terrors abated but didn't stop. What did ebb, and quite quickly, was my uncle's patience.

I don't blame him. He had surrendered enough to me that summer: his privacy, his social life. But I stopped calling him at night, smothered my screams, clammed up at the breakfast table, because I couldn't bear the weight of his impatience. His impatience was obvious and caustic; it erased the glow of Hubble's approval and cast me back on my own troubled past.

He left me alone more often. Usually Evangeline was in the house, and on rare occasions we were allowed to borrow the car. We saw Hollywood, Sunset Boulevard, the pier at Santa Monica. Mostly, though, I wandered through the house while Evangeline worked in the kitchen. I watched KTLA from Mt. Wilson on my uncle's TV set, played Sinatra on his hi-fi rig, raided his library. (I read Huxley's *The Perennial Philosophy* and *Beyond the Mexique Bay* and understood neither.) At lunch I assembled mile-high sandwiches and took them into the backyard, sequestered myself under an acacia tree with a magazine or just let the California sunshine make me drowsy.

My father phoned once a week. I told him I was having a great time. Had "the problem" come back? No, I said, and I don't think Carter contradicted me.

And by my own impoverished standards I *was* having a good time. "The problem" was at least in remission. Perhaps I was lulled into susceptibility.

I think Carter was lulled, too. I think that's why he left me alone in the house that August night.

Carter was an astronomer on a day schedule. Most of his work involved the tedious comparison of photographic plates, and I think he chafed at his junior status at Palomar. He must have needed a night life, God knows; if not with the stars then with the constellations of human bodies at certain clubs along the Sunset Strip.

But he left me alone, and even after fifty years I find it difficult to forgive him.

He called an hour after Evangeline had served dinner and driven herself home, and though there was still plenty of daylight, the sun was westering; the shadows were longer, and I had begun to feel nervous. On the phone he sounded strange, maybe a little drunk. He wouldn't be back until tomorrow, he said, and would I be all right?

And what could I say to that? I wanted to beg him not to leave me alone, but that would have been abject, cowardly. So I said I would be okay, probably, and hoped the quaver in my voice would communicate some of the terror I was feeling. But he didn't hear it, or didn't choose to hear it. He thanked me lugubriously and hung up the phone. And that was that.

What do you do in an empty house, when you're alone and you don't want to be?

The obvious things. I turned on all the lights, plus the TV set. Messed up the kitchen making popcorn. Watched *All-Star Revue* and *Your Show of Shows* and *Hit Parade*, by which time it was eleven o'clock and the street outside was quiet and I could hear crickets in the garden and the nervous whisper of my own breath. I stayed up later, smoked one of Carter's cigarettes and tried to enjoy a Charlie Chan movie but dozed in spite of myself. I remember deciding that I really truly ought to go to bed, but that was as far as I got. I slept on the sofa with my head on a velveteen cushion. And woke again, and the house was still ablaze with light, but my watch said it was two A.M., and the television was all snow and static, radio noise, cosmic rays, random electrons. I turned it off.

I remember thinking I should have closed the window blinds, that the house would be more secure that way. I stood up, yawned, and went to the big picture window. Outside, the date palms danced in a fierce, dry midnight wind, a Santa Ana wind. No human life was visible.

I tried to think of something nice, something comforting. I called up the memory of Hubble, of Hubble telling me I was "a bright girl." But that only reminded me of our conversation, which had been, to tell the truth, a little creepy. The universe was expanding, or I was shrinking, "the statements are commutable," and the future was inside me, and what if I could look in that direction?

What would I see, if I could turn my eyes inside out?

I would see the future into which I was dwindling. A blackness as illimitable as death, a dark consuming nothingness.

Or would it be full of stars?

Or would it be a looking-glass world, like Alice's: deceptively familiar, except for. . . .

For what?

And then I heard a noise from the kitchen.

The wind had blown open the back door. I closed it and locked it. If Carter had forgotten his keys, he could pound on the door. Maybe I'd let him in. Maybe I wouldn't.

I turned at a suggestion of a shift in the light, and saw—

(The words are impotent. Powerless.)

Saw one of *them*.

It came through the wall. This was the kitchen wall where Carter had hung a Monet print and where Evangeline kept, lower down, a rack of hanging copper pans. It came through all these things without disturbing them, though one of the pans bumped gently against its neighbor as if a breeze had touched it. The creature was indifferent, gray, only a little taller than myself. For a moment, I stared transfixed. It moved through the wall as if against a trivial resistance, like a man walking through surf. Then it was wholly in the room, and its head rotated in an oiled motion, and its vast black deep sad eyes locked on mine.

I drew a breath but didn't scream. Who would hear?

Instead I ran from the kitchen.

Not that there was anywhere to go, any safer place. Maybe I could have fled the house altogether, but if I opened the big front door what might be waiting outside? The night was too large; it would swallow me.

The visitor didn't instantly follow me into the living room, and that gave me a space to think, although the house was suddenly full of minor, deeply ominous noises. I wanted tools, weapons, barricades. But there was only my uncle's black telephone and, next to it, his Rolodex of personal numbers.

To my credit, I did the sanest thing first: I called Evangeline's number. There was no answer. Evangeline had found somewhere to go this Saturday night, or else she was a very deep sleeper.

I thought about dialing the operator and asking for the police—I could say I'd seen a prowler—but I knew the police would come and listen with dreary patience and tell me to lock the doors, and then I'd be alone again.

From the direction of the bedroom I heard a rustling sound, the sound of leaves in autumn, restless mice, cat's claws on glass.

I had reached the state of calm that borders on panic, when thoughts are crisp and weightless and nerves light up like neon tubes. I flipped through the Rolodex again, found Edwin Hubble's home number and dialed with a trembling finger.

Grace answered after seven rings. She was in no mood to comfort a frightened teenage girl. Nor would she put her husband on: "This is completely inappropriate, Sandra, and I'm sure your uncle would agree," and I was about to give up and run, just run, when Hubble's deep voice displaced hers: "Sandra? What's wrong?"

Suddenly it seemed possible the whole thing had been a humiliating mistake. I had dreamed the monster in the kitchen. And even if not, what could I tell the stern and unforgiving Edwin Hubble, how could I enlist his sympathy for what he would almost certainly consider an adolescent fantasy?

But I needed someone in the house. Above all else, that.

I mumbled something about my uncle being away and "there's something wrong here, and I'm sorry, but I don't know what to do, and there's no one else I can call!"

"What sort of problem?"

Big silence. I listened for monsters. "It's hard to explain."

I think he heard in my voice what Carter hadn't: the sweaty tremolo of fear.

Miraculously, he said he'd be right over. (I heard Grace protesting in the background.)

"Thank you," I said.

And put down the phone reluctantly. No voice now but my own. The house all echos and shadows and stubborn clocks.

I was in a frenzy of embarrassment when, some twenty minutes later, Hubble's big Ford pulled into the driveway. The kitchen was empty: I asked Hubble to look, and then I looked myself.

We didn't talk about what I thought I had seen, or if we did it was only in the most indirect, delicate way. He seemed to know without being told. I wondered if Carter had already briefed him on "my problem."

He cased the house, and then we sat at opposite ends of my uncle's long living room sofa. I asked him whether he was ever scared, perched in his supernaturally powerful telescope at the top of a mountain and staring into the bottomless deeps of space.

He smiled. "You know, Edith Sitwell once asked me the same thing. I was showing her some photographic plates. Galaxies millions of light-years distant. It terrified her. The immensity of it. To be such a mote, less than dust among the stars. To see oneself from that perspective."

I had no idea who Edith Sitwell was. (An English writer; she had been in Hollywood to consult on a script about Anne Boleyn.) "What did you tell her?"

"That it's only terrifying at first. After a time you learn to take comfort from it. If we're nothing, then there's nothing to be frightened of. The stars are indifferent."

The words were not especially soothing, but his presence was. Even at the end of his life, Hubble was still the former athlete, six-foot-two, almost two hundred pounds. A guardian, powerful and benign. I wondered why he had come so willingly. He was supposed to despise children and he had little sympathy for weakness.

I wonder now if he was suddenly conscious of his own mortality. He must have known he was nearing the end of his life. This visit might have been the random kindness of a dying man. Or maybe he just missed late nights, mysteries, the hours before sunrise. Maybe he'd been away from the telescope for too long.

Certainly he remembered what it was like to be alone and afraid. He told me about a summer job he'd held when he was seventeen ("Only three years older than you!"), working with a survey crew in northern Wisconsin, trekking into what was then a virgin forest. He talked about the campfires and canvas tents and sextants and the way the sky opened like a book in the silence of the great woods. "Sometimes," he admitted, "I saw things. . . ."

"What kind of things?"

But he wouldn't say. He changed the subject. "Time for bed," he told me. "Past time."

"But you'll be here?"

"I'll be here. It won't be the first dawn I've seen, you know, Sandra."

I slept while Edwin Hubble kept watch for me.

I slept in the dark, and woke to a harsh and terrible light.

The palace of light.

Should I call it a flying saucer? An unidentified object? I don't know if it's either of those things; I've never seen it objectively, as a sky-ship, a vehicle, though there have been accounts (and I do recognize the details) in which people describe it that way. Still, the words trivialize the experience. Was I taken up into a "flying saucer"? Surely not; surely it wasn't one of those silver-domed art-deco totems from the cover of *Fate* magazine.

No, it was . . . the palace of light.

The palace of light.

I was taken up through the beams and tiles of the house, lifted above the roof in a slow delirium of terror, and then I was in the palace of light. I had been here before, but every visit is as fresh and terrifying as the first. The light was soulless, sullen, and everywhere at once. It hurt my eyes. They gathered around me, a dozen or more; they turned their sad and quizzical eyes on me, queried my body with probes and syringes of solid light.

The ordeal was endless, worse because there seemed to be no malevolence in it, only a bland curiosity. And of course the sadness. I wondered: Why don't they weep?

This time, though, the experience was different. My body was paralyzed, my eyes were not, and when I looked to my left I was astonished to see Edwin Hubble next to me on a pedestal of shadows, equally helpless, equally bound and paralyzed. But his eyes were open.

I remember that. His eyes were wide open, and he seemed . . . not afraid.

He seemed almost at home with these creatures, with their sadness and their curiosity.

But I was not. I closed my eyes and prayed for dawn, begged for unconsciousness, begged for a door back into my daylight life.

When I woke, Edwin Hubble had gone.

What woke me was the sound of the front door. It was Carter, home from the night's revels. The window was full of sunshine and fresh with the smell of jasmine and acacia and a few warm ions from the distant sea.

I spent the day in a frenzy of apprehension. Hubble would say something to Carter, lodge a complaint; I would be disgraced, humiliated, sent home to another round of psychiatric torture.

But I don't think Carter ever found out Hubble had visited that night; or if he did, he was too ashamed to make an issue of it. He was the one who had been AWOL, after all. I was only a child.

But I don't think he knew. When he came home from Palomar the next day he was as incommunicative as ever.

And I was, as ever, frightened of the dark. . . .

But here is the strange fact: *they didn't come back*.

Not that night, or the night after, or any other night in California or in the decades since.

(Except lately. . . .)

They didn't come back. I had lost them, somehow. I had learned to evade them.

I had learned not to let my eyes turn inside out.

I didn't see Edwin Hubble again that summer—not until the last day (the last hour, in fact) of my visit.

It was a Saturday, end of August. Uncle Carter drove me to the airport. I sat in the passenger seat of the car whispering a silent good-bye to the dwarf palms and the tindery hills and the bobbing duck-billed oil rigs. We arrived at the terminal half an hour early.

I was astonished—though less astonished, I think, than Carter—when Edwin Hubble met us at the luggage check-in, gave us a wide grin, and steered us into the lunch counter while we waited for my flight to be called.

Hubble said he hoped I had enjoyed my stay and my visit to the Hale Observatory. Pleasantries all around, but there wasn't really much to say or time to say it. At last my bewildered uncle excused himself and lined up for a second cup of coffee.

And I sat at the table with the famous astronomer.

He touched his finger to his lips: I was not to speak.

"If you look into the uncreated world," he said quietly, "it looks back at you. Maybe you think, why me? How did they find me? But it's a mirror world, Sandra. Maybe they didn't find you. Maybe you found them."

"But—!"

"*Shh*. It isn't wise to speak about this. You have a knack for turning your eyes inside out, so you see them. And they see you. And you're afraid, because they're from the uncreated future, from a place, I think, where the human race has reached its last incarnation, from the end of the material world. Perhaps the end of all worlds. And they're sad—melancholy is the better word—because you're like an angel to them, the angel of the past, the angel of infinite possibility. Possibility lost. The road not taken."

My uncle was heading back to the table, too soon, with tepid black coffee in a waxed-paper cup.

Suddenly I wanted to cry. "I don't understand!"

Hubble touched his lips again. He was solemn. "One doesn't have to understand in order to look. One has to look, in order to understand."

Carter stood beside the table glancing between the old astronomer and myself. "They're calling your flight," he said. "Did I miss something?"

Edwin Hubble died that autumn, still making plans for the Hale Observatory, still probing the limits and implications of the red shift. He suffered a fatal heart attack at the end of September— the twenty-seventh, if I recall correctly. He had been on the mountain for the first time in many weeks, making long photographic exposures of NGC 520, and he was looking forward to another run. I cried when I heard the news.

My uncle continued his career in astronomy, eventually left Palomar for a tenured position at Cal Tech. He died, too, prematurely, halfway through Reagan's second term.

George Adamski, who owned the diner up the mountain, went on to publish several accounts of gaudy flying-saucer jaunts around the solar system. Crank books, clearly, though I sometimes wonder what prompted his change of career.

Aldous Huxley, whom I had met briefly at my uncle's party, experimented with mescaline and wrote *The Doors of Perception*, his own inquiry into what he called "the antipodes of the mind." His book dwells at length on light, the quality of light, the intensity of light. He died of throat cancer on November 22, 1963, the day John F. Kennedy was shot.

And I went back to Toronto, finished school, left home, married a petroleum chemist, raised two children, and nursed my beloved husband through his own long struggle with cancer.

I live alone now, in a world 1953 might not recognize as its linear descendant. The multiethnic, information-intensive, post-industrial present day. The Great Metrollopis of the World. The world is full of frightening things.

But I am not afraid to look at what I see.

———

Lately they have come back.

They have come back, or, Hubble might say, I have gone back to them.

There is no explanation. They are the perennially anticlimactic, the ever-unknown. The world expands, or I am shrinking, and sometimes my less than 20/20 vision turns inside out, and in the long nights I see them moving through the walls. I have even visited the palace of light, and the palace of light is as terrible and enigmatic as ever.

And they are as sad as ever, their eyes more poignant than I remembered, but—is it possible?—they seem, in their alien fashion, somehow pleased with me.

Pleased, I think, because I'm not afraid of them anymore.

I look, in order to understand. The understanding is elusive, but I suppose it will come, perhaps at the moment I reach the final dwindling point, the event-horizon of my own life, when the universe expands to infinity . . . and will they be there?

Waiting?

I don't know. I understand so very little. But I am not afraid to look: I am a good observer at last. My eyes are open, and I am not afraid.

PROTOCOLS OF CONSUMPTION

The question, now as always: Do I belong here?

F-wing invites doubt. You're never quite alone in F-wing, but it's not a place anyone actually belongs. There are no waiting rooms in F-wing, just these barely upholstered chairs scattered along the hallway. Not much in the way of magazines, either. I'd learned to buy my own at the hospital gift shop. *Time, Newsweek*: barricades of choice for the antisocial outpatient. But when I saw Mikey Winston barrelling toward me with all the blind momentum of a runaway tractor-trailer, I knew with that no mere magazine would daunt him.

I didn't know his name at that point. He was only vaguely familiar, a face I'd seen somewhere, not here. Mikey waddled along the corridor in a striped T-shirt that didn't quite meet the waist of his thrift-shop trousers, trouser cuffs turned up over tattered low-top Nikes. Fixed grin, pig-narrow eyes, a high forehead merging into black hair that ran in strings to his dandruff-dusted shoulders. Gray teeth, not a complete set. He found the chair next to me.

"Meds?" he asked.

I put down *Time*. "Pardon me?"

His voice had the penetrating power of a veterinary syringe. "You're here for Dr. Koate, right? Tuesday group, right? New guy?"

All those things, Heaven help me.

"So," he said, "what meds are you on?"

I wasn't prepared for this frontal assault. I made the mistake of answering him. "Lithium," I admitted.

"Just lithium?"

Yeah, just. Babe in the woods, me.

"So you're, uh, bipolar?"

"Uh-huh."

"That's nothing much. That's no big deal. I've done Librium, Elavil, Prozac, Paxil . . . a couple of anxiolytics for a while . . . Tofranil for years, but I hated it. Made me sweat. Now I'm on the new one."

"The new one?"

"Thallin. You gotta know about that. New one. Hey, I recognize you," he said.

"Do you?"

"Yeah. What's your name?"

"Zale," I said. "Bob Zale."

"Zeal. Laze."

"What?"

"Anagrams. Zale. Mix up the letters, you know, like the Jumble cartoon in the newspaper. You're on the mailbox!"

"Mailbox?"

"In the lobby. We live in the same building. That's where I saw you."

Come to think of it, that was where I'd seen Mikey: a gnome on the stairway, forging his way through drifts of cigarette butts to the lobby mailbox. I live in a four-story brick apartment building on a busy street near Sunnybrook Hospital, the sort of building that houses single mothers, immigrants working night shifts, recluses, marginal cases of all sorts. My new fraternity.

Mikey introduced himself. "I'm at the other end of the basement! B-13! We're neighbors!"

I was less than overjoyed.

Dr. Koate thought group would be good for me, so I was invited to her biweekly 10 A.M. with a half dozen of the walking wounded. I won't dwell on this. Suffice to say that I was introduced to Estelle, of the Thorazine twitch and raw-chewed fingers; Mikey, obsessive-compulsive and subject to schizophrenic interludes; Daniel, who had been arrested while masturbating during the New Year's Eve celebration at Nathan Philips Square, which must have been a chilly exercise; Kip, a reformed heroin addict and incompletely reformed paranoid, age eighteen; and two other women so pathologically withdrawn that I never did learn their names.

Dr. Elizabeth Koate sat in the midst of this zoo, her smile as unflagging as her blouse was neatly pressed. No lab coats in F-wing. We're all just folks here. Actually, I admired Dr. Koate's unshakable calm, her lucid and benevolent presence. I often wondered what it cost her, in emotional terms. Did she go home at night and bite the cat?

She introduced me to the group, or rather encouraged me to introduce myself. I ran down the salient facts. Thirty years old, newly single, ex-electrical-engineer (ex-several-things by now), suffering a bipolar "mood disorder," as I've been encouraged to think of it, probably since adolescence but only lately diagnosed.

Estelle, the finger-chewer, asked what had finally brought me to therapy.

Every human instinct resists these confessions. Anyway, it was a tricky question. Where do you start? The money wasted senselessly, the suicidal impulses, the drinking binges, the failed marriage?

"My daughter," I said finally.

Dr. Koate gave me a meaningful and gently interested look. "Your daughter told you to go into therapy?"

"No. I went into therapy when I figured out that my daughter was afraid of me."

No further questions.

Dr. Koate asked Mikey how he was responding to his meds. He glowed at the attention. Six months on Thallin, our Mikey, and liking it. "It's not heavy. It doesn't load down the body. Less pushy than Prozac, and I'm not sleepy all the time."

And so around the circle. Prozac, Limbitrol, Elavil, Triavil; Thallin, Thallin, Thallin. I felt like a novice, a parvenu, with my simple chemical salt, though the list of potential side-effects ap-

pended to the small brown bottle of Lithotabs has a nicely ominous ring: dry mouth, blurred vision, loss of coordination; in a
worst-case scenario, blackouts, blurred speech, seizures, coma.

We psychonauts expect these hazards. They are the tigers in
our jungle, the anacondas of our private Amazon.

Naturally, Mikey didn't drive. Naturally, he begged a ride with
me. Rain came down in torrents, glazing the Sunnybrook parking
lot and making even a polite refusal impossible.

Mikey nestled into the passenger seat, exuding his own odd
chem-lab smell. Nervous at first, he entertained me by rearrang-
ing the letters on the traffic signs. (*"Pots! Texi!"*) Then, a gambit
on my part, we talked about the apartment building. I thought
of it as an affordable rat hole. Mikey claimed to like living there.

"Basement at the back," he said, "not bad, close to the laundry
room, storage, not bad. Close to the furnace. Warm in winter.
Not bad at all."

"The bugs don't bother you?"

"Bugs?"

"The ants."

"Oh, ants. Well, you know, *ants*—I don't mind 'em."

The building was a unique property. The problem wasn't cockroaches, though I had found one or two prospecting the bathroom walls, but ants. They boiled up from under the basement
floorboards, ignored all propriety, invaded shoes, clothing, sleeping bodies. I had reached a kind of armed truce by way of liberal
applications of Crack 'n Crevice Raid, which was probably con-
taminating my food and causing my testicles to shrink. I told
Mikey I'd complained to the superintendent. Mikey was unex-
pectedly upset.

"Mr. Saffka, Mr. Saffka, he won't do anything. Maybe put
down more roach powder in the halls. Make life difficult. Did
you *have* to complain?"

"Yeah, I think I did."

"Make life more difficult. I'll talk to them."

"Who, the ants?"

But Mikey didn't answer.

My ex-wife, Corinna, had been granted custody of my daughter, Emily in the divorce settlement. I hadn't contested the issue. I trusted Corinna, I didn't trust myself, and in any event I knew what the courts would make of a male parent with bad debts and a psychiatric condition.

I told Mikey good-bye and retreated to my own apartment—a "bachelor" apartment, or more accurately a closet with a toilet. There was e-mail from Em. Bless the Internet for letting me exchange these semaphores with my daughter, ions darting between two synapses in the World Brain. Em, twelve years old, had mastered the electronic mysteries. Her note was chatty and peppered with happy-face emoticons.

Her class had gone on a field trip to the Humber River Valley—one of those glorious late-May rock-turning expeditions, I gathered. Many and various were the small things that lived in the pitch-black riverside muck: water striders, mayflies, eggs and larvae and protozoa. Em was excited because she'd found a rock with the image of a trilobyte frozen in it. "It is even older than you, Dad! :-)"

The river of time, I told her in a return note, is the oldest river of all, rich with life. Em was my contribution to that river, my own ripple in the stream: I the sinking stone, Em the perfect golden wave shimmering in the sunlight.

(Dr. Koate calls this kind of thinking "fatalistic" and wants me to avoid it.)

We arranged to meet on the weekend, brunch at McDonald's and maybe a movie in the afternoon. Saturday was my regular day with Em. Lately she had stopped cringing at the sight of me, and for that thank Lithium, thank Dr. Koate, thank even Biweekly Group.

Which left only the evening to kill. Bless television, while we're counting our blessings. Television talks to you when there's no human voice but your own, when your own voice is an abusive whine that hums in your head like a dynamo. God bless lithium and Raid and cable TV, and God bless me, if I should wake before I die.

I work four days a week at a downtown used-book shop, shelving and stocking and making sales for the obese owner, who lives upstairs with his collection of brocaded smoking jackets and his Oscar Wilde first editions. His last employee had gone mad or fled to the wilds of British Columbia, depending on which version of the story he chose to tell. Either scenario had begun to seem plausible.

Holding a job means keeping regular hours, unfortunately. Mikey learned when to look for me in the building's tiny lobby. Usually I could forestall his hints and invitations with a wave or a complaint about how busy I was, perhaps the world's most pathetic lie. But Mikey had the doggedness of a true obsessive-compulsive.

I came home Thursday too tired to fend him off and accepted the offer of coffee at his apartment. "Good!" he exclaimed. "Hey, *fine!* Roll out the red carpet!"

Mikey may or may not have been capable of sarcasm—I've never been sure.

He turned the key in his lock—he had locked his apartment even for a stroll down the corridor—with all the pomp and circumstance of a bank president cracking a vault. A peculiar odor wafted out as he opened the door, the acrid smell of ancient laundry and unaired rooms, but under that a cloying sweetness, as if he had spilled a jar of honey once long ago. I drew a precautionary breath and stepped inside.

The obsessive-compulsive is doomed to display his mania. Mikey, at least, was an orderly O-C. The floor was naked parquet, the sofa and chair shabby but positioned symmetrically: I was certain the distance to each adjacent wall would match within a millimeter. There were no visible books except for a set of the *Encyclopaedia Britannica* in relentless order on a shelf.

And bugs. Insects, rather. Mikey was an amateur entomologist, or at least a bug collector. The specimens framed and mounted on the walls were nothing exotic, only what you might find on the streets any average summer: June bugs, ladybugs, cicadas; even cockroaches, centipedes, silverfish. Creatures more often scraped off the sole of the shoe than admired under glass.

But I admired them, or at least pretended to. Mikey, for once, was unresponsive, wouldn't talk about his collection, just measured coffee by the level teaspoonful into an immaculately washed percolator and whistled nervously to himself. When we sat down on his clean but ragged, ancient sofa all he wanted to talk about was Dr. Koate and the Group.

Mikey admired Dr. K. "She's a genius. Good with meds. Best meds of any doctor. You're still just doing lithium, right?"

"That's all I need, Mikey."

"Don't be so sure." He tapped his shining forehead. "Things hide. It's a complicated system. Serotonin, epinephrine, norepinephrine, dopamine: every brain cell like a gun with a thousand bullets, a thousand fingers on a thousand triggers. Brain cells talk in chemistry, did you know that?" His coffee cup rattled on his trembling knee. "Like insects. Pheromones. Hormones. Chemicals. The same way insects talk. Like in an anthill or a beehive, little chemical messages, it's the first kind of communication, the most basic."

"I'm okay with the lithium."

"An elementary salt."

"It gets the job done."

"Our problem is communication. A little Prozac, a little Thallin, it gets the cells talking. They communicate in new ways. Lithium just, you know, damps things down."

This was oppressive, and so was Mikey's apartment, its junkstore sterility and sealed windows, its dry and overheated air. "I have to go."

Mikey took my cup and placed it next to his on the kitchen counter, symmetrically.

"The whole earth is full of messages," he said brightly.

I watched an ant cross the countertop, probing our empty cups for whatever messages we had left there.

Picking up a daughter from the home of an estranged wife: always a comedy of humiliation.

Em was playing in the backyard when I arrived. Corinna took me into the kitchen. From the window I could see my daughter rolling her Barbie camper among the tall weeds by the fence.

"I'd like her back by four-thirty," Corinna said. "Early supper. And she has a Social Studies project due Monday."

"Okay," I said. "Sure." The difficult part about being a manic-depressive–in–remission is that one inhabits the ruins of a life. The lens of sanity is merciless. Around Corinna I was reduced to the role of a penitent, sin-stained and humbled and hair-shirted.

Corinna is a short, compact, dark-haired woman, an account-ant for a Bay Street firm, devastatingly good-looking when she isn't encased in her professional armor. She smiled, a good sign, and asked how I was doing.

"Even keel," I said.

"Still taking the lithium?"

"I don't think that's going to change."

"Is it still working for you?"

"More or less."

This was leading up to a confession. "I've been getting some counseling myself." There was a defiant note in her voice, as if she expected me to mock her for the decision. God help me, there might have been I time when I would have. (Seeing people flinch from me has become a mode of recognition, like seeing one's own face in a mirror.)

I said, "Does it help?"

"Well, I think so. I like my shrink. She wants me to consider medication."

"Medication?"

"Just an antidepressant. Prozac, probably, or Thallin. What do you think?"

I understood that she wanted an opinion from someone al-ready "on meds," an insider. I said, weakly, "Whatever works for you, Corinna. There's no guarantee with this sort of thing."

"No, I know. It's just been kind of hard lately, keeping every-thing together, with Em's school and all."

"Trouble at school?"

"She won't sit still. Talks over the teacher. Kid stuff, really, but the school nurse has been using the H-word. Hyperactivity. Or attention-deficit disorder."

"Em's not hyperactive."

"You get different manifestations of ADD. At least, that's what they tell me."

"She's just restless."

"She won't keep quiet in class, apparently."

Not my Em, I thought. My Em is a quiet, thoughtful little girl. Occasionally sullen, it's true, and sometimes moody . . . or maybe that's just the effect I have on her.

She picked up her Barbie camper and shook a dozen ladybugs out the back. They flew off like tourists evicted from a tour bus. Em looked at me brightly. "What movie are we seeing?"

We saw *James and the Giant Peach* at a review theater. Em had seen it on videotape, but she enjoyed the popcorn and the big-screen ambience. She laughed at the right places but seemed thoughtful, afterward, in the car. "Real bugs don't act like that," she said. "Well, I mean, of *course* they don't, but what they really do is a lot more interesting."

The combined physical weight of all the insects on earth, Em said, outweighed all other living things put together. "Think of all that," she said, "all hidden under the dirt or inside things. All those insects, talking to each other."

"They can talk?"

"To each other," Em said firmly. "Not like in the movie. They talk with chemicals."

The cell phone buzzed. Corinna, asking how we'd liked the movie.

I said we'd liked it fine.

"Good. Great. Listen, I know I said I wanted Em back early—"

"We're on the way."

"Well, would it be okay if you kept her little longer? For the evening, maybe?"

It took me a moment to work out the implication. "Date, Corinna?"

"Just a chance to get out of the house. I mean, if it's all right with you, if you don't have other plans."

"No plans. I'd be happy to spend an evening with Em. When do you want her back?"

"By ten, say? If I'm not here I'll have Natalie put her to bed."

"Natalie?"

"The teenager next door. Baby-sitter. Is ten all right?"

"Sounds fine."

Em was silent, listening.

Comes a time when coincidence is heaped upon coincidence until the mind screams: Pattern, for Christ's sake, there's a *pattern* here.

Maybe if I'd reached that point sooner—

No, that's bad thinking. Depressive thinking.

I have to be linear about this. Coherent. Objective.

I made dinner in my minuscule kitchen, hamburgers and baked potatoes for Em and I. While she waited for the food she cruised cable, finally abandoned the remote control and settled down with a Harry Potter book. Not my idea of hyperactivity, and are ADD kids usually such attentive readers?

She seemed to enjoy dinner, though she complained about the lack of ketchup. She went to the refrigerator for a Coke, took a glass from the cupboard, paused to inspect the bottle of Lithotabs I'd left on the counter. "Is this your medicine?"

"Yup."

"Looks different from mine."

"From yours? What medicine are you taking, pumpkin?"

"Ritalin. At school. Little round yellow pills."

Ritalin is the brand name for methylphenidate, a central nervous system stimulant often prescribed for kids with attention-deficit disorder. Helps the brain cells talk to each other, Mikey would have said. A talk-talk chemical. I was bothered by the idea of someone modifying my daughter's brain chemistry without my knowledge or permission, perhaps even without Corinna's. "I guess the school nurse gives you Ritalin?"

"Uh-huh."

"Did she clear this with Mom?"

"Yeah."

I sat at the table and regarded my daughter: her golden hair askew, her nails still dark with backyard dirt because she'd forgotten to wash her hands before dinner.

"So do you think the Ritalin helps?"

"I don't want to talk about it." She looked at me solemnly. "Can we rent a videotape tonight?"

Days passed. I quizzed Corinna about the Ritalin and she confessed to signing a permission form. "She takes a minimal dose, and it hasn't harmed her in any way. Helped, if anything. Her grades are up and her teacher has stopped complaining. If I notice any kind of side effect I'll take her off it, of course."

"You should have told me."

"I almost did—you know, when you came to pick her up."

"But?"

"But I wasn't sure how you'd react."

"I don't throw things anymore, Corinna."

"Old habits die hard."

Hers or mine? My emotional volatility or her conditioned flinch?

Either way, my fault. One night last year, unemployed, drunk, nearly suicidal, I had come home and demolished the kitchen. I broke bottles, trashed the microwave, threw a full jug of Javex through the French doors. Creating, of course, one of those memories that throbs periodically like an old war wound. Chilling forever any impulse Corinna might have once possessed to confide in me.

And frightening Em, who had stood in the kitchen doorway twisting her nightgown in her small fists, crying soundlessly.

I had described the scene to Dr. Koate a few months ago. Dr. Koate listened with barely a furrowing of her thoughtful brow. "Your remorse is appropriate," she had said. "But you mustn't let it lock you in place. Apologize and move on."

I appreciated Dr. Koate's advice, but what I really liked about her was her cool receptivity—her implacable, wise smile, as if she were privy to some ancient wisdom of the earth.

———

Mikey's fondness for Thallin began to fade. Coincidentally, up-beat stories about the drug were suddenly everywhere: newspa-pers, TV. It was the psychiatric miracle Prozac had only hinted at, an antidepressant that was also an anxiolytic and antipsy-chotic and reducing pill and sleep aid, and safer than salt. Your basic all-round medicine for melancholy.

But Mikey was backsliding, and that was obvious at the next Tuesday Group. He looked unhealthy and withdrawn. He hadn't washed his hair in recent memory; his skin was sallow, his teeth the color of weathered ivory. When Dr. Koate asked him how he was doing, he hesitated and then launched into one of his monologues.

"Whenever they find something new, something powerful, they always think it's medicine. But they're wrong."

"Who are *they*, Mikey?"

"Scientists. Doctors. Did you know, Dr. K., that when they brought back tobacco from the New World lots of Europeans thought it was a medicine? There was a guy invented a machine, he went around pumping tobacco smoke up the rear ends of the crowned heads of Europe. As medicine! That's a true story, you can look it up. And radium! That guy Kellogg, the corn flake guy, he had a sanatorium back at the turn of the century where he made people inhale radium gas, for a cure! But it's a force of nature, Christ, *radium*, it's atoms decaying, matter turning into energy, radiation, tumors, disease!"

"That was a long time ago, Mikey."

"They poured X rays into people's *feet*, just to figure out their *shoe size!*"

"Perhaps that's true, but—"

"But you think I should talk about me. But I am, Dr. K. This *is* about me."

"In what way, Mikey?"

He hung his head. "Thallin."

"Thallin isn't radium. It isn't radioactive."

"Not *just* Thallin. All those chemicals we dump all the time, dioxin, methporine, you get those frogs in Michigan with two heads or one eye or six legs, you get alligators in Florida with no testicles, you get birds dying out because their eggs are soft as

Jell-O. Because there's no such thing as just a chemical, Dr. K. I read all about this. The planet is talking to itself, the planet has been talking to itself for a million years, and chemicals are the language, and we keep dumping weird messages into the dirt, the rivers—into our own bodies!"

"Do you think the Thallin is bad for you?"

"That's not the problem!"

"Let's not shout at each other."

"Good, bad, that's not the *problem!* The problem is messages, don't you get it? All these chemicals are fake code, bad letters, words all scrambled up! If you could listen you'd hear trees talking, flowers, insects, they talk in chemicals as complicated as anything you can cook up in a laboratory, but we're killing their language, and it's *our* language, too, the oldest language, body language, and it's written in dopamine, serotonin, testosterone, estrogen, a million chemicals that don't even have names!"

"We could consider a different medication. That might be a good idea."

"You're not listening!"

"Maybe we should listen to each other, Mikey."

"Everything's talking to everything else, every chemical is a word or a sentence or a book, but what are we *saying*, Dr. Koate? Nobody knows—*that's* what scares me!"

Dr. Koate let a silence fall, a reverberant and calming silence. Then she spoke. "Mikey has concerns about his medication. Would anyone else like to share some thoughts on this?"

I left, as politely as possible, ahead of the other outpatients, made my way quickly down the F-wing corridor past the nursing station and the pastel watercolor prints in protective glass, past academic offprints posted on the bulletin board like souvenirs: *SSRI Interaction at 5-HTa Receptor Sites, Dopamine Depletion and Renal Function in Chronic Schizophrenia.* Past the pharmacy, auditorium, lunch cart, at last into the open air. Into a fine, early-summer noon.

Mikey somehow reached the car ahead of me.

"Zeal," he muttered. "Laze."

I groaned. "Need a ride, Mikey?"

"Okay."

He filled the car with the stink of his sweat-drenched clothing, acrid and terrible. Mikey wasn't shy about his pheromones. I rolled my window down. "Where'd you learn all that stuff, Mikey?"

"What stuff?"

"Hormones, chemicals, all that jazz."

"I can read," he said sullenly. Then: "First-year biology. The endocrine system. Plus stuff in the newspapers."

"You went to university?"

"For a year. I'm not stupid." He pouted like an infant. "I wasn't always like this."

And I understood that Mikey, in his lucid moments, knew that some terrible and debilitating condition had overtaken him, that he had fallen from the sunny aristocracy of the sane into that twilight world whose citizens might mumble or scream but seldom communicate. As if he had wandered into a hidden city of tenements and madhouses and couldn't find his way out.

(I know that city, Mikey. Look: Here are its windowless walls and towers, here's the rust-scabbed WELCOME sign, here are the mossy cobbles under my own weary feet.)

He was quiet for the rest of the ride, quiet until we pulled into the building's tiny parking lot. I parked and turned off the ignition. Mikey opened his door a crack, then paused and looked back at me.

"You be careful," he said. "Don't attract attention. Don't trust Dr. K—she's not what she seems. And tell Em to be careful, too."

"What?"

He shrugged and moved to leave the car.

"Mikey," I said. "Wait."

"Thanks for the ride and all—"

"Mikey. Get back in here and shut that fucking door."

He froze. "Don't yell at me."

"You said to tell Em to be careful."

"Yeah. . . ."

"Do you mean my daughter? Is that who you mean?"

"Emily. The little girl."

"I don't recall introducing you to Emily. I don't recall mentioning her name." In fact I kept those two worlds scrupulously separate: my family, Tuesday Group. I would never have mentioned Em to Mikey or vice versa. "How do you know Emily?"

"Maybe the ants told me."

"I don't want to hear that. No more crazy shit, Mikey: Are you spying on me?"

"Just tell her to be careful!" He sprang out of the car and then leaned back through the window, his hair hanging in strings across his brick-red face. His breath smelled like the air that wafts from trashcans on hot August afternoons. "I don't owe you anything, Mr. Fucking Big-Shot Zale!"

"Stay away from my family, Mikey."

"Fuck your family!"

He slammed the door and scurried away.

I phoned Corinna. No answer, but maybe she was still at work. I waited an hour, gazing vaguely at CNN and wondering what the limits of Mikey's psychosis might be. He was unhappy with his meds, had probably stopped taking Thallin, and he was capable of anger: he had demonstrated that.

Another call. This time Corinna picked up the phone. Suddenly I was in the position of admitting that I might have attracted the attention of lunatic, that the lunatic might be stalking Em. I started by describing Mikey and asking Corinna whether she'd seen anyone like that recently.

"No," she said.

"You sure? This could be important."

"Well, not somebody new, anyway. It does sound kind of like Mikey Winston."

I gripped the phone. "You *know* him?"

"Heck, everybody on the street knows Mikey. He does yardwork, rakes leaves, that kind of thing. I gather it's what he does for a living, though it can't be much of one. He's retarded or something."

"Not exactly."

"So what's this all about?"

"Maybe just the long arm of coincidence. Corinna, did you hire Mikey?"

"He straightens up around the property once a month or so. Mowed the lawn for me last weekend. He's slow, but he's meticulous, and he charges half what the professional services charge. The front yard looks practically vacuumed—I'm surprised you haven't noticed."

"Does Em know him?"

"To wave at, I guess. Hey, you're starting to scare me. Is there something I should know about Mikey?"

"How long has he been working for you?"

"Off and on, maybe six months. Since January, anyway. I remember he shoveled snow after that big storm."

January. Well before I ran into him in F-wing. Mikey must have seen me at the house one weekend and made the connection.

(*I recognize you*, Mikey had said when we met.)

Which meant I had accused him groundlessly. Worse, I'd made it obvious that I thought of him as a leper, a subhuman whose company I might be forced to keep but who was too unclean to meet my family.

Just what Mikey needed when his medication was failing.

"Hey," Corinna said. "Are you still there?"

"Still here."

"Anything wrong?"

"Nope. But I owe somebody an apology."

Story of my life.

Mikey wasn't home, but his door, unusually, was unlocked and ajar. It drifted open when I knocked.

"Mikey?"

I stepped inside, then closed the door behind me when I heard heavy footsteps from the basement stairwell. When I squinted out Mikey's peephole into the corridor I saw Mr. Saffka, our aging superintendent, shaking roach powder onto the hallway carpet. He wore rubber gloves and a hardware-store respirator.

Mikey must have left in a hurry. There were papers scattered

over his parquet floor, as if he had filled a pad of typewriter paper
and torn out the pages one after the other.

I picked one up.

THALLIN, it said at the top, and in the center of the otherwise
blank page, this:

```
          ANT
            H
        A     A
     ANTHILL
     ANTHILL
      A  THALLIN
     ANTHILL  N
    ANTHILL
      THALLIN
        ILL
         L
       ILL
```

I looked at several more pages, each with similar cryptic anagrams, messages struggling to emerge from the noise inside
Mikey's head. I found this:

```
     THE RED QUEEN
     THE RED ANT
     QUEEN EMILY
     ANTY EM
```

And on the sheet beneath it:

```
     PROZAC
     ELAVIL
     AMITRIPTYLINE
        ZA EL MYLIE
         MY ZEAL LIE
           LIE LAZY EM
             ZALE EMILY
     EMILY ZALE
```

Here is a litany for Dr. Koate, should she ever read this. Here are some things I know. Some sane and sober facts.

I know insects don't talk to each other.

I know insects don't talk to Mikey Winston.

I know there is not a vast, slow conversation taking place between the human and the invertebrate world.

I know that dioxin and methporine and serotonin and fluoxetine are not dialects, words, syllables or signifiers in a global chemical language.

And I know—give me credit, Dr. Koate—that insects don't develop pharmaceuticals for Pfizer or Eli Lily, even though insect pheromones are a hot new source of bioactive drugs and tweakable molecules such as Thallin.

See, Dr. Koate? No hedging. No doubts. I don't *need* the new meds.

I barreled out of Mikey's apartment past Mr. Saffka, who gaped at me, eyes wide above his respirator, like a startled June bug. Ran for the car.

The afternoon light was getting long, but the air was warm and full of early-summer smells: fresh leaves, mown lawns, diesel exhaust from the sighing Bayview buses. Traffic, thank God, wasn't bad. It was a quick drive to Corinna's house, which I still sometimes thought of as "our house."

We had bought it during one of my rare prosperous years, when interest rates plummeted after the '87 stock market adjustment. Even so, it was mortgaged to the teeth. It backed onto a ravine. We had rear-window views of forest and a quaint pedestrian bridge.

Corinna was all smiles when she answered the door. The first giddy flush of a Prozac prescription, I guessed. I asked her if she'd seen Mikey.

"What is this about Mikey Winston? Are you stalking him or something?"

Or maybe she'd been drinking. "Corinna, it's probably nothing. Is Em at home?"

"Just home from school. She's playing in the backyard. This isn't your day with her, though."

"I just want to say hi to her." Reassure myself? Warn her?

"Okay," Corinna said dubiously, "but—"

A voice from inside the house: "Corrie? What's up?"

Male voice.

"I can't ask you to stay for dinner," Corinna finished.

"That's okay."

Everything's okay with me. I'm an okay kind of guy.

"But you can say hello to Em if you want." She frowned. "And explain this to me sometime, all right?"

I promised I would.

I went around back. The house shadowed the yard. The cedar fences I had installed a few years ago were starting to look shabby. The lawn could have used work, too, but I guessed that was Mikey's department.

Emily was nowhere visible. But the back gate was standing open.

The gate opened onto a trail, a kid trail leading gently down past birches and silver maples into the deeper shadows of the ravine. We had taught Em to stay out of the ravine on general principle, but it wasn't known to be dangerous; Corinna used the trail for jogging when weather permitted. Farther downslope there were paved city trails, wooden stairs, kilometer distances posted for dedicated runners.

The woods were deep. Young plants had covered last year's mulch. Anything off the trail was a tangle of old and new life. The spring had been warm and wet; undergrowth crowded the margin of the path; mushrooms thrived on the scabbed trunks of fallen trees. There was nothing human to see: no joggers today, no furtive teenage couples. Almost as if the woods had been evacuated; as if a warning sign had been posted.

No trespassing. Here there be tygers. Keep out—this means *you*.

I called for Emily. Odd how tentative, how lost a human voice can sound, even a few yards into the woods. The tall trees creaked and whispered among themselves. I called again.

There seemed to be an answer this time: a muted sound, choked but human—too deep, I thought, to be Emily's voice, but frightening in its inarticulate panic. Maybe an animal; a raccoon, say, sick or wounded. Or maybe not. I hurried down the path calling Emily's name, pausing to listen for a response.

The path forked into blind alleys, doubled around boulders, paralleled the creek at the bottom of the ravine but seemed never to approach it. Gnats hovered between the trees in blinding clouds.

I found a shoe at one crook in the path—a girl's shoe, scuffed but fresh, leather still shiny, and it looked familiar, but was it Em's? I couldn't be sure.

Then I heard the muffled cry again, much closer now. I had doubled back on myself without realizing it: I was approaching Corinna's house from the south, upslope. I saw the cedar fence directly above me.

A willow grew where the slope eased out to an escarpment. Its branches reached almost to the trail, enclosing the space around the trunk as neatly as a tent. Concealment, I thought. Camouflage. Other people must have thought so, too. There was a flurry of ancient condoms and crumpled cigarette packs among the fallen leaves.

I didn't call for Em again. Every instinct demanded stealth. I parted the willow branches like a hunter.

More gnats fluttered against my face; then flies, dozens of them, hard as raisins, bumping toward the light.

I cannot describe the smell under that shadowed tree: acrid, sharp, bitter, earthy . . . overwhelming. My eyes adjusted to the dim green nimbus. I made out two human figures.

Human. Approximately.

I won't hedge this, Dr. Koate. There's no point in lying, as you've said so often yourself. I'll try to be objective. Dispassionate.

Two human figures, both swarming with flies, with ants.

But not corpses. They were alive.

One lay on the ground, writhing, mouth choked with insects, gasping stertorously. Mouth open and—well, *full*.

The other figure stood over the first with apparent complacency, apparently watching; but this figure, too, was covered in a skin of crawling insects, covered so deeply that I couldn't distinguish any human features.

(Am I calm enough, Dr. Koate?)

I don't know how long I stood there. The cliché turns out to be painfully accurate: it might have been centuries; was probably seconds.

I moved at last when the standing figure shifted its attention to me. Eyes moved under that coat of ants, that armor of silverfish, beetles, flies, wasps. Eyes that might have been two more insects, shiny and cool and inscrutable.

The figure on the ground gagged and screamed, and I ran for the house.

This differs from what you may have seen on the local news.

I told the news people and the police I'd found an insect-covered body under the willow while looking for my daughter, and I was honest about what I did next. I ran up the hill, arrived panting and incoherent at Corinna's back door, told her to phone 911; then I hooked up the garden hose, the sixty-footer that reached both front and back yards, tossed the coil over the cedar fence and unwound it downslope. Turned the garden faucet counterclockwise as far as it would go and hurried back down to the willow.

Under the willow I found not two figures now but one, just one, the one that had been writhing on the ground; but it was motionless, and the insects were twining back into the mulch even before I turned the water on them.

I washed the body clean.

I couldn't make out the face in the fading light until I leaned close enough to scoop a mass of wriggling larvae out of the open mouth.

Then I recognized him.

Mikey Winston. He was still alive, though barely.

There was not much left of his clothing or, in places, his skin. His body was grotesquely swollen. His eyes were gone, and I don't know how he recognized me. Maybe by my smell. But he grasped my sleeve, turned to vomit more insects and bloody granulae from his throat; then he said, a nearly soundless wheeze, "Thank you."

I told Mikey to lie still, that help was coming. Not that I imagined he had more than minutes to live.

"They loved me," he said.

"Don't talk, Mikey."

"They used to! And I protected them. No pesticides on the lawns. Not on *my* lawns."

He took my hand. I felt the abraded tissue of his palm, the bony clench of his fingers.

"But the meds don't work right. I smell bad to them now. They want a new king." He turned his eyeless face toward mine. "A new *queen*."

I stayed with him until the paramedics arrived, but he was beyond help. The medics made a half-hearted attempt at resuscitation, but even they seemed repulsed by what Mikey had become.

He died, they tell me, of shock, both physical and anaphylactic. If his wounds hadn't killed him, the multiple venoms and poisons in his bloodstream surely would have.

"At least," one cop told me later, "we can be sure it wasn't murder."

"Regicide," I said.

"Regicide? What the fuck's that, some brand of bug spray?"

"Just thinking out loud," I said. "Never mind."

Emily, Corinna said, had been in her room all along.

But she came downstairs during all the commotion.

Came down barefoot.

Later that evening, I retrieved her missing shoe and returned it to her. She looked at it, and then at me, and I don't care to recall the depths of hatred and suspicion in her eyes.

Turnabout is fair play, right, Dr. Koate? Once my daughter was afraid of me.

Now I'm frightened of my daughter.

She took the shoe sullenly and turned to carry it up to her room. In the space where she had been standing, a dozen glossy black ants scurried away.

Maybe it was a mistake to tell Dr. Koate the story. Plainly she didn't believe me, though she was relentlessly sympathetic, reserved, calm. Deep as the earth, that calm, and weighty as all the insects in the world.

Dr. Koate prescribed Thallin to go with the Lithotabs. Ostensibly to suppress what she views as my alarming slide into paranoia, but there is, I think, a subtext: an invitation to join in the invisible protocols of the planet, take my place in the new and shifting global chemical discourse.

I have the bottle now. I have it in my hand. An innocuous brown pharmacy bottle with my name and dosage and doctor printed on the label. Open the lid, and I can see sixty daily doses of Thallin: small crosshatched pills the same shade of purple as those Flintstone vitamins we used to give Emily.

The ants are worse since Mikey died. They come up between the floorboards. Mr. Saffka has stopped putting down roach powder, for reasons he won't divulge. The roaches are getting worse, too.

But it's the ants that circle around me like an anxious audience.

They want me to take the pills.

Corinna, is there really a secret language? Em, have you learned to speak it?

Do I belong here?

If I take the pills, will I be able to hear my daughter's voice?

Only one way to find out. A cup of water, a toss of the hand, a simple swallow . . . peristalsis, the transit of molecules, the infiltration of atoms in the blood. . . .

Now wait for morning.

ULYSSES SEES THE MOON IN THE BEDROOM WINDOW

Paul Bridger invited me to his home to see the unusual thing he'd dug out of his garden. I accepted the invitation because I meant to seduce his wife.

Let me clarify. "Something out of the garden" was Paul's shorthand for any new item he added to the random collection of objects that decorated (if that's the word) his house. His wife was Leah, a small woman of forty with a trim figure and green eyes that had grown more deliciously melancholy over the last ten years, and "seduce" is shorthand, too. I believed I had already seduced Leah Bridger; all that remained was to consummate the seduction. To speak the necessary words and arrange to see her while Paul was off at some academic conference in Reykjavik or Brisbane. We would open a future together (I imagined) like a great, joyous book.

I parked in the gravel drive of Paul and Leah's unfailingly tasteful Rosedale property. The night was warm for October, a big three-quarter moon rising in a sky still luminous with dusk. Paul's house backed onto a ravine, and I heard something calling from the woods, a cat or a raccoon; some animal in heat, anyway. I came up the beveled-stone walk carrying a bottle of white wine. Leah opened the door before I knocked.

It was always Leah who did hostess duty at the Bridger house, answering the door or the phone, serving drinks. Paul himself had long ago settled into a placid domesticity untroubled by such peasant chores. "He's in the front room," Leah whispered into my ear, and I gave her a quick embrace.

Which she did not enthusiastically return. When I tried to meet her eyes, she looked away.

"Close the door," she said briskly. "Before Ulysses gets out."

She had been drinking, I thought.

She took the wine bottle to the kitchen.

Leah had restrained her husband's decorative instincts in the more public parts of the house. Here in the spacious front room, the only concessions to Paul's eclecticism were a framed Hopi weaving of no particular merit or value, an audio system cobbled out of fifty-year-old black and chrome vacuum-tube components, and an African ritual mask that looked very *Bell, Book and Candle* against the textured buff-orange wall. As a decor statement, it announced Genteel Eccentricity Held Within Acceptable Bounds.

And here, in a large but fashionable easy chair, was Paul Bridger himself, smiling benignly.

I didn't dislike Paul Bridger. My designs on Leah had nothing to do with Paul, or so I told myself. Paul and I had been friends since our undergraduate days. If I resented anything about Paul, it was that he had achieved virtually everything he wanted in life and had accepted this good fortune, not exactly arrogantly, but as his due . . . That is, yes, he *knew* he was lucky, and wasn't it mildly amusing that so much had come his way so easily?

But then, he wasn't exactly Bill Gates. His needs were simple and he satisfied them on a regular basis; he enjoyed a modest but secure tenure at the University of Toronto, which was exactly as it should be; a little family money made possible the amenities, such as this house. And he had married the perfect wife. Leah occasionally mentioned the possibility of children (forlornly), but that had never happened, probably because children wouldn't have fit into Paul's schematically ideal existence.

Does that make him sound boring—a Babbitt, a nebbish? Don't be deceived. He had a quick and open mind and a grasp of history (both mainstream and off-trail) that made him a popular guest at faculty barbecues. And he loved to talk.

I said, "What have you got to show me?"

He smiled. "You know better than that, Matthew. There has to be an overture before the curtain goes up. Have a seat."

I settled at the near end of the sofa, hoping Leah might join me there for a little illicit knee-touching. But when she came into the room she just offered aperitifs and wandered off again. She seemed preoccupied, abstracted.

Paul talked about the old days.

"I think about Ulysses sometimes," Paul Bridger said. "*Leah?* Where is the old reprobate at the moment?"

Leah's voice came from the kitchen but seemed much farther away. "I saw him up in the bedroom a little while ago. He was looking at the moon."

Ulysses was Paul's cat, ten years old, a fat mongrel (can you call a cat a mongrel?) with some Siamese in his ancestry. As if on cue, or maybe he heard his name, Ulysses came stalking through the room with his tail in the air. His fur was spotted with orange, his eyes were as green and bright as a go light—a patch-work quilt of a cat. "He's nervous tonight," Paul said. "All that ruckus outside," meaning the female-animal-in-heat I had heard from the walk. "Ulysses is neutered, of course, but he knows something's up, and it interests him."

But Ulysses wasn't allowed outside. Traffic on one side of the house, a ravine full of foxes and skunks on the other, bad news for an animal as thoroughly domesticated as Ulysses.

Ulysses padded through the hallway to the front door and yowled. Leah called "Hush!" from the kitchen, where she was still fixing food or sneaking a drink.

"Sometimes," Paul said, "I look at Ulysses and think about those dormitory bull sessions we used to have. You remember that, Matthew?"

Of course I remembered that. I remembered sitting up often until dawn, Paul and I and a circle of friends in the dormitory commons, sorting out life, the universe, and everything. My parents were the kind who worried that I'd go to college and end up smoking fortified cigarettes and using words like "empowered" and "patriarchal," and I had been perfectly happy to fulfill their expectations. Those of us who reach middle age without children of our own are allowed to own up to these things. We call them fond memories.

"There was that engineering student," Paul said, "remember Ken Schroeder? The one who read science fiction and was always going on about the next stage of evolution, the Superior Being . . . ?"

Yes, and we had pilloried him for it. The *ubermensch*: it had seemed such a quaintly totalitarian notion, reeking of eugenics and Nordic Purity. Also, it was easy to make Schroeder blush. He had bad gums and dandruff. Homo superior, right. (I had actually run into Ken Schroeder a couple of months ago. He does industrial design for a major architectural firm now, pulls in a couple of hundred K a year. Balding, but his teeth are perfect.)

"Well," Paul said, "I've been thinking about that off and on for, what is it, almost twenty-five years now? More often when I'm around Ulysses. Because it's an interesting question, if you ask it the right way. Matthew, are you an animal-rights person?"

I shrugged. "I eat meat. I refrain from clubbing baby harp seals."

"Because I don't want to be misunderstood. If I say we are, as a species, *superior* to Ulysses and his kind, I'm not presuming a *moral* superiority. Human beings aren't necessarily the crown of creation and Ulysses may not be a lesser creature than you or I, in the grand scheme of things. Still, there is indisputably a wide range of things we can do, as a species, that Ulysses can't. Write poetry, map the stars, do calculus, build bridges. All of this is beyond the ken of our four-footed cousin, yes?"

"Granted."

"So let's reconsider the old dorm room debate. What if there was a creature superior to us in all the ways we are superior to Ulysses? Would we even know such a being existed?"

I didn't really care. My appetite for this kind of sophomore philosophy had waned with middle age. What I wanted was some time with Leah. I needed to find out what had changed since Paul's last party, when she had taken me into the cedar-scented darkness back of the garden and kissed me and cried a little at the strangeness of her betrayal.

But she came in with a plate of carrot sticks and sour cream and sat listlessly in a dim corner of the room. She gave the window an uneasy look, then rose to draw the curtain against the moonlight.

Ulysses continued to complain of his confinement in eerie Siamese wails.

Paul wanted me to play along. I said, "I read all those stories, too. Somebody who can do higher math in his head, interpret Mozart, read minds. And gets to forgive brutal mankind its adolescent folly as he's burned at the stake. Homo superior. *That* guy."

"Do you suppose that's how Ulysses sees *us*?"

I shrugged. "In his terms, maybe."

"Clearly not. Show me the cat who believes he lives in the midst of superior beings. Nonsense. Bullshit. In point of fact, Ulysses doesn't find us in the least frightening or intimidating— we're far less scary than the Doberman down the block. And why would a cat consider us *superior* when in all the things that matter to cat-kind—chasing and killing things and fucking and establishing territory—we're barely capable?"

Leah, who had contributed nothing to the conversation up to this point, said: "But we *do* chase and kill things. As a species. We're incredibly good at it, actually."

"Certainly, but it all takes place in a realm Ulysses can't penetrate or comprehend. And that's the point. Ninety percent of what we consider vitally important is, to Ulysses, either imperceptible or completely trivial."

I tried to sort this out. "You're saying a superior being wouldn't be *obviously* superior."

He grinned. "Exactly. The opposite, in fact. As far as Ulysses is concerned, Leah and I are actually more catlike than the other creatures he encounters. We groom him; we feed him. We're about as unpreposessing, in his eyes, as that sofa you're sitting on."

"Okay," I said, "and this means . . . ?"

"Well, to draw the most vulgar inference first, it means the Superior Being could be walking among us today and not attracting attention."

Leah shook her head. "Not necessarily. We're reasoning beings, which Ulysses isn't. We would know."

"Ulysses reasons all the time. He figured out how to spring the latch on the pantry, remember?"

"But," Leah insisted, "he doesn't *know* he reasons."

"Is that important? Maybe we really are the pearl of evolution and there is nothing that can outthink or outperceive us—maybe sentience has a ceiling, and we've reached it. But maybe not. We can at least consider the alternative."

"Well," Leah conceded darkly, "it's not like it matters or anything."

Paul ignored her. I said, "If this being exists, and if he's essentially imperceptible, Leah's right. It doesn't matter; it *can't* matter."

"Except for two things," Paul said. "Artifacts and sleight of hand."

Could Paul have found out about Leah and I? Had she said something to him? It was at least possible. Paul was capable of many things, perhaps even of maintaining this glib insouciance while plotting to stab me with a pickle fork.

But it hardly seemed likely.

I looked at Leah, feeling a rush of warmth that was hard to conceal. I thought I loved her. Yes, *that* word. It had occured to me only lately that I loved Leah Bridger, though we had flirted for years and I had always liked her immensely. She was, I thought, a little martyred by her marriage; she cared for Paul, but their relationship hadn't evolved the way she'd hoped. He was too self-sufficient to really love anyone. She delighted him—he made that plain enough—but delight isn't love.

Leah owned a degree in visual arts but had never worked outside the home. That was Paul's preference. And she had kept her figure; that was Paul's preference, too, I think. Once, years ago, he had told me he liked women "underfed and underfoot."

(When I ragged him about the gross incorrectness of this he smiled innocently but never repeated the phrase. At least not in my presence.)

So my ambitions may not have been especially noble, but I wasn't here just to get laid, either. I *did* care about Leah. I had been telling myself so on a daily basis.

I looked at her, trying to shoot a warmth-and-comfort vibe across the room. She regarded me distantly and lit a cigarette.

Leah had stopped smoking in 1987. I remembered the ordeal. When had she started again?

She waved out a match and exhaled a blue halo of smoke. Paul wrinkled his nose.

"Artifacts?" I said. "Sleight of hand?"

"Here's the question. When, if ever, does Ulysses suspect that human beings are more than they seem? When does our uniqueness impinge on *him* in some way?"

"When we talk about having him put down," Leah said.

Paul looked hurt. "No, and anyway we wouldn't do a thing like that. Shame on you. No, but he gets freaked out by our artifacts once in a while. You remember your Sylvester slippers?"

Leah had gotten a pair of slippers one Christmas (a gift from some demented uncle) in the likeness of Sylvester the Cat. Big rolling plush-toy eyes, black fur, nylon whiskers.

Paul turned to me. "Ulysses could not *abide* those slippers. It was as if Leah's feet had been taken over by aliens. His fur would bristle; he'd growl and arch his back. We had to throw the slippers out, and it still took him a good day to settle down. We—human beings—had manufactured an artifact that sent all the wrong cat signals. Ulysses' experience of a higher being is therefore an experience of the *unnatural*, the eerie.

"Likewise sleight of hand. When Ulysses was a kitten, I would roll a rubber ball for him to chase. Great game. He loved it. Except when I cupped the ball in my hand and *pretended* to throw it. He'd jump up, follow the trajectory, and—no ball! Hey, presto! It's a trick that wouldn't fool a two-year-old more than once, but Ulysses always fell for it. And it bothered him. You could tell. He'd let out this quizzical little mewling sound and scratch at the carpet."

"So," I said, "the only evidence we would have of a Superior Being would be things that make us feel . . . quizzical?"

"Things that aren't natural," Leah interpreted. Her voice was cold. The cat emitted another yowl from some far-off room of the house. "Things that make the hair on your neck stand up."

"Arm," I said.

She frowned. "What?"

"People always say, 'The hair on your neck.' I mean, I know the feeling. But it's the hair on my arms that prickles. Not the neck."

Paul looked at me as if he forgave this unfortunate descent into trivia. (Nevertheless, it's something I've noticed about myself. A good campfire story makes the hair on my arms stand at attention. This was explained to me once: something about the arrector pili muscles and the fight-or-flight reflex.)

Leah gave Paul a long evaluating stare. "Why don't you just show him the rock?"

Paul went off to rummage in his study (presumably for "the rock") while Leah poured herself yet another drink. I waylaid her in the kitchen. It was one of those chrome kitchens, all mirror surfaces. Our reflections glared back at us from a dozen angles.

I put my hands on her shoulders. She said, "Matthew, don't."

I backed off and looked, I guess, hurt.

We may not have been lovers, but we had known each other a long time. The unspoken question was obvious and I didn't have to ask it.

She looked briefly ashamed. "There's nothing between us, you know, but a little loneliness."

"It could be more."

She shook her head firmly. "No, Matthew. No, it couldn't. People like us, we're like shadows orbiting a vacuum. We have nothing to give each other."

I was too hurt to react sensibly. "How very Sylvia Plath," I said.

Which made her angry. "Fuck you," she muttered.

I went back to the living room.

"It *is* a rock," I said.

Paul was holding it in his hand. The rock was about the size of a potato. "I told you so."

"You told me you dug it out of the garden, too, but I assumed that was some kind of metaphor."

"There you have me, Matthew. No, I didn't literally dig it out of the garden, though it looks just about that prosaic, doesn't it? I bought it at Finders, as a matter of fact. As a paperweight."

Finders was the name of a run-down secondhand bookshop near the University. Paul loved the place. I had been there, but it didn't impress me. It offered a few blowsy first editions, a big section of occult nonsense in the Madame Blavatsky tradition, forgotten junk novels from the fifties. And a little knickknack shelf cluttered with fake Wedgwood and cracked china dolls and Victorian mirrors and, evidently, rocks. I said, "You bought a *rock?*"

"It's a scrying rock."

It was a smooth lump of whatever it is commonplace rocks are made of, lusterless gray with a few chunks of quartz randomly embedded. "You paid money for this?"

"Don't be facetious. I got change back from a dollar. But the appearance of the artifact is consistent with our thesis, Matthew. Ulysses, for instance, has no way of distinguishing a man-made object from a natural object. The distinction between a rubber ball and a pebble is not *categorical*, in the cat's mind. Both are round; one is hard and one is soft; they have distinguishing smells, and so on, but as for their purpose or provenance—he can't even phrase the question."

"So the artifact of a Superior Being might look to us like a fucking *rock?*"

"As well a rock as something else. The point is, what makes *this* rock special would be instantly obvious to our Superior Being and vague, at best, to the rest of us."

I said, "Vague if not imaginary. My arm hairs aren't standing up, Paul."

He smiled benignly and said, "Hold it in your hand."

I understand about the power of suggestion.

It was a moonlit night in autumn. Ulysses was wailing like a lost soul, and something out there in the dark was answering him. Leah had turned away from me for no apparent reason. And Paul insisted on ghost stories.

But it had stopped being frightening. The evening had grown tedious and bitter and I wanted to leave. Why stay?

I took the rock in my hand.

It was not warm. It did not radiate a strange electricity.

"Hold it a while," Paul said. "Close your eyes."

I closed my eyes and heard Paul settling into his chair, Leah bumping around in the kitchen, Ulysses walking the stations of his discontent. No more. No dreamlike images sprang to mind. No unusual sensations, only the usual minor discomforts. (I had cinched my belt a notch too tight in an effort to impress Leah with my youthful waistline. My shoes pinched.)

Given that Paul's exegesis had lead up to this stunning anti-climax, I let my thoughts drift to Leah.

Had her drinking become a problem? She had always had a thing for what we euphemistically call "substances," including an expensive cocaine habit when that was still fashionable. Much of this I had put down to her unhappiness with Paul, from which I had lately longed to rescue her . . . but some of it must have been intrinsic to her nature, some unacknowledged and unProzac'd darkness out of her childhood. There are people for whom un-happiness is a default state. Maybe Leah had stayed with Paul all these years because with Paul she could be *functionally* unhappy. He made room for her depression. He tolerated it. Indulged it. Remained impervious to it. He was, above all else, reliable.

Change the equation and everything might topple. Her alco-holism might expand to engulf her; a new lover might prove fickle or even hostile; she would be exposed to a world she found deeply threatening.

And where did I fit into this equation? Or rather, where had I innocently imagined I might fit? Leah's small erotic gestures, the touch of her lips in the dark, were as inevitable and as meaningless as her fourth drink. Fifth drink. I might actually have contrived to fuck her, if I hadn't stupidly fallen in love.

That was the forbidden threshhold, the door into chaos.

And what would we have been together, Leah and I? I imagined the two of us locked in a tightening spiral of need and contempt—not the tidy impersonal orbit she had worked out with Paul, but a slow dive into the abyss. She would come to hate me. The feeling would probably be mutual.

I visualized a future as long and dry as a desert horizon.

There was nothing here for me.

I dropped the rock.

Paul was apologetic over dinner.

"I'm sorry, Matthew. It seemed to me there *was* something unusual about the stone. That's why I called it a scrying rock. Just a touch of—the future? The past? But that must sound absurd."

"A little," I said.

"So the thesis is unsupported."

"I guess the Superior Being isn't with us tonight."

"I guess not," Paul Bridger said amiably.

He excused himself when the meal was finished, and I was briefly alone with Leah once more.

The steady flow of cocktails had left her sullen and remote. She hadn't eaten much of the dinner she'd prepared—charred veal medallions and asparagus abandoned too long in the steamer.

She said, "You're kidding, right?"

"About what?"

"I know what you saw." She wagged a finger at me. The nail polish was chipped. "I saw it too, Matthew. Last night. With the stone. You and I. Dead in the water. One big joyless pity fuck. And then not even that. *There's nothing there for us.*"

I said carefully, "Is it so obvious?"

"Not much fun having your daydreams stripped away, is it, Matthew? Not much fucking fun."

No fun at all.

So the evening ended.

Leah, one drink past her limit, fell asleep on the sofa, strands of lank hair across her face. Paul showed me to the door.

He was smiling. He always smiled, and I wondered how he did it. The smile was by all appearances genuine, a benign amusement that seemed never to fade. "Don't worry about Leah," he said confidently. "She'll perk up in the morning."

It did not occur to me to wonder why Paul had invited me here or what he imagined he had accomplished.

There was another yowl from the darkness outside. Why do cats make such tortured sounds when they're in heat?

Ulysses came hurtling down the stairs as Paul opened the door for me. I stepped outside quickly and said good night. Paul thanked me for coming.

The screen door was still open a crack when Ulysses bumped into it, mewling. Paul reached down in a practised motion and picked up the unhappy animal, latching the door with calm authority and separating Ulysses from whatever it was Ulysses so plainly longed for out in the unsilent dark.

"You know better than that, Ulysses," I heard him whisper. "There's nothing out there for you."

And the hair stood up on my arms.

PLATO'S MIRROR

1.

"You don't know me," she said, eyes wide. "But I got this for you."

It was a package about the size of a coffee-table book, flat, wrapped in brown paper and tied with butcher's twine. "You're right," I said, blocking the doorway. "I don't know you."

She smiled. "I'm Faye," she said. "Faye Constance."

She stood as tall as my collar, wide mouth, small nose, eyes a stunning shade of green—sunny clover, summer lawn. (*Beware all green-eyed girls*, my father used to say. A drunk's advice.) She was, she told me later, all of twenty-two years old.

"I don't know you, Faye Constance, so I have to ask: what do you want? And what's in the package?"

"Oh my God!" She put a hand to her mouth, mock-horrified. "You must think it's like a *letter bomb* or something! Oh God! No—what happened is, I read your book. The back cover said you lived in town. So when I came across *this* I knew I had to look you up and give it to you. It's not as weird as it sounds . . . don't look at me like I'm from another planet or whatever."

"I'm not sure I follow."

She thrust the package at me. "It's a present, that's all. From an admirer."

The package was heavier than it looked. Downright hefty. She turned away.

"Wait," I said. "I can't accept this." Adding, against my own better judgment, "Not from a stranger."

"You know who I am."

"I know your name. That's different." I checked my watch. "You can have fifteen minutes of my time."

"I'm not buying time."

"My time you can't buy. Come in. If you want."

Her smile broadened. The glare was blinding.

Faye gazed at my apartment, which Helen had once called my "seduce-atorium." The walls were lined with books, many of which I had read. The bay window was tall and relatively sunny, for a fifth-story one-bedroom buried in a canyon of condo towers. Two potted cacti braced the window and cast faintly green reflections across the ceiling. The room was done in green: in what the paint-chip and upholstery-sample folks called sea foam, ochre, and mist. The sofa was large and inviting if somewhat checkered with coffee stains.

Not that I meant to seduce Faye Constance. I was still a little afraid of her.

My work attracts the emotionally damaged. I had met them, at "psychic fairs" and Chapters signings, clutching copies of *Plato's Mirror* and peering at me through smudged lenses murky as millponds. They believed, these people, believed with all their stilted hearts and inadequate minds, that I had tapped the wisdom of the ancients and was dispensing it one volume per annum through an American paperback press. A loyal crowd, but not necessarily stable.

So I laid it out for her. Counting my fingers: "One. Everything I know about history I learned auditing a classics course at the University. Two. The book is fiction. I made it up. For money. Three. Meeting me won't make you a better person. Probably the opposite. I drink and I smoke dope and I have a lot of shitty friends."

"That's supposed to discourage me, right?"

"Only if you're smart."

She laughed, which was disarming. "Look, I don't want to

marry you. I just like your writing. I was rummaging around the thrift shops and I found . . . well, something that made me think of you. So I was a little impulsive. It's no big deal. Anyway," checking her watch, "you can have your time back. I have to be somewhere."

As suddenly as that, I didn't want her to leave.

"Look, I'm sorry if I was harsh. Give me a number, Faye Constance. In case I want to say thanks."

"You don't have to thank me. The number is in the package."

She smiled good-bye and headed for the door. From behind she looked like some Botticelli angel who had just discovered the possibilities of gender. The seduce-atorium was sorry to see her go.

I opened the package—wouldn't you?

It was, of course, a mirror. An "antique" mirror, the sort you find in shops where any object sufficiently motheaten and older than Sarah Michelle Gellar is deemed to be an antique. (By which definition, wasn't I one?)

The frame was pinholed Victorian gingerbread with flakes of gilt still clinging to it, held together with blackened finishing nails and backed with brittle brown paper. The glass itself was probably older than the frame, and where the silvering had corroded there were patches of quivery distortion, the effect you get passing a magnet in front of a TV tube. The mirror reflected my own homely face, no more and no less. (Had Faye been disappointed by the face behind the book? But I create illusions and dispel them: that's what I do.)

Tucked between glass and frame was a note in Faye's childish handwriting.

PLATO'S MIRROR? You never know!!

Signed, *Your admirer*. Plus name, address, telephone number.

"But it's ugly," Conrad said.

"Is that a problem? I like *you*, don't I?"

"Mm. But you don't hang me on the wall, notice."

"Not that I haven't thought of it."

Conrad, my neighbor-three-doors-down, grimaced at his reflection. I had put Faye's mirror in the hallway adjacent to the
bathroom. The light was dim here, making the mirror (I hoped)
more decorative and less obviously trashy. Conrad disagreed. His
image moved in the surface of the glass like a dolphin attempting
to surface. "Your taste is unfailing, Donald. Everything you own,
it's all so—*rec room*."

"Ugly but fun?"

"Ugly, anyhow." He bent closer to my ear. The noise of the
party had already reached deafening and was approaching traumatic. "By the way. Word of caution. Watch out for Helen. She's
not a happy camper."

"Fuck," I said.

"Judging by her mood, not tonight."

Fifteen people in my apartment was a crowd; twenty was practically coitus. Maybe twenty-five had arrived for the weekly zoo.
Oh, we were a motley crowd: five writers, three contract
programmers, a dozen unemployed intellectuals and aging students, a couple of hookers, my dentist, my drug dealer, and my
girlfriend. Helen. Girlfriend, I suspected, for not much longer.
She was allergic to tobacco smoke, pot smoke, perfume, and red
wine, which begged the question: what was she doing here?

At the moment she was engaged in a raging argument with
Conrad's partner William, a writer of small-press fiction. The
subject had been literary to begin with but the conversation had
deteriorated when William, waxing impatient, described T. S. Eliot as "a closet queen, sewn up so tight he couldn't fart authen-
tically." Helen's graduate thesis had been a feminist defense of
T. S. Eliot. Eliot was her red flag. I had learned to wince at the
sound of his name.

I put my hand on her shoulder. "William's baiting you, Hel.
Ignore him."

She whirled on me. Her eyes—brown—flashed. "Stop defending me!"

"I don't think that's what I'm doing."

"Then stop defending your asshole friends!"

Things had been going bad for weeks. Helen was, as they say, conflicted. She liked me, we got along well (when we got along at all), but underneath all that me-too bohemianism was a fragile Bishop Strachan debutante still yearning for cashmere and clean forks.

Or else—looking at it from her point of view—she had fallen in with a crowd whose appetites and poverty had turned out to be more dismal than stylish.

In other words, we embarrassed her.

Later, she took me into the bedroom and closed the door against a crush of bodies. For reprimands, not a quick fuck. Times change. "I'm leaving," she said. "I mean it. I'm tired of beer on the rug and puke in the kitchen sink and I'm tired, frankly, of you, Donald, and your self-loathing and your pussy-chasing and the crappy way you treat people."

"About covers it," I said.

"*And* that self-serving ironic *tone* you take whenever you feel *threatened*."

"Anything else?"

"Yes. This. For every time you stood me up while you diddled some young ignoramus."

She raked her nails across my cheek and wrestled her way down the hallway to the door. Helen slammed doors for punctuation. Slam: period. Full stop.

The mirror was full of restless shapes. I headed for the kitchen. On the way I turned up the music. Polyrythmic, agressive, dangerous. Like me.

What I had neglected to tell her was how much I loved her.

The crowd faded around three, spilling out into the empty street. Conrad and William stayed behind to share a spliff. They were practically home already.

Conrad was a city-bred white boy and William was a Nova Scotia black, but they had developed, in tandem, similar voices, similar mannerisms. At ease, they draped their arms across each other's shoulders and inclined together like lazy willows. I envied them.

I had told them the story of the mirror. (Stroking my wounded vanity with images of Faye.) Conrad said sleepily, "Well, what if she's right?"

"Right about what?"

"The mirror."

"The *mirror?*"

"Sure the mirror. How do you know it doesn't show, ah—what was it you called them in your book? Architects?"

"Archons. Archons and Essences."

William stirred from his nestling place at Conrad's shoulder. "What are Archons?"

"Shush. It's a Greek word."

"Right," I said. "It's a Greek word for 'bullshit.' Come on, Conrad, I get enough of that crap from the public at large."

"Donald, hon, I know you're a fraud; you don't have to remind me. But, heck, magic mirrors, can't we even play?"

"Busman's holiday. You play with it if you want. Just don't break it."

"You really do like the ugly thing!"

"No. I like the pretty young thing who brought it to me."

"I see. And how exactly did it work in your little book?"

In my "little book," Plato's Mirror was the long-forgotten secret of the Eleusinian rites—the ancient Greek Demeter cult that survived, in one form or another, for almost two thousand years. The Eleusinian mysteries remain shrouded in secrecy, but according to most scholars they involved an annual pageant at an underground spring. "Happy is he who, having seen these rites, goes below the hollow earth; for he knows the end of life and its beginning." Pindar.

The mirror was my own invention. It was the mirror, I claimed, that had inspired Plato's fable of the cave. You know the story? If a man lived out his life in a cave with only the narrowest of pinhole openings and no way in or out, he would experience the world as shadows projected on a wall. And if this hypothetical cave dweller were to be transported outside for the first time, the experience would be overwhelming, instant immersion in a madly hyperreal universe of colors and shapes and textures.

Plato's Mirror, I claimed, provided that glimpse of an unmediated world. Created by Greek alchemists, the mirror had been banished to the lightless underground, where it became the secret icon of the Eleusinian Mysteries, to be experienced only by devotees and even then only briefly. The human mind, after all, can bear only so much reality.

I had adduced my evidence from Gnostic manuscripts and freshly discovered Dead Sea scrolls which only I had seen. Documents, in other words, that didn't exist. The book was punctuated with pseudo-scholarly footnotes but all the references were blind, unavailable in any real-world library.

Fold in a little Atlantis lore, a bit of Masonic paranoia, and a soupçon of New Age millenarianism; yield: one not-quite-beststelling addition to the crackpot rack of your local bookstore. I had contracted for three more volumes. Carlos Castaneda, watch your ass.

Conrad wouldn't leave it alone. "It works," he said, "the mirror I mean, only in the dark, right?"

"Conrad, if you want to turn off the lights and look at your absence of a reflection, be my guest."

"Vampires," William chimed in. "Vampires have a mirror thing, don't they?"

"Vampires you *can't* see in a mirror. I think what Donald is talking about are monsters you can *only* see in a mirror."

"Are there such things?"

"No," I said, "for Christ's sake, it's pretend, all right?"

"Shall we prove it?" Conrad wouldn't let this go; he was off on some coy, stoned trajectory of his own.

"If it'll shut you up, I'll turn off the lights and dance nude."

"I am," he said haughtily, "not tempted. Geez, Donald, did Helen leave with your sense of humor in her purse?"

So I turned off the lights and sat back down.

"This is," William announced, "already spooky."

"Draw the blinds," Conrad said. "The streetlights are glaring."

"Draw them yourself."

He did, eliminating everything but a dim green glow. I couldn't see my hand in front of my face—couldn't see anything but the faint silhouettes of the cacti, each tall as a man. There was a brief flare as Conrad toked once more before setting off for the hall-way. We had all smoked enough to make it seem like a long trip. And yes, there was some of that giggly thrill about the occasion: just us kids, up past our bedtime, stealing Mom's cigarettes and telling ghost stories.

"Donald!"

Conrad's voice sounded hollow and small, as if he had gone much too far away. "What?"

"Your mirror is broken!"

"Broken?"

"Must be! I can't see a thing!"

"Stop torturing me, Conrad. Shouldn't you and William be asleep by now?"

"Spoilsport." I heard his shoes scuffling along the linoleum, his small laugh. "All right, we'll—ah—"

Long pause.

"Conrad?"

Nothing.

Annoyed, I switched on the lamp next to the sofa. William sat up, still playing along but faintly uneasy. Conrad was out of sight around the corner, all of three feet down the hall. He stumbled back into the living room, frowning. "Not funny, Donald. . . ."

"What's not funny?"

"Practical jokes." He seemed genuinely hurt. "You set me up, didn't you? So what is it really—some kind of computer display back of the glass? One of those LCD things?"

"Who's setting who up, exactly?"

"Ah, well . . . I don't grudge a joke at my expense. Kudos, Donald, and good night. Thank you for a lovely party. Sorry about Helen."

"Don't kid a kidder," I said to the closing door.

Helen called in the morning—far too early. Her voice on the phone was wistful. "Maybe," she said, "I was out of line last night. I meant what I said. But I didn't have to say it like that."

"Don't apologize. You were right."

"I was right? Is this a first? Donald Wilcox admits he might have acted like a jerk from time to time?"

"Right about us, I mean. Maybe we're not, as they say, a viable option."

"You don't like hearing the truth about yourself, do you?"

"I did kind of hope we'd finished that part of the conversation."

"What's her name this time?"

"Pardon me?"

"I swear to God, Donald, when I met you I thought I saw something fundamentally good about you. Was it all an act? A little seductive innocence, just enough to get you laid? Like some, I don't know, *spider,* spinning out those psycho books and devouring any woman you happen to catch. . . ."

"You must have the wrong number, Hel. This isn't the Verbal Abuse Club."

And she was gone, as quick as that. I didn't know whether to cheer or weep.

I made a pot of coffee. Then I called Faye Constance.

2.

"Of *course* it works," Faye said.

"Didn't we make a rule? No feng shui, no crop circles, and no magic mirrors?"

"What are you so afraid of?"

Two months had passed, during which time I had learned some things about Faye Constance. Under that lovely oxymoron of a name was a young woman of fierce enthusiasms and grave gullibility; a believer, but not a fanatic; not a virgin, but enthusiastically and youthfully adventurous in bed; a self-proclaimed poet, apt to leap up at midnight full of odes and couplets, unpublishable; by day, a transcriptionist at some dreary Provincial Ministry or other. "You never *leave* this place," she had complained, so we'd been doing dinners out, sentimental movies, head-cracking concerts. Tonight, however, we dined in. Faye had rented *Emma*. But she seemed more interested in the mirror.

"I'm not afraid of anything," I said, "except maybe your obsession with that slab of glass."

"Obsession, great, thank you very much. But, Donald—it *does* work. I tried it last night, when you went out for roti."

"I wish you could hear yourself. Faye, it *works?* What's that even mean?"

"I'm not saying it's necessarily the Plato's Mirror in your book. Just that it does the same thing."

"The book is crap, my love, and there's no such thing as a magic mirror."

"Or Archons, or Essences? You didn't make those up."

"No. I borrowed them from the Gnostic writers. Who *did* make them up."

"There's some truth in every religion, I think."

"Faye. Come on. What are you saying here?"

"Let me show you."

"No. No games. I'm not in the mood."

"Just let me *show* you!"

And I agreed, because I remembered Conrad's performance, and that made me a little afraid, and I was mad at myself for being afraid and I didn't want Faye even to suspect that I took any of this seriously. Helen was gone for good and Faye had become the significant female presence in my life, and without Faye's adulation what would I be? A lonely con artist, a writer without a text, a congenital liar.

Faye was afraid of nothing. I think she was born without the fear gene. She got a double dose of puppy-dog enthusiasm instead. Uneasy as I felt, it was a joy to watch her fuss around the apartment, pulling curtains, even switching off the air conditioner because it might emit hostile technological vibrations. She brough the mirror into the bedroom. "Now we take off our clothes," she said. "We have to be pristine."

Could she have been *more* pristine, stripped to pure pale geometry, nipples royally erect? She braced the mirror on a dresser and against the wall, angled slightly up. From where I stood I could see her reflection, knees to crown, muzzy in the age-frosted glass. And she could see mine. My hairy-legged and paunchy male nudity. "Now turn off the light," she said.

I flipped the switch.

I looked toward Faye and saw nothing but whirly retinal static. I looked in the direction of the mirror and saw—

Must I say this?

I would much rather lie.

Saw an angel.

Hyperbole in the service of truth isn't my strong suit. No, I don't know what an angel looks like. But her reflection in the mirror was awe-inspiring. I drew a quick, frightened breath. Frightened, because how can there be a reflection in a dark mirror? And how can a reflection make its own light, especially this cool mother-of-pearl radiance fractured to rainbows in the still air?

Seconds ticked away in the silence. Faye said breathlessly, "Donald?" In the mirror, an angel-mouth moved. "What do you *see?*"

The distilled liquor of a thousand stained-glass windows. The glow of a cloudless summer day, compacted into human form. Sum of all the wide-eyed, wide-legged girls I had ever convinced to take off their clothes, innocence flaring into soft night breezes. Starlight in amber. "I see," I said, "I think, it's *you*, Faye, only, only. . . ."

"Yes," she said, meaning *I know*. "And I see you."

Instantly, I turned my face away.

"Donald?"

I switched on the light.

Her face was bright with tears. "But you're so—so fucking *beautiful!* Oh, Donald! Donald!"

"You know what we saw," she said as we lay together in bed.

I had turned the mirror to the wall. "Trick of the light."

"You can't be serious."

"What else?"

"That's a lie," Faye said, turning her back to me. "A *cruel* lie."

I'm a liar by trade. The cruelty is just a bad habit.

———

That summer Faye took me to the shop where she'd bought the mirror—not an antique store but a cramped secondhand bookstore on Harbord Street called Finders. The mirror had been taking up space along a side wall; the pale silhouette where it had hung was still visible against the yellowed paint.

Faye said she had asked the owner if the mirror was for sale and he had shrugged and agreed to take ten dollars for it. The woman behind the cash counter claimed to know nothing about the deal, and the owner, she told us, "doesn't like to be disturbed."

Apart from that, I didn't discuss the mirror with Faye. She knew what she had seen; she smiled obliquely whenever I dodged the subject.

But I knew what I had seen, too.

I just didn't like to think about it.

I ran into Helen at the Starbucks near my building.

She was amiable, if a little wary, when I joined her at the table. She was seeing someone, she announced. And so, of course, was I. With these admissions we relaxed into the past tense of "us," a surprisingly comfortable space.

"Yeah," Helen said, "Conrad told me about your current. A little young, he seems to think."

"Not as young as she looks. And Conrad is a gossip."

"You think it'll last?"

I shrugged.

"In other words, no."

"I didn't say that, Helen."

"Poor Donald." She looked genuinely sympathetic. "It never goes away, does it? That picture in the back of your head. Daddy drunk and mom all bruises. The nightmares."

The trouble with women is that sometimes I confide in them. "I'm not sure this is something I want to talk about in Starbucks on a Saturday morning."

Helen scrunched up her paper cup. "Somebody ought to warn that girl, Donald. Maybe even you."

———

Turned out Conrad had befriended Faye; the two of them had gone thrift-shop trawling together. Conrad collected vintage Barbie dolls and accessories. Faye liked to pick up any old piece of colored glass: bottles, paperweights, vases. Sunlight through a prism could keep her fascinated for hours. She had magpie instincts.

I went with them on one of these weekend flea-market expeditions. Had no idea there were so many Thrift Villas and Salvation Army shops in the city. And they all smelled the same: of old clothes and rust, Lysol and mildew. Faye and Conrad shopped knowingly, pawing through trash for gems while I scanned the book racks, the literary equivalent of the Elephant's Graveyard, last stop for Edgar Cayce, Carl G. Soziere, Lobsang Rampa, and someday, perhaps, my humble self. Sun-faded spines all uniform yellow. This, too, a sort of mirror.

We lunched at a suburban fried-chicken factory. Faye was off at the washroom when Conrad said, "You ought to keep this girl, Donald."

"You think?"

"I'm serious. She's a sweet, bright, gentle little thing. She doesn't deserve the usual Donald treatment—six months fucking and a fare-thee-well."

"I'll treasure your advice."

"There is," he said meaningfully, "a little magic about that girl."

"Magic?"

"Well? She gave you the mirror, didn't she?"

"Ah—the *magic* mirror."

"I've seen it, remember? Plus we looked at it again one night. Last week. When you were out."

"Did you."

"A little functional magic in your life at last, and all you can do is grind your teeth."

"There's no such thing as magic, Conrad."

"Oh, I don't imagine there's anything special about that old mirror, but the magic, *that's* authentic. Comes by way of Faye, I suspect. Is that why it scares you so much? There's nothing *bad* in the mirror, you know."

"Let's talk about something else, shall we?"

He rolled his eyes. "Too late to slam that barn door, Donald. Those horses are *out*."

The experience of making love to Faye, the nights she stayed over, was indescribably sweet, subtle, and gratifying. No impatience marred the act and the only selfishness was mutual and guiltless. In bed, she set me free. How then to describe, how even to admit to myself the occasional impulse, at the height of our passion, to take her guileless head into my hands and twist it until something snapped?

"Who is it," Helen used to ask, "who is it, Donald, who lives inside you, who knows how to do or say exactly the thing that hurts the most? What kind of monster has instincts like that?"

No monster. I speak from the heart.

Faye says I write from the heart, too: that's how I know things I don't think I know.

3.

The sequel to *Plato's Mirror* was called *The Book of Lies*. Due in September, and it wasn't going well. Which made me irritable. Which made me say things to Faye I shouldn't have said. Which she forgave, with bravery and wounded eyes. Which led me to think our days together were numbered.

Hot summer that year. Late asphalt-scented nights, fan-cooled sheets, long showers. August storms rolled out of the west in gray-tumbled waves. For four nights in a row dry lightning flickered over the lake.

It was storming when our last August Friday party broke up, leaving behind the usual overturned bottles, aggrieved neighbors, and Conrad and William and Faye to appreciate the four A.M. calm.

Four *ante meridiem*, and the night cool enough that I turned off the air conditioner and threw open the windows, letting gusts of damp air flush away memory and smoke. We were all four of us beyond sleep, our private clocks lurching toward sunrise. There was no rain but plenty of distant lightning and fitful thunder. In the dark street outside, window awnings flapped like captive birds.

We didn't mention the mirror—Faye and Conrad were too much in awe of it to raise the subject lightly; William remained gently agnostic, and I despised the thing—until a great flash of lightning filled the apartment with purple light and thunder rattled the casements. A nearby strike. A transformer or hydroelectric substation had taken the hit, I guessed, because the lamplight dimmed and died and didn't come back.

The darkness made our shared space smaller. Faye, Conrad, and William huddled on the sofa while I rummaged for a tea candle in the kitchen drawer. The thought of the mirror struck them simultaneously while I was out of the room.

"Mirrors are funny things," William was saying, gossamer-eyed by candlelight. "When I was little there was a game we played. Like a dare-you thing: who's brave enough? You go into the bathroom and you turn off the light and you stare into the mirror, and there was this little chant, like *I want to see the ghost of Lizzie Borden* or some shit. So you think, hey, I'm not that stupid, and you do it, but you know what? Not five minutes go by before there's old Lizzie Borden staring back at you with her crazy eyes all lit up. It's imagination and bullshit, and you know that, but . . . there she is."

"Who's Lizzie Borden?" Faye asked.

"Axe murderess," Conrad said. "Before your time."

"Hey," I said. "Ghost stories. Shouldn't we roast a marshmallow or something?"

"Donald is reinforcing his little wall of rationality. I think he wants us to help."

Maybe. I had played that game too, the mirror game, when I was young, and William was right. Try as you might not to see it, the monster would always show up, raise your hackles, scare you into the light. I dislike mirrors. I dream about them from

time to time. The notion for *Plato's Mirror* had come straight
from a nightmare, and that was a factoid I had neglected to share
with Helen or Faye.

"But it's a perfect opportunity!" Faye said fervently. "Look,
Donald, the whole *city* is dark."

And so it was. The blackout had quenched every light for
blocks around. There were only occasional headlights down
along Bathurst Street, and not many of those. In the apartment
tower across the alley, one or two flashlights flickered behind the
windows. Otherwise, dark. But so what?

"The mirror!" Faye said. "We can see the whole city—I mean
the *essence* of the city."

"If we hurry," Conrad added. "They usually fix these things
pretty quick."

"Gimme the candle," Faye said. "I'll fetch the mirror."

I said, "You can't be serious."

"Yes!" A chorus. "We can!"

I burned my indignation in a joint and watched them go about
their little game. Faye took the mirror out onto the minuscule
balcony that adjoins the kitchen and balanced it on the Adirondack chair. Their voices were nervous and enthusiastic: children's voices. Faye had found the Christmas candles and they
each carried one, like monks with gaudy votive candles, red green
white, initiates into the Mystery. But no Dionysian underground,
only this fifth-story pigeon perch.

The hush of the four A.M. city was shocking. Live in a city long
enough, you forget about quiet. Stepping out onto the balcony
(reluctantly, with a candle of my own) I heard all the sounds
normally lost under the pressure of daylight: dripping eaves and
drawn breath and even a train whistle, some CN freight crossing
the Don. Tag ends of lightning flickered far away.

"Now blow out the candles," Faye said solemnly.

Out they went.

"Yours too, Donald."

"I like the light. Helps keep me from falling down."

"Don't be a pig! You'll ruin it."

So I blew out the candle.

But I didn't look at the mirror. In the dark, would Faye see this small act of cowardice?

I should have covered my ears, too. There was, at first, nothing to hear, only the steady drip of rainwater and a breath of wind. Then, finally, their voices, hushed with awe: *So beautiful* and *It can't be* and *oh God!*

So I looked, despite my best intentions.

At first the mirror seemed merely opaque, the same fogged-silver Victorian grotesque that might have been salvaged from any condemned Toronto boardinghouse or crumbling semidetached—junk, in other words. But then the glass misted and roiled like fog on a lake, and images surfaced, faintly at first, then suddenly crisp. From where I stood the mirror reflected the city skyline, towers immersed in cloud made bright and intricate as cowry shells in clear water, and every brick a prism.

"It's," William stuttered, *"heartbreaking. . . ."*

And it was. In the absence of light every object glowed with its own essence, radiated purer colors than any rainbow. How can a color you've never seen be so achingly familiar?

"And the people," Faye whispered.

People?

"Look hard," she urged me. "Let it in."

Yes. Behind stone walls, brick walls, and forests of rusted re-bar: people. People sleeping, mainly. People like small galaxies, constellations suspended in the night. "So beautiful," Faye sighed again. No two alike, yet all the same, as if souls had fallen from the clouds and drifted through open windows, the banked windrift of humanity.

Conrad and William had found each other's reflections. I saw them, too. They were in love, and love has its own spectrum, its own unearthly color. Something bright and gauzy (ectoplasm? passion?) floated between them, delicate as lace. Their bodies had been unclothed by the mirror. They had become bright vortices of energy, knots of life on a rope of spine. Bones like pastel coral.

Now Faye stepped into view. I felt the heat of her attention on my skin. She said, "Oh, Donald!" Words rippled the air. Her eyes were at once fierce and gentle, lenses focusing the light of distant suns. "Look at yourself!"

I meant to. I swear I did. But something else caught my attention.

"Faye?" I said.

". . . yes . . . ?"

"Some of those people out there—they're not—"

I felt her frown. "Not what? I don't know what you mean."

Not *Essences*. Oh, I saw the Essences, jewel-bright in their beds and sleeping the sleep of children. But also—*look harder*—the others. The ugly, intelligent ones. Call them Archons. They float (*look harder, Faye, look as hard as you can*) between the buildings, patroling the night in clockwork formation, skeletal, big-headed, hairy and malevolent as spiders. . . .

I backed up a step.

You look at them, they look at you. Their attention is caustic and demanding.

"Donald, what is it?"

"Can't you see them?"

Maybe she couldn't. Bless her green eyes: maybe only the good light got through. She started to say, "Look at *yourself*, Donald, and then—" But I lashed out, kicked the slats of the Adirondack chair, which collapsed spectacularly, the mirror shattering against the concrete floor of the balcony, each fragment flashing briefly bright as lightning before it chimed into darkness.

4.

Conrad and William went home—shocked, dazed, breathless. They had shared a memory they might never discuss—it really did beggar language—but it would always be there between them, for better or worse, a mystery that would echo whenever they touched.

Faye stayed behind—for a while.

She didn't say much. I did the talking.

I won't repeat the obscenities here. I cursed her at length for finding the mirror and for bringing it into my home and for mind-fucking my friends with it. When she began to cry I didn't let that stop me; I called her brainless, gullible, illiterate, an eager slut.

I was aware of hurting her. The urge to hurt her, to humiliate her, ultimately to drive her away, was palpable, a weight in my throat, a buzz behind my eyes. I watched her sink to her knees, sobbing, and felt gratified.

She said she would leave. I said, "About fucking time."

But before she left she went to the balcony and gathered what she could of the broken mirror, harvesting glass by candlelight. Came back with sharp silvered fragments and splintered wood and bloodied fingers. Taking back her gift, I thought, but then she did the unexpected.

She held up the largest fragment of the mirror, and blew out the candle, and said into the expanding darkness, "If only you could *see*, Donald!"

She wanted me to see that I was an angel—an Essence—as bright and full of color as the rest of them. To see my goodness, I suppose.

And I did see that. (I'm not blind.)

But I saw the *other*, too. I saw what Faye could not: the Archon, the one who had been with me all along, spindly arms close to mine, black-mandibled skull bobbing in back of my own. I'm not alone. I know this too well, Faye: I think I've always known it, glimpsed this image in too many dream-mirrors. The Archon is every day a little closer, close as a shadow now, close as a lover, and it will have me soon enough; and if it has me then it will have Faye or whoever replaces Faye. And the voice shouting obscenities, the shrill voice accusing her of ignorance and stupidity, the voice trying so fervently to drive her away, now, now before it's too late—

It's the voice of the angel.

She left, at last, in tears, for good.

I waited for sunrise. But the room was dark.

Angels wept. And I was not alone.

DIVIDED BY INFINITY

1.

In the year after Lorraine's death I contemplated suicide six times. Contemplated it seriously, I mean: six times sat with the fat bottle of clonazepam within reaching distance, six times failed to reach for it, betrayed by some instinct for life or disgusted by my own weakness.

I can't say I wish I had succeeded, because in all likelihood I did succeed, on each and every occasion. Six deaths. No, not just six. An infinite number.

Times six.

There are greater and lesser infinities.

But I didn't know that then.

I was only sixty years old.

I had lived all my life in the city of Toronto. I worked thirty-five years as a senior accountant for a Great Lakes cargo broker-age called Steamships Forwarding, Ltd., and took an early retirement in 1997, not long before Lorraine was diagnosed with the pancreatic cancer that killed her the following year. Back then she worked part-time in a Harbord Street used-book shop called Finders, a short walk from the university district, in a part of the city we both loved.

I still loved it, even without Lorraine, though the gloss had dimmed considerably. I lived there still, in a utility apartment

over an antique store, and I often walked the neighborhood—
down Spadina into the candy-bright intricacies of Chinatown, or
west to Kensington, foreign as a Bengali marketplace, where the
smell of spices and ground coffee mingled with the stink of sun-
ripened fish.

Usually I avoided Harbord Street. My grief was raw enough
without the provocation of the bookstore and its awkward memories. Today, however, the sky was a radiant blue, and the smell
of spring blossoms and cut grass made the city seem threatless.
I walked east from Kensington with a mesh bag filled with onions
and Havarti cheese, and soon enough found myself on Harbord
Street, which had moved another notch upscale since the old
days, more restaurants now, fewer macrobiotic shops, the palm
readers and bead shops banished for good and all.

But Finders was still there. It was a tar-shingled Victorian
house converted for retail, its hanging sign faded to illegibility.
A three-legged cat slumbered on the cracked concrete stoop.

I went in impulsively, but also because the owner, an old man
by the name of Oscar Ziegler, had sent an elaborate bouquet to
Lorraine's funeral the previous year, and I felt I owed him some
acknowledgment. According to Lorraine he lived upstairs and
never left the building.

The bookstore hadn't changed on the inside, either, since the
last time I had seen it. I didn't know it well (the store was Lorraine's turf and as a rule I had left her to it), but there was no
obvious evidence that more than a year had passed since my last
visit. It was the kind of shop with so much musty stock and so
few customers that it could have survived only under the most
generous circumstances—no doubt Ziegler owned the building
and had found a way to finesse his property taxes. The store was
not a labor of love, I suspected, so much as an excuse for Ziegler
to indulge his pack-rat tendencies.

It was a full nest of books. The walls were pineboard shelves,
floor to ceiling. Free-standing shelves divided the small interior
into box canyons and dimly lit hedgerows. The stock was old
and, not that I'm any judge, largely trivial, forgotten jazz-age
novels and belles-lettres, literary flotsam.

I stepped past cardboard boxes from which more books overflowed, to the rear of the store, where a cash desk had been wedged against the wall. This was where, for much of the last five years of her life, Lorraine had spent her weekday afternoons. I wondered whether book dust was carcinogenic. Maybe she had been poisoned by the turgid air, by the floating fragments of ivoried Frank Yerby novels, vagrant molecules of *Peyton Place* and *The Man in the Gray Flannel Suit*.

Someone else sat behind the desk now, a different woman, younger than Lorraine, though not what anyone would call young. A baby-boomer in denim overalls and a pair of eyeglasses that might have better suited the Hubble space telescope. Shoulder-length hair, gone gray, and an ingratiating smile, though there was something faintly haunted about the woman.

"Hi," she said amiably. "Anything I can help you find?"

"Is Oscar Ziegler around?"

Her eyes widened. "Uh, Mr. Ziegler? He's upstairs, but he doesn't usually like to be disturbed. Is he expecting you?"

She seemed astonished at the possibility that Ziegler would be expecting anyone, or that anyone would want to see Ziegler. Maybe it was a bad idea. "No," I said, "I just dropped by on the chance . . . you know, my wife used to work here."

"I see."

"Please don't bother him. I'll just browse for a while."

"Are you a book collector, or—?"

"Hardly. These days I read the newspaper. The only books I've kept are old paperbacks. Not the sort of thing Mr. Ziegler would stock."

"You'd be surprised. Mysteries? Chandler, Hammett, John Dickson Carr? Because we have some firsts over by the stairs. . . ."

"I used to read some mysteries. Mostly, though, it was science fiction I liked."

"Really? You look more like a mystery reader."

"There's a look?"

She laughed. "Tell you what. Science fiction? We got a box of paperbacks in last week. Right over there, under the ladder.

Check it out, and I'll tell Mr. Ziegler you're here. Uh—"

"My name is Keller. Bill Keller. My wife was Lorraine."

She held out her hand. "I'm Deirdre. Just have a look; I'll be back in a jiff."

I wanted to stop her but didn't know how. She went through a bead curtain and up a dim flight of stairs while I pulled a leathery cardboard box onto a chair seat and prepared for some dutiful time-killing. Certainly I didn't expect to find anything I wanted, though I would probably have to buy something as the price of a courtesy call, especially if Ziegler was coaxed out of his lair to greet me. But what I had told Deirdre was true; though I had been an eager reader in my youth, I hadn't bought more than an occasional softcover since 1970. Fiction is a young man's pastime. I had ceased to be curious about other people's lives, much less other worlds.

Still, the box was full of forty-year-old softcover books, Ace and Ballantine paperbacks mainly, and it was nice to see the covers again, the Richard Powers abstracts, translucent bubbles on infinite plains, or Jack Gaughan sketches, angular and insectile. Titles rich with key words: Time, Space, Worlds, Infinity. Once I had loved this sort of thing.

And then, amongst these faded jewels, I found something I did not expect—

And another. And another.

The bead curtain parted and Ziegler entered the room.

He was a bulky man, but he moved with the exaggerated caution of the frail. A plastic tube emerged from his nose, was taped to his cheek with a dirty Band-Aid and connected to an oxygen canister slung from his shoulder. He hadn't shaved for a couple of days. He wore what looked like a velveteen frock coat draped over a T-shirt and a pair of pinstriped pajama bottoms. His hair, what remained of it, was feathery and white. His skin was the color of thrift-shop Tupperware.

Despite his appearance, he gave me a wide grin.

"Mr. Ziegler," I said. "I'm Bill Keller. I don't know if you remember—"

He thrust his pudgy hand forward. "Of course! No need to explain. Terrible about Lorraine. I think of her often." He turned to Deirdre, who emerged from the curtain behind him. "Mr. Keller's wife. . . ." He drew a labored breath. "Died last year."

"I'm sorry," Deirdre said.

"She was . . . a wonderful woman. Friendly by nature. A joy. Of course, death isn't final . . . we all go on, I believe, each in his own way. . . ."

There was more of this—enough that I regretted stopping by—but I couldn't doubt Ziegler's sincerity. Despite his intimidating appearance there was something almost wilfully childlike about him, a kind of embalmed innocence, if that makes any sense.

He asked how I had been and what I had been doing. I answered as cheerfully as I could and refrained from asking after his own health. His cheeks reddened as he stood, and I wondered if he shouldn't be sitting down. But he seemed to be enjoying himself. He eyed the five slender books I'd brought to the cash desk.

"Science fiction!" he said. "I wouldn't have taken you for a science fiction reader, Mr. Keller."

(Deirdre glanced at me: *Told you so!*)

"I haven't been a steady reader for a long time," I said. "But I found some interesting items."

"The good old stuff," Ziegler gushed. "The pure quill. Does it strike you, Mr. Keller, that we live every day in the science fiction of our youth?"

"I hadn't noticed."

"There was a time when science seemed so sterile. It didn't yield up the wonders we had been led to expect. Only a bleak, lifeless solar system . . . half dozen desert worlds, baked or frozen, take your pick, and the gas giants . . . great roaring seas of methane and ammonia. . . ."

I nodded politely.

"But now!" Ziegler exclaimed. "Life on Mars! Oceans under Europa! Comets plunging into Jupiter—!"

"I see what you mean."

"And here on Earth—the human genome, cloned animals,

mind-altering drugs! Computer networks! Computer *viruses!*"
He slapped his thigh. "I have a *Teflon hip*, if you can imagine
such a thing!"

"Pretty amazing," I agreed, though I hadn't thought much
about any of this.

"Back when we read these books, Mr. Keller, when we read
Heinlein or Simak or Edmond Hamilton, we longed to immerse
ourselves in the strange . . . the *outre.* And now—well—here we
are!" He smiled breathlessly and summed up his thesis. *"Immersed in the strange.* All it takes is time. Just . . . time. Shall I
put these in a bag for you?"

He bagged the books without looking at them. When I fumbled out my wallet, he raised his hand.

"No charge. This is for Lorraine. And to thank you for stopping by."

I couldn't argue . . . and I admit I didn't want to draw his attention to the paperbacks, in the petty fear that he might notice
how unusual they were and refuse to part with them. I took the
paper bag from his parchment hand, feeling faintly guilty.

"Perhaps you'll come back," he said.

"I'd like to."

"Anytime," Ziegler said, inching toward his bead curtain and
the musty stairway behind it, back into the cloying dark. "Anything you're looking for, I can help you find it."

Crossing College Street, freighted with groceries, I stepped into
the path of a car, a yellow Hyundai racing a red light. The driver
swerved around me, but it was a near thing. The wheel wells
brushed my trouser legs. My heart stuttered a beat.

. . . and I died, perhaps, a small infinity of times.

Probabilities collapse. I become increasingly unlikely.

"Immersed in the strange," Ziegler had said.

But had I ever wanted that? *Really* wanted that?

"Be careful," Lorraine told me one evening in the long month
before she died. Amazingly, she had seemed to think of it as my
tragedy, not hers. "Don't despise life."

Difficult advice.

Did I "despise life"? I think I did not; that is, there were times when the world seemed a pleasant enough place, times when a cup of coffee and a morning in the sun seemed good enough reasons to continue to draw breath. I remained capable of smiling at babies. I was even able to look at an attractive young woman and feel a response more immediate than nostalgia.

But I missed Lorraine terribly, and we had never had children, neither of us had any close living relations or much in the way of friends; I was unemployed and unemployable, confined forever-more within the contracting walls of my pension and our modest savings . . . all the joy and much of the simple structure of my life had been leeched away, and the future looked like more of the same, a protracted fumble toward the grave.

If anything postponed the act of suicide it wasn't courage or principle but the daily trivia. I would kill myself (I decided more than once), but not until after the nightly news . . . not until I paid the electric bill . . . not until I had taken my walk.

Not until I solved the mystery I'd brought home from Finders.

I won't describe the books in detail. They looked more or less like others of their kind. What was strange about them was that I didn't recognize them, although this was a genre (paperback science fiction of the 1950s and '60s) I had once known in inti-mate detail.

The shock was not just unfamiliarity, since I might have missed any number of minor works by minor writers; but these were major novels by well-known names, not retitled works or variant editions. A single example: I sat down that night with a book called *The Stone Pillow*, by a writer whose identity any science fiction follower would instantly recognize. It was a Signet paperback circa 1957, with a cover by the artist Paul Lehr in the period style. According to the credit slug, the story had been serialized in *Astounding* in 1946. The pages were browned at the margins; the glued spine was brittle as bone china. I handled the book carefully, but I couldn't resist reading it, and in so far as I was able to judge it was a plausible example of the late author's well-known style and habits of thought. I enjoyed it a great deal and went to bed convinced of its authenticity. Either I had missed it, somehow—in the days when *not* missing such things meant a great deal to me—or it had slipped out of memory. No other explanation presented itself.

One such item wouldn't have worried me. But I had brought home four more volumes equally inexplicable.

Chalk it up to age, I thought. Or worse. Senility. Alzheimer's. Either way, a bad omen.

Sleep was elusive.

The next logical step might have been to see a doctor. Instead, the next morning I thumbed through the yellow pages for a used-book dealer who specialized in period science fiction. After a couple of calls I reached a young man named Niemand who offered to evaluate the books if I brought them to him that afternoon.

I told him I'd be there by one.

If nothing else, it was an excuse to prolong my life one more interminable day.

Niemand—his store was an overheated second-story loft over a noisy downtown street—gave the books a long, thoughtful examination.

"Fake," he said finally. "They're fake."

"Fake? You mean . . . counterfeit?"

"If you like, but that's stretching a point. Nobody counterfeits books, even valuable books. The idea is ludicrous. I mean, what do you do, set up a press and go through all the work of producing a bound volume, duplicate the type, flaws and all, and then flog it on the collector's market? You'd never recoup your expenses, not even if you came up with a convincing Gutenburg Bible. In the case of books like this, the idea's doubly absurd. Maybe if they were one-off from an abandoned print run or something, but, hell, people would know about that. Nope. Sorry, but these are just . . . fake."

"But—well, obviously, somebody did go to the trouble of faking them."

He nodded. "Obviously. It's flawless work, and it can't have been cheap. And the books are genuinely old. *Contemporary* fakes, maybe . . . maybe some obsessive fan with a big disposable income, rigging up books he wanted to exist . . ."

"Are they valuable?"

"They're certainly odd. Valuable? Not to me. Tell you the truth, I kind of wish you hadn't brought them in."

"Why?"

"They're creepy. They're too good. Kind of *X-Files*." He gave me a sour grin. "Make up your own science fiction story."

"Or live in it," I said. We live in the science fiction of our youth.

He pushed the books across his cluttered desk. "Take 'em away, Mr. Keller. And if you find out where they came from—"

"Yes?"

"I really don't want to know."

Items I noticed in the newspaper that evening:

GENE THERAPY RENDERS HEART BYPASS OBSOLETE

BANK OF ZURICH FIRST WITH QUANTUM ENCRYPTION

SETI RESEARCHERS SPOT "POSSIBLE" ET RADIO SOURCE

I didn't want to go back to Ziegler, not immediately. It felt like admitting defeat—like looking up the answer to a magazine puzzle I couldn't solve.

But there was no obvious next step to take, so I put the whole thing out of my mind, or tried to; watched television, did laundry, shined my shoes.

None of this pathetic sleight of hand provided the slightest distraction.

I was not (just as I had told Deirdre) a mystery lover, and I didn't love this mystery, but it was a turbulence in the flow of the passing days, therefore interesting. When I had savored the strangeness of it to a satisfying degree, I took myself in hand and carried the books back to Finders, meaning to demand an explanation.

Oscar Ziegler was expecting me.

The late-May weather was already too humid, a bright sun bearing down from the ozone-depleted sky. Walking wasn't such a pleasure under the circumstances. I arrived at Finders plucking my shirt away from my body. Graceless. The woman Deirdre looked up from her niche at the rear of the store. "Mr. Keller, right?" She didn't seem especially pleased to see me.

I meant to ask if Ziegler was available, but she waved me off: "He said if you showed up you were to go on upstairs. That's, uh, really unusual."

"Shouldn't you let him know I'm here?"

"Really, he's expecting you." She waved at the bead curtain, almost a challenge: Go on, if you must.

The curtain made a sound like chattering teeth behind me. The stairway was dim. Dust balls quivered on the risers and clung to the threadbare coco-mat tread. At the top was a door silted under so many layers of ancient paint that the molding had softened into gentle dunes.

Ziegler opened the door and waved me in.

His room was lined with books. He stepped back, settled himself into an immense overstuffed easy chair, and invited me to look at his collection. But the titles at eye level were disappointing. They were old cloth volumes of Gurdjieff and Ouspenski, Velikovsky and Crowley—the usual pseudo-gnostic spiritualist bullshit, pardon my language. Like the room itself, the books radiated dust and boredom. I felt obscurely disappointed. So this was Oscar Ziegler, one more pathetic old man with a penchant for magic and cabalism.

Between the books, medical supplies: inhalers, oxygen tanks, pill bottles.

Ziegler might be old, but his eyesight was still keen. "Judging by the expression on your face, you find my den distasteful."

"Not at all."

"Oh, fess up, Mr. Keller. You're too old to be polite and I'm too old to pretend I don't notice."

I gestured at the books. "I was never much for the occult."

"That's understandable. It's claptrap, really. I keep those volumes for nostalgic reasons. To be honest, there was a time when I looked there for answers. That time is long past."

"I see."

"Now tell me why you came."

I showed him the softcover books, told him how I'd taken them to Niemand for a professional assessment. Confessed my own bafflement.

Ziegler took the books into his lap. He looked at them briefly and took a long drag from his oxygen mask. He didn't seem especially impressed. "I'm hardly responsible for every volume that comes into the store."

"Of course not. And I'm not complaining. I just wondered—"

"If I knew where they came from? If I could offer you a meaningful explanation?"

"Basically, yes."

"Well," Ziegler said. "Well. Yes and no. Yes and no."

"I'm sorry?"

"That is . . . no, I can't tell you precisely where they came from. Deirdre probably bought them from someone off the street. Cash or credit, and I don't keep detailed records. But it doesn't really matter."

"Doesn't it?"

He took another lungful from the oxygen bottle. "Oh, it could have been anyone. Even if you tracked down the original vendor—which I guarantee you won't be able to do—you wouldn't learn anything useful."

"You don't seem especially surprised by this."

"Implying that I know more than I'm saying." He smiled ruefully. "I've never been in this position before, though you're right, it doesn't surprise me. Did you know, Mr. Keller, that I am immortal?"

Here we go, I thought. The pitch. Ziegler didn't care about the books. I had come for an explanation; he wanted to sell me a religion.

"And *you*, Mr. Keller. You're immortal, too."

What was I doing here, in this shabby place with this shabby old man? There was nothing to say.

"But I can't explain it," Ziegler went on; "that is, not in the depth it deserves. There's a volume here—I'll lend it to you—" He stood, precariously, and huffed across the room.

I looked at his books again while he rummaged for the volume in question. Below the precambrian deposits of the occult was a small sediment of literature. First editions, presumably valuable.

And not all familiar.

Had Ernest Hemingway written a book called *Pamplona*? (But here it was, its Scribners dust jacket protected in brittle mylar.) *Cromwell and Company*, by Charles Dickens? *Under the Absolute*, by Aldous Huxley?

"Ah, books." Ziegler, smiling, came up behind me. "They bob like corks on an ocean. Float between worlds, messages in bottles. This will tell you what you need to know."

The book he gave me was cheaply made, with a utilitarian olive-drab jacket. *You Will Never Die*, by one Carl G. Soziere.

"Come back when you've read it."

"I will," I lied.

"I had a feeling," Deirdre said, "you'd come downstairs with one of those."

The Soziere book. "You've heard of it?"

"Not until I took this job. Mr. Ziegler gave me a copy. But I speak from experience. Every once in a long while, somebody comes in with a question or a complaint. They go upstairs. And they come back down with *that*."

At which point I realized I had left the paperbacks in Ziegler's room. I suppose I could have gone back for them, but it seemed somehow churlish. But it was a loss. Not that I loved the books, particularly, but they were the only concrete evidence I had of the mystery—they *were* the mystery. Now Ziegler had them back in his possession. And I had *You Will Never Die*.

"It looks like a crank book."

"Oh, it is," Deirdre said. "Kind of a parallel-worlds argument, you know, J. W. Dunne and so on, with some quantum physics thrown in; actually, I'm surprised a major publisher didn't pick it up."

"You've read it?"

"I'm a sucker for that kind of thing, if you want the truth."

"Don't tell me. It changed your life." I was smiling.

She smiled back. "It didn't even change my mind."

But there was an odd note of worry in her voice.

Of course I read it.

Deirdre was right about *You Will Never Die*. It had been published by some private or vanity press, but the writing wasn't crude. It was slick, even witty in places.

And the argument was seductive. Shorn of the babble about Planck radii and Prigogine complexity and the Dancing Wu-Li Masters, it came down to this:

Consciousness, like matter, like energy, is preserved.

You are born, not an individual, but an infinity of individuals, in an infinity of identical worlds. "Consciousness," your individual awareness, is shared by this infinity of beings.

At birth (or at conception; Soziere wasn't explicit), this span of selves begins to divide, as alternate possibilities are indulged or rejected. The infant turns his head not to the left or to the right, but both. One infinity of worlds becomes two; then four; then eight, and so on, exponentially.

But the underlying essence of consciousness continues to connect all these disparate possibilities.

The upshot? Soziere says it all in his title.

You cannot die.

Consider. Suppose, tomorrow afternoon, you walk in front of a speeding eighteen-wheeler. The grillwork snaps your neck and what remains of you is sausaged under the chassis. Do you die? Well, yes; an infinity of you *does* die; but infinity is divisible by itself. Another infinity of you steps out of the path of the truck, or didn't leave the house that day, or recovers in hospital. The you-ness of you doesn't die; it simply continues to reside in those remnant selves.

An infinite set has been subtracted from infinity; but what remains, remains infinite.

The subjective experience is that the accident simply doesn't happen.

Consider that bottle of clonazepam I keep beside the bed. Six times I reached for it, meaning to kill myself. Six times stopped myself.

In the great wilderness of worlds, I must have succeeded more often than I failed. My cold and vomit-stained corpse was carted off to whatever grave or urn awaits it, and a few acquaintances briefly mourned.

But that's not *me*. By definition, you can't experience your own death. Death is the end of consciousness. And consciousness persists. In the language of physics, consciousness is conserved.

I am the one who wakes up in the morning.

Always.

Every morning.

I don't die.

I just become increasingly *unlikely*.

I spent the next few days watching television, folding laundry, trimming my nails—spinning my wheels.

I tossed Soziere's little tome into a corner and left it there.

And when I was done kidding myself, I went to see Deirdre.

I didn't even know her last name. All I knew was that she had read Soziere's book and remained skeptical of it, and I was eager to have my own skepticism refreshed.

You think odd things, sometimes, when you're too often alone.

I caught Deirdre on her lunch break. Ziegler didn't come downstairs to man the desk; the store simply closed between noon and one every weekday. The May heat wave had broken; the sky was a soft, deep blue, the air balmy. We sat at a sidewalk table outside a lunch-and-coffee restaurant.

Her full name was Deirdre Frank. She was fifty and unmarried and had run her own retail business until some legal difficulty closed her down. She was working at Finders while she reorganized her life. And she understood why I had come to her.

"There's a couple of tests I apply," she said, "whenever I read this kind of book. First, is it likely to improve anyone's life?

Which is a trickier question than it sounds. Any number of people will tell you they found happiness with the Scientologists or the Moonies or whatever, but what that usually means is they narrowed their focus—they can't see past the bars of their cage. Okay, *You Will Never Die* isn't a cult book, but I doubt it will make anybody a better person.

"Second, is there any way to test the author's claims? Soziere aced that one beautifully, I have to admit. His argument is that there's no *subjective* experience of death—your family might die, your friends, your grade-school teachers, the Princess of Wales, but never *you*. And in some other world, you die and other people go on living. How do you prove such a thing? Obviously, you can't. What Soziere tries to do is *infer* it, from quantum physics and lots of less respectable sources. It's a bubble theory—it floats over the landscape, touching nothing."

I was probably blushing by this time.

Deirdre said, "You took it seriously, didn't you? Or half seriously. . . ."

"Half at most. I'm not stupid. But it's an appealing idea."

Her eyes widened. *"Appealing?"*

"Well—there are people who've died. People I miss. I like to think of them going on somewhere, even if it isn't a place I can reach."

She was aghast. "God, no! Soziere's book isn't a fairy tale, Mr. Keller—it's a horror story!"

"Pardon me?"

"Think about it! At first it sounds like an invitation to suicide. You don't like where you are, put a pistol in your mouth and go somewhere else—somewhere better, maybe, even if it is inherently less likely. But take you for example. You're what, sixty years old? Or so? Well, great, you inhabit a universe where a healthy human being can obtain the age of sixty, fine, but what next? Maybe you wake up tomorrow morning and find out they cured cancer, say, or heart disease—excluding you from all the worlds where William Keller dies of a colon tumor or an aneurism. And then? You're a hundred years old, a hundred and twenty—do you turn into some kind of freak? So unlikely, in

Soziere's sense, that you end up in a circus or a research ward? Do they clone you a fresh body? Do you end up as some kind of half-human robot, a brain in a bottle? And in the meantime the world changes around you, everything familiar is left behind, you see others die, maybe millions of others, maybe the human race dies out or evolves into something else, and you go on, and on, while the universe groans under the weight of your unlikeliness, and there's no escape, every death is just another rung up the ladder of weirdness and disorientation. . . ."

I hadn't thought of it that way.

Yes, the *reductio ad absurdum* of Soziere's theory was a kind of relativistic paradox: as the observer's life grows more unlikely, he perceives the world around him becoming proportionately more strange; and down those unexplored, narrow rivers of mortality might well lie a cannibal village.

Or the Temple of Gold.

What if Deirdre was too pessimistic? What if, among the all the unlikely worlds, there was one in which Lorraine had survived her cancer?

Wouldn't that be worth waiting for?

Worth *looking* for, no matter how strange the consequences might be?

News items that night:

NEURAL IMPLANTS RESTORE VISION IN FIFTEEN PATIENTS

"TELOMERASE COCKTAIL" CREATES IMMORTAL LAB MICE

TWINNED NEUTRON STARS POSE POTENTIAL THREAT, NASA SAYS

My sin was longing.

Not grief. Grief isn't a sin, and is anyway unavoidable. Yes, I grieved for Lorraine, grieved long and hard, but I don't remember having a choice. I miss her still. Which is as it should be.

But I had given in too often to the vulgar yearnings. Mourned youth, mourned better days. Made an old man's map of roads not taken, from the stale perspective of a dead end.

Reached for the clonazepam and turned my hand away, freighted every inch with deaths beyond counting.

I wonder if my captors understand this?

I went back to Ziegler—nodding at Deirdre, who was disappointed to see me, as I vanished behind the bead curtain.

"This doesn't explain it." I gave him back *You Will Never Die.*

"Explain," Ziegler said guilelessly, "what?"

"The paperbacks I bought from you."

"I don't recall."

"Or these—"

I turned to his bookshelf.

Copies of *In Our Time, Our Mutual Friend, Beyond the Mexique Bay.*

"I didn't realize they needed explaining."

I was the victim of a conjuror's trick, gulled and embarrassed. I closed my mouth.

"Anomalous experience," Ziegler said knowingly. "You're right, Soziere doesn't explain it. Personally I think there must be a kind of critical limit—a degree of accumulated unlikeliness so great that the illusion of normalcy can no longer be wholly sustained." He smiled, not pleasantly. "Things leak. I think especially books, books being little islands of mind. They trail their authors across phenomenological borders like lost puppies. That's why I love them. But you're awfully young to experience such phenomena. You must have made yourself very unlikely indeed—more and more unlikely, day after day! What have you been *doing* to yourself, Mr. Keller?"

I left him sucking oxygen from a fogged plastic mask.

Reaching for the bottle of clonazepam.

Drawing back my hand.

But how far must the charade proceed? Does the universe gauge intent? What if I touch the bottle? What if I open it and peer inside?

(These questions, of course, are answered now. I have only myself to blame.)

I had tumbled a handful of the small white tablets into my hand and was regarding them with the cool curiosity of an entomologist when the telephone rang.

Pills or telephone?

Both, presumably, in Soziere's multiverse.

I answered the phone.

It was Deirdre. "He's dead," she told me. "Ziegler. I thought you should know."

I said, "I'm sorry."

"I'm taking care of the arrangements. He was so alone . . . no family, no friends, just nothing."

"Will there be a service?"

"He wanted to be cremated. You're welcome to come. It might be nice if somebody besides me showed up."

"I will. What about the store?"

"That's the crazy part. According to the bank, he left it to *me*." Her voice was choked with emotion. "Can you imagine that? I never even called him by his first name! To be honest—oh, God, I didn't even *like* him! Now he leaves me this tumbledown business of his!"

I told her I'd see her at the mortuary.

I paid no attention to the news that night, save to register the lead stories, which were ominous and strange.

We live, Ziegler had said, in the science fiction of our youth.

The "ET signals" NASA scientists had discovered were, it turned out, a simple star map, at the center of which was—not the putative aliens' home world—but a previously undiscovered binary neutron star in the constellation Orion.

The message, one astronomer speculated, might be a warning. Neutron-star pairs are unstable. When they eventually collide, drawn together by their enormous gravity, the collision produces a black hole—and in the process a burst of gamma rays and cosmic radiation, strong enough to scour the Earth of life if the event occurs within some two or three thousand light-years of us.

The freshly discovered neutron stars were well within that range. As for the collision, it might happen in ten years, a thousand, ten thousand—none of the quoted authorities would commit to a date, though estimates had been shrinking daily.

Nice of our neighbors to warn us, I thought.

But how long had that warning bell been ringing, and for how many centuries had we ignored it?

Deirdre's description of the Soziere book as a "bubble theory" haunted me.

No proof, no evidence could exist: that was ruled out by the theory itself—or at least, as Ziegler had implied, there would be no evidence one could share.

But there *had* been evidence, at least in my case: the paperback books, "anomalous" books imported, presumably, from some other timeline, a history I had since lost to cardiac arrest, a car accident, clonazepam.

But the books were gone.

I had traded them, in effect, for *You Will Never Die*.

Which I had returned to Oscar Ziegler.

Cup your hands as you might. The water runs through your fingers.

There was only the most rudimentary service at the crematorium where Ziegler's body was burned. A few words from an Episcopal minister Deirdre had hired for the occasion, an earnest young man in clerical gear and neatly pressed Levis who pronounced his consolations and hurried away as if late for another function. Deirdre said, afterward, "I don't know if I've been given a gift or an obligation. For a man who never left his room, Mr. Ziegler had a way of weaving people into his life." She shook her head sadly. "If any of it really matters. I mean, if we're not devoured by aliens or God knows what. You can't turn on the news these days. . . . Well, I guess he bailed out just in time."

Or moved on. Moved someplace where his emphysema was curable, his failing heart reparable, his aging cells regenerable.

Shunting the train Oscar Ziegler along a more promising if less plausible track. . . .

"The evidence," I said suddenly.

"What?"

"The books I told you about."

"Oh. Right. Well, I'm sorry, but I didn't get a good look at them." She frowned. "Is *that* what you're thinking? Oh, shit, that fucking Soziere book of his! It's *bait*, Mr. Keller, don't you get it? Not to speak ill of the dead, but he loved to suck people into whatever cloistered little mental universe he inhabited, misery loves company, and that book was always the bait—"

"No," I said, excited despite my best intentions, as if Ziegler's cremation had been a message, his personal message to me, that the universe discarded bodies like used Kleenex but that consciousness was continuous, seamless, immortal. . . . "I mean about the evidence. You didn't see it—but someone did."

"Leave it alone. You don't understand about Ziegler. Oscar Ziegler was a sour, poisonous old man. Maybe older than he looked. That's what I thought of when I read Soziere's book: Oscar Ziegler, someone so ridiculously old that he wakes up every morning surprised he's still a human being." She stared fiercely at me. "What exactly are you contemplating here—serial suicide?"

"Nothing so drastic."

I thanked her and left.

The paradox of proof.

I went to Niemand's store as soon as I left Deirdre.

I had shown the books to Niemand, the book dealer. He was the impossible witness, the corroborative testimony. If Niemand had seen the books, then I was sane; if Niemand had seen the books they might well turn up among Ziegler's possessions, and I could establish their true provenance and put all this dangerous Soziere mythology behind me.

But Niemand's little second-story loft store had closed. The sign was gone. The door was locked and the space was for lease.

Neither the jeweler downstairs nor the coffee-shop girl next door remembered the store, its clientele, or Niemand himself.

There was no Niemand in the phone book. Nor could I find his commercial listing. Not even in my yellow pages at home, where I had first looked it up.

Or remembered looking it up.

Anomalous experience.

Which constituted proof, of a kind, though Ziegler was right; it was not transferable. I could convince no one, ultimately, save myself.

The television news was full of apocalypse that night. A rumor had swept the Internet that the great gamma-ray burst was imminent, only days away. No, it was not, scientists insisted, but they allowed themselves to be drawn by their CNN inquisitors into hypothetical questions. Would there be any safe place? A half-mile underground, say, or two, or three? (*Probably not*, they admitted; or, *We don't have the full story yet.*)

To a man, or woman, they looked unsettled and skittish.

I went to bed knowing she was out there, Lorraine, I mean, out among the plenitude of worlds and stars. Alone, perhaps, since I must have died to her—infinities apart, certainly, but enclosed within the same inconceivably vast multiuniverse, as alike, in our way, as two snowflakes in an avalanche.

I slept with the pill bottle cradled in my hand.

The trick, I decided, was to abandon the charade, to *mean* the act.

In other words, to swallow twenty or thirty tablets—a more difficult act than you might imagine—and wash them down with a neat last shot of Glenlivet.

But Deirdre called.

Almost too late.

Not late enough.

I picked up the phone, confused, my hands butting the receiver like antagonistic parade balloons. I said, or meant to say, "Lorraine?"

But it was Deirdre, only Deirdre, and before long Deirdre was shouting in an annoying way. I let the phone drop.

I suppose she called 911.

2.

I woke in a hospital bed.

I lay there passively for more than an hour, by the digital clock on the bedstand, cresting waves of sleep and wondering at the silence, until I was visited by Candice.

Her name was written on her lapel tag. Candice was a nurse, with a throaty Jamaican accent and wide, sad eyes.

"You're awake," she said, barely glancing at me.

My head hurt. My mouth tasted of ashes and quicklime. I needed to pee, but there was a catheter in the way.

"I think I want to see a doctor," I managed.

"Prob'ly you do," Candice agreed. "And prob'ly you should. But our last resident went home yesterday. I can take the catheter out, if that's what you want."

"There are no doctors?"

"Home with their families like everybody else." She fluffed my pillow. "Only us pathetic lonelyhearts left, Mr. Keller. You been unconscious ten days."

Later she wheeled me down the corridor—though I insisted I could have walked—to a lounge with a tall plateglass window, where the ward's remaining patients had gathered to talk and weep and watch the fires that burned fitfully through the downtown core.

Soziere's curse. We become—or we make ourselves—less "likely." But it's not our own unlikeliness we perceive; instead, we see the world growing strange around us.

The lights are out all over the city. The hospital, fortunately, has its own generator. I tried to call Deirdre from a hospital phone, but there was no dial tone, just a crackling hiss, like the last groove in an LP record.

———

The previous week's newspapers, stacked by the door of the hospital lounge, were dwindling broadsheets containing nothing but stark outlines of the impending gamma-ray disaster.

The extraterrestrial warning had been timely. Timely, though we read it far too late. Apparently it not only identified the threatening binary neutron stars—which were spiraling at last into gaudy destruction, about to emit a burst of radiation brighter than a billion galaxies—but provided a calculable time scale.

A countdown, in other words, which had already closed in on its ultimate zero. Too close to home, a black hole was about to be born.

None of us would survive that last flash of annihilating fire.

Or, at least, if we did, we would all become extremely unlikely.

I remember a spot of blue luminescence roughly the size of a dinner plate at arm's length, suspended above the burning city: Cherenkov radiation. Gamma rays fractured molecules in the upper atmosphere, loading the air with nitric oxides the color of dry blood. The sky was frying like a bad picture tube.

The hard, ionizing radiation would arrive within hours. Cosmic rays striking the wounded atmosphere would trigger particle cascades, washing the crust of the Earth with what the papers called "high-energy muons."

I was tired of the ward lounge, the incessant weeping and periodic shouting.

Candice took me aside. "I'll tell you," she said, "what I told the others. I been into the medicine cupboard. If you don't want to wait, there are pills you can take."

The air smelled suddenly of burning plastic. Static electricity drew bright blue sparks from metal shelves and gurney carts. Surely this would be the end: the irrevocable death, the utter annihilation, if there can ever be an end.

I told Candice a nightcap might be a good idea, and she smiled wanly and brought me the pills.

3.

They want me to keep on with my memoirs.

They take the pages away from me, exchange them for greater rations of food.

The food is pale, chalky, with the claylike texture of goat cheese. They excrete it from a sort of spinerette, white obscene lumps of it, like turds.

I prefer to think of them as advanced machines rather than biological entities—vending machines, say, not the eight-foot-long centipedes they appear to be.

They've mastered the English language. (I don't know how.) They say "please" and "thank you." Their voices are thin and reedy, a sound like tree branches creaking on a windy winter night.

They tell me I've been dead for ten thousand years.

Today they let me out of my bubble, let me walk outside, with a sort of mirrored umbrella to protect me from the undiluted sunlight.

The sunlight is intense, the air cold and thin. They have explained, in patient but barely intelligible whispers, that the gamma ray burst and subsequent bath of cosmic radiation stripped the earth of its ozone layer as well as much of the upper atmosphere. The oxygen that remains, they say, is "fossil" oxygen, no longer replenished. The soil is alive with radioactive nuclei: samarium 146, iodine 129, isotopes of lead, of plutonium.

There is no macroscopic life on Earth. Present company excepted.

Everything died. People, plants, plankton, everything but the bacteria inhabiting the rocks of the deep mantle or the scalding water around undersea volcanic vents. The surface of the planet—here, at least—has been scoured by wind and radiation into a rocky desert.

All this happened ten thousand years ago. The sun shines placidly on the lifeless soil, the distant blue-black mountains.

Everything I loved is dead.

———

I can't imagine the technology they used to resurrect me, to re-create me, as they insist, from desiccated fragments of biological tissue tweezed from rocks. It's not just my DNA they have recovered but (apparently, somehow) my memories, my self, my consciousness.

I suppose Carl Soziere wouldn't be surprised.

I ask about others, other survivors reclaimed from the water-less desert. My captors (or saviors) only spindle their sickeningly mobile bodies: a gesture of negation, I've come to understand, the equivalent of a shake of the head. There are no other survivors.

And yet I can't help wondering whether Lorraine waits to be salvaged from her grave—some holographic scrap of her, at least; information scattered by time, like the dust of an ancient book.

There is nothing in my transparent cell but bowls of water and food, a floor soft enough to serve as a mattress, and the blunted writing instruments and clothlike paper. (Are they afraid I might commit suicide?)

The memoirs run out. I want the extra food, and I enjoy the diversion of writing, but what remains to be said? And to whom?

Lately I've learned to distinguish between my captors.

The "leader" (that is, the individual most likely to address me directly and see that others attend to my needs) is a duller shade of silver-white, his cartilaginous shell dusted with fine powder. He (or she) possesses many orifices, all visible when he sways back to speak. I have identified his speaking orifice and his food-excreting orifice, but there are three others I haven't seen in use, including a tooth-lined maw that must be a kind of mouth.

"We are the ones who warned you," he tells me. "For half of a million years we warned you. If you had known, you might have protected yourself." His grammar is impeccable, to my ears anyway, although consonants in close proximity make him stumble and hiss. "You might have deconstructed your moon, created a shield, as we did. Numerous strategies might have succeeded in preserving your world."

The tocsin had sounded, in other words, for centuries. We had simply been too dull to interpret it, until the very end, when nothing could be done to counter the threat.

I try not to interpret this as a rebuke.

"Now we have learned to transsect distance," the insectile creature explains. "Then, we could only signal."

I ask whether he could re-create the Earth, revive the dead.

"No," he says. Perhaps the angle of his body signifies regret. "One of you is puzzle enough."

They live apart from me, in an immense silver half-sphere embedded in the alkaline soil. Their spaceship?

For a day they haven't come. I sit alone in my own much smaller shelter, its bubble walls polarized to filter the light but transparent enough to show the horizon with vicious clarity. I feel abandoned, a fly on a vast pane of dusty glass. And hungry. And thirsty.

They return—apologetically—with water, with paper and writing implements, and with a generous supply of food, thoughtfully pre-excreted.

They are compiling, they tell me, a sort of interstellar database, combining the functions of library, archeological museum, and telephone exchange. They are most grateful for my writings, which have been enthusiastically received. "Your cosmology," by which they must mean Soziere's cosmology, "is quite distinctive."

I thank them but explain that there is nothing more to write— and no audience I can even begin to imagine.

The news perplexes them. The leader asks, "Do you need a human audience?"

Yes. Yes, that's what I need. A human audience. Lorraine, warning me away from despair, or even Deirdre, trying vainly to shield me from black magic.

They confer for another day.

I walk outside my bubble at sunset, alone, with my silver umbrella tilted toward the western horizon. When the stars appear, they are astonishingly bright and crisp. I can see the frosted breath of the Milky Way.

"We cannot create a human audience for you," the leader says, swaying in a chill noon breeze like a stately elm. "But there is perhaps a way."

I wait. I am infinitely patient.

"We have experimented with time," the creature announces. Or I think the word is "experimented." It might as easily have been the clacking buzz of a cricket or a cicada.

"Send me back," I demand at once.

"No, not you, not physical objects. It cannot be done. Thoughts, perhaps. Dreams. Speaking to minds long dead. Of course, it changes nothing."

I rather like the idea, when they explain it, of my memoirs circulating through the Terrestrial past, appearing fragmented and unintelligible among the night terrors of Neanderthals, Cro-Magnons, Roman slaves, Chinese peasants, science fiction writers, drunken poets. And Deirdre Frank, and Oscar Ziegler. And Lorraine.

Even the faintest touch—belated, impossible—is better than none at all.

But still. I find it difficult to write.

"In that case," the leader says, "we would like to salvage you."

"Salvage me?"

They consult in their own woody, windy language, punctuated by long silences or sounds I cannot hear.

"Preserve you," they conclude. "Yourself. Your soul."

And how would they do that?

"I would take you into my body," the leader says.

Eat me, in other words. They have explained this more than once. Devour my body, hoc est corpus, and spit out my soul like a cherry pit into the great galactic telephone exchange.

"But this is how we must do it," the leader says apologetically.

I don't fear them.

I take a long last walk, at night, bundled against the cold in layers of flexible foil. The stars have not changed visibly in the ten thousand years of my absence, but there is nothing else familiar, no recognizable landmarks, I gather, anywhere on the surface of the planet. This might be an empty lake bed, this desert of mine, saline and ancient and, save for the distant mountains, flat as a chessboard.

I don't fear them. They might be lying, I know, although I doubt it; surely not even the most alien of creatures would travel hundreds of light years to a dead planet in search of a single exotic snack.

I do fear their teeth, however, sharp as shark's teeth, even if (as they claim) their bodies secrete an anesthetic and euphoriant venom.

And death?

I don't fear death.

I dread the absence of it.

Maybe Soziere was wrong. Maybe there's a teleological escape clause, maybe all the frayed threads of time will be woven back together at the end of the world, assembled in the ultimate library, where all the books and all the dreams are preserved and ordered in their multiple infinities.

Or not.

I think, at last, of Lorraine: really think of her, I mean; imagine her next to me, whispering that I ought to have taken her advice, not lodged this grief so close to my heart; whispering that death is not a door through which I can follow her, no matter how hard or how often I try. . . .

"Will you accept me?" the leader asks, rearing up to show his needled mouth, his venom sacs oozing a pleasant narcotic.

"I've accepted worse," I tell him.

PEARL BABY

The first cramp hit her just ten minutes before Nick Lavin was due to arrive with his daughter Persey. Deirdre ignored it. She didn't want to be sick right now. She hadn't seen Nick for more than five years and she wanted to make a good impression. So she hung stoically over the rusty basin of the bathroom sink, wondering whether she would vomit, while her belly knotted in long, dry peristaltic waves.

She hated this bathroom. It might have been quaint, with its clawfoot tub and porcelain water closet and peeling Victorian wallpaper. It wasn't. It was dark, it was narrow, and it reeked of genteel poverty. Like so many of the furnishings of her life, it was not something she had chosen; it was something she had arrived at.

But the pain diminished at last. Funny how familiar pain was when you were suffering, how distant it seemed afterward. Pain was like some little animal that lived in a burrow in your stomach and came out every now and then to take the air. The cold sweat dried and she washed her face with a washcloth. The pain had left no visible evidence. She looked at herself in the mirror. Pushing sixty, Deirdre thought. How had *that* happened? And how old would Nick be these days—forty-eight, forty-nine? With a teenage daughter. Persephone. Only Nick would name a child Persephone. On the phone he had called her "Persey."

Deirdre's hair was gray but long and full. She wore faded blue-jeans and a batiked blouse from the Goodwill. The heavy lenses of her eyeglasses had slipped down her small nose again. She bumped them back up with her thumb.

She hid in an upstairs bedroom and rolled a joint to take away the lingering residue of discomfort. This was the resinous cannabis she had grown in the subcellar, potent but strange-tasting, dark as peat moss. It expanded into her lungs like a hot balloon and left behind its peculiar halo of strangeness and ease. She remembered reading somewhere that the ancient Scythians had smoked pot. Burned the seed clusters inside a communal hut. A sweat lodge for stoners. Had she done that herself, in some former life?

Far away, there was a woodpecker sound. Nick and Persey at the door. Oh, God. She hid her soapstone pipe in a drawer and hurried down the stairs to let them in. A residue of pain beat in her abdomen like a hummingbird's wings.

She led them through the dim warren of the bookstore, through the bead curtains and up to the kitchen. Nick and Persey sat at the Ikea table while Deirdre put the kettle on for tea. "Interesting digs," Nick said, which she supposed was his attempt to be tactful. Tact had never been Nick's long suit.

He sat there smiling at her, looking like any other middle-aged man. The years had erased his individuality. Back in the commune days he had dressed like a hirsute backwoodsman, his full beard framing his face, his smile quick and generous. Plaid timberjack jackets, long blond hair, dirty fingernails. Now he looked like every other millennium prole. Without the casement of his beard his lips were too full, his chin too small. He had shaved his head to disguise, or acknowledge, his hair loss. He wore a tiny gold ring in the lobe of one ear. He taught undergraduate English literature and had just landed a position at the University of Toronto, back from his decades-long exile at some women's college or other in the American hinterland.

"I inherited the bookstore," Deirdre said. "The old man who owned it had no family. I was his only employee. He willed the property to me. Much to my astonishment. One of these days I'll put it up for sale. Been planning to. But it brings in a little bit of profit most months. It's not labor-intensive and it's, you know, a place to live."

She had fixed up the upstairs living quarters, had sold or given away Oscar Ziegler's cloying Mauve Decade furniture and replaced it with generic but modern equivalents. She had meant to paint the walls and carpet the creaking wooden floors . . . she just hadn't gotten around to it.

"It's really interesting," Persey observed, "in a fucked-up way."

She didn't mean anything by it, but Deirdre was faintly shocked to hear her use the f-word in front of adults. Not that Deirdre herself was particularly dainty about it. Fuck, no. But Persephone was a good-looking and well-scrubbed fifteen-year-old, the sort people called "wholesome." Times change, Deirdre supposed; most of the young people she met these days couldn't order breakfast or make change without using the f-word.

Nick gave his daughter a sharp look, but Deirdre said, "It *is* fucked up. It's an old building and you can bet it's not up to municipal code. The plumbing is ridiculous and I had to put new wiring in the basement just to run the washer and dryer." Not to mention the thousand-watt metal-halide grow-light in the subcellar.

"Lots to read, though," Persey said, hastening to repair the faux pas. "It must be great living over a secondhand bookstore."

"Persey's a bookworm," Nick said.

"What do you like to read, Persey?"

"All kinds of things." The last book she had read, Persey said, was *I Know This Much Is True*, by Wally Lamb. Pretty ambitious for a teenager, Deirdre thought.

Nick said, "She likes Oprah books."

"Not just," Persey said, blushing.

"If you want to," Deirdre told her, "you can go downstairs, switch on the lights and look at the books. Pick out something you want. On the house."

"To keep?" Persey asked hopefully.

"To keep."

"Don't get anything out of order," Nick said as his daughter made for the stairs, her tear-away pants brushing the kitchen door, her ridiculous disco heels knocking the floorboards.

Deirdre poured tea for herself and Nick. She sat across the table from him trying to smile but wanting, obscurely, to cry. Was it just because this meeting with Nick had made her feel so fucking old? So old, now, that there was no disguising it? In the commune days—the days when five unmarried young persons sharing a downtown apartment could pronounce themselves a "commune," as if the French Revolution had broken out—Nick had been twenty-three, twenty-four, twenty-five; Deirdre had been nine years older. Even then, they had occasionally called her "Earth Mother," and it wasn't always a compliment. On the other hand, because everybody was sleeping with everybody else, no one wanted to push the maternal metaphor too far.

Yes, she had slept with Nick. It had been quite passionate for a few months. Now, by some silent mutual agreement, neither of them would mention it.

"She seems real nice," Deirdre said, meaning Persey.

"A little outspoken," Nick said, "at least since her mom re-married. She spends a month out of every year with Patrice and Joseph in Ann Arbor, getting spoiled rotten."

"No, she seems great. And literate, which is kind of a rarity."

"I found her reading a Tom Clancy novel last week. I thought, where have I failed?"

"Bullshit. You're proud of her."

"From time to time."

"You should be."

And they talked about Patrice and Annie and Carl and the rest of that crowd, how they were doing and where they were, until they had exhausted the shortlist of mutual acquaintances and there was nothing left to say. Deirdre began to feel weirdly superior to Nick, as if in her poverty she had retained some authenticity he had lost. Still, that made him one of the last of the good ones, broad-minded enough to be bashful about his own success. Nowadays, when you outperformed an old friend, you were supposed to make a notch in your gunstock or some damn thing.

A slice of summer moonlight found its way into the alley behind the shop, her kitchen window. Persey remained downstairs, rummaging and reading. Deirdre felt mischievous. "So," she said, "you want to share a joint?"

Nick grinned—a ghost of the old Nick inhabiting his face. "Still smoking, Deirdre?"

"Off and on. You?"

"Not for years. But it's only a joint, right? What the hell."

She had rolled one for herself last night and left it in a kitchen drawer. She took it out. "The kids Persey's age," she said, "it's all, what, Ecstasy? GHB?"

"All I know is what I read in the papers. Lots of drugs, but it sounds like frat-party shit to me. Nothing profound about it."

"Whereas *we*. . . ." Deirdre teased.

"We were on a *spiritual quest*."

They both laughed. But the irony wasn't lost on Deirdre. She was laughing at herself. Nick, like most people of her class and generation, had put away the Tibetan Book of the Dead, donated *Zen and the Art of Motorcycle Maintenance* to the yard sale, filled the empty shelf space with Windows guidebooks and *Listening to Prozac*. Only Deirdre had gone on questing after the fabled enlightenment . . . but no, not that, not the usual discount guru bullshit; something else; something strange, elusive, unworldly.

Nick took the joint to the open window so the warm July breeze would draw away the smoke. Persey might come back upstairs at any moment. "We used to hide this from our parents," he said. "Now we hide it from our kids."

"As a rule," Deirdre said, "I don't hide it."

Nick inhaled cautiously but deeply. A plume of white smoke rose past the hanging dream-catcher and out into the wide world. "Tastes peculiar."

"It's one of the new strains. Some hybrid Dutch Indica, supposedly."

"Whoa," he said. "Enough of *that*. I have to drive."

Deirdre took the joint from him, and for one pellucid moment she was aware of his uneasiness, the way he avoided her eyes.

He was uncomfortable with what she had become, what he had once felt about her.

She thought, *I embarrass him*.
Fresh pain coiled in her belly.

Persephone surprised Deirdre by coming upstairs with a recent book about Martian nanofossils, the hints of ancient life lately discovered in an Antarctic meteorite. "Persey sees herself as a biologist," Nick said. Not *wants to be* but *sees herself as*, trivializing the ambition. Persey winced faintly and shot her father a look. It was the first hint of family discord Deirdre had seen, evidence perhaps of some deeper, buried rift.

"Smart choice," Deirdre said. "Everything is . . . you know . . . older than it seems." Which meant what? The pain was distracting her.

She ushered Nick and Persephone to the door, told Nick how great it was to see him, told him not to be a stranger, told Persey it was really nice meeting her. When they were gone the store seemed suddenly cavernous. She locked up front and back and retired upstairs, taking the steps slowly because she hurt again. Hurt worse than before. She rummaged through the bathroom cabinet until she found the old bottle of Percodan left over from her gallbladder operation. She popped one, then two, then—for insurance—a third.

And so to bed.

The pain woke her sometime in the quiet hours before dawn. She came out of a claustrophobic dream nauseated with pain and vaguely aware that the mattress under her thighs was slick and warm. *My period*, she thought vaguely, but it had been years since her last menstrual flow. She groped for the switch on the lamp beside her bed, threw back the bedsheet and saw blood.

Then more pain, cruel hot blades of it. She bit back a cry and hunched to the bathroom, where she ate four more Percodan and promptly fell to the floor, weak with shock. The blood between her legs was only a trickle, but the pain . . . the pain rose in a great swelling crescendo, and this time she screamed, and the pain clamped her peritoneal muscles impossibly tight, and her legs arched, and she delivered *something*. . . .

Something she didn't want to see.

She wanted to sleep. To faint. To die. But she didn't. Already the pain had begun to abate; and without looking at the thing on the tiled floor she was able to raise herself up, strip off her soiled nightgown, wad some toilet paper between her legs to serve as a pad. She was dizzy, confused. Should she call 911? Probably— almost certainly—she should, but she didn't want to, couldn't face the humiliation of an army of helpful paramedics, would rather die, if she must, though the bleeding had stopped short of outright hemhorrhage. She could see a doctor in the morning, after she cleaned up, after she came to terms with this awful thing, this midnight delivery of, of *what?* A blood clot, a tumor? She let her eyes creep toward the dark mass on the floor.

She could not have been pregnant, unless it was some weird parthenogenic pregnancy, so this blood-drenched mass must be a token of disease, probably something advanced and eventually deadly, like the ovarian cancer that had killed her mother forty years ago. God, she thought, *look* at it. In her mind's eye she had pictured some mutant abortion, some crudely human cut of meat, but the reality was in fact much less disgusting. The lump was about the size and shape of a lemon, and under the skein of adhesive blood it looked white, *shiny* white, white as a button.

As if, Deirdre thought wildly, I had fucked an elephant tusk and delivered a cue ball.

"Sick," she muttered to herself.

She touched the mass with her toe. It was heavy. It rolled to one side. It made a clinking sound against the ceramic tile.

"Oh," she said out loud, "oh, this is too much. Too much."

She washed her hands. She dampened a washcloth and dabbed the blood off her thighs, her legs, the bathroom floor. At last—tentatively, cautiously—she bent over the tumorous white lump, picked it up and dropped it into the sink under the rushing warm water. Blood swirled into the basin and down the drain. She ran the water until the water ran red, then pink, then clean. The glittering white object sat in the rusty basin like a river rock. She had collected such rocks when she was little. Rocks worn smooth by water. Warmed by sunlight. The Percodan was kicking in.

The Percodan was kicking in big time, and Deirdre stumbled back to her bed. She retained barely enough presence of mind to peel away the stained sheets, not enough to redress the bare mattress. She simply fell onto it. Her eyes registered the first light of dawn past the window blind. She closed her eyes and made it dark again.

The secondhand bookstore Deirdre had inherited was called Finders, and the name had proved apt: she was always finding peculiar things.

Prior to moving in she had gone through the store and the apartment above it meticulously, exorcising the shade of Oscar Ziegler. Nice of the old man to drop this fossilized property in her lap, but she had, to tell the truth, never *liked* him. Not that he was hostile or angry; he had been too frail for that. But he radiated an old strangeness she might once have called "bad magic," a contagious atmosphere of bleak resignation. So she had rented a van and trucked his stuff to the Goodwill drop-off, his ridiculous smoking jackets, his 78-rpm platters featuring Caruso and Dame Nellie Melba, his dozen matching copies of the crank book *You Will Never Die*. His jar of nineteenth-century Austrian coins. His Quaker quilt bedspread with hex signs woven into the pattern, yellow-stained. His perforated Oxford shoes and matching shoe trees. His silver-handled shaving brush and straight razor. His rack of tarry, stinking meerschaums.

Some of this kibble might have been worth money, but Deirdre didn't care. The point was to get it out, to replace it with something clean, something new.

And still, a year later, evidence of Oscar Ziegler surfaced from time to time. From a cupboard long ago obstructed by bookcases: a rude wooden chess board, a child's tattered cloth jacket with a copy of *The Time Machine and Other Stories* jammed into one pocket, a litter of strange glass needles of various colors.

She had found the subcellar just six months ago. The entrance was a hinged wooden door so obscured with dust that she had mistaken it for part of the basement wall. A narrow flight of stairs led down to an earthen-floored space roughly seven feet high by fifteen wide. The room contained nothing but a rotted wooden shelf on which resided six sealed mason jars wrapped in dust as white as spider silk. One of the jars was labeled APPLE CHUTNEY OCT 3 '99 in crabbed fountain-pen script. One hundred years of chutney. She threw the jars away.

A week later she braced the subcellar stairs, laid down a crude plank flooring, whitewashed the walls, and installed a grow light. She germinated a batch of British Columbia pot seeds ("Shiva Shanti X Northern Lights," according to the mail-order ad) and transplanted them to fifteen-liter ice-cream buckets filled with potting soil, vermiculite, and shrimp compost. She installed a fan to circulate the air and she tended the plants three evenings a week. It had been a good crop. No whiteflies, no fungus gnats. The female buds had looked a little strange, gnarled and golden, as if she had overfertilized, but otherwise healthy and sticky with resin glands.

She had dried her first harvest carefully and stored the buds in a fresh set of mason jars. She resisted the temptation to make her own labels: BC ORGANIC INDICA AUG '02.

Deirdre recovered quickly from the strange birth.

She stayed in bed for a day, didn't eat, only limped to the kitchen for tall glasses of ice water. Finders was closed for the duration and that was okay with Deirdre. She felt no pain now, just a subsiding ache that was almost pleasant, a *healing* ache, she chose to think.

The next day she was up on her feet with a single Percodan and thinking more clearly.

She decided not to see a doctor. This was not the advice she would have given anyone else. But it felt right. Right for her, anyway. If the thing she had delivered was a tumor, then it was either benign or malignant. If malignant, it had surely already planted its seeds throughout her body. If benign, no problem.

But of course it wasn't a tumor. She had never heard of a tumor as white and hard as that. And if it wasn't a tumor, then it was a mystery. Bless me, Deirdre thought, I have made a pearl from a grain of sand.

She retrieved the thing from the bathroom sink, fighting her queasiness. But it was pleasant to the touch. It was warm, it was heavy, and it was as smooth as if it had been polished. It reflected the daylight from the window blinds in a bright miniature rectangle. If she looked at it closely she saw her own long-nosed reflection, just the way she used to see her reflection in Christmas-tree balls when she was a child.

Well, she thought, didn't I hunt this all my life, this *strangeness*? Wasn't it what she had looked for in blotter hits of LSD and in the collected works of Gurdjieff and Ouspensky, in Vedanta Buddhism and in that fucking brown rice diet that had nearly killed her? People talked about "enlightenment," but "enlightenment" was the wrong word. Really, it was the limits of the material world she had been hunting. The borders of reality, the place where *is* met *might be*.

And here it was, Deirdre thought, and it had come to her in a way uniquely humiliating, appeared as an object she could neither understand nor discuss with others, and wasn't that somehow appropriate? That her epiphany should be *unspeakable*?

Three days later she noticed that the pearl baby had grown protuberances that resembled the stumps of arms and legs, and on the top a rounded nub that could have been a head.

The day after that, the pearl baby opened its shiny black eyes.

Persey wanted to be a marine biologist. Her great ambition was to work at the Woods Hole Oceanographic Institute. At her last school she had taken two advanced courses in biology and was certain she could get into one of the good universities, especially if she improved her math.

She felt okay talking about this with Deirdre, she said, because Deirdre knew about science and didn't think it was stupid.

Nick, Deirdre gathered, harbored the old contempt of the humanities people for the sciences. He dismissed her interests as "bugs and germs." He didn't actually, you know, *mind* it, Persey said, but he was obviously unimpressed. "I can't talk about it to him, the way I can talk to you. . . . Uh, Deirdre? What's that sound?"

Deirdre looked up sharply.

The sound was a staggered but somehow rhythmic knocking that came up through the joists of the building. It was louder than Deirdre had hoped, but she had prepared an explanation in case something like this happened.

"Raccoons," she said. "They get up under the eaves of old buildings like this. Get into the space behind the wall and make nests. You see a lot of young ones this time of year."

Raccoons moved at night, and it was night now, a blossomy summer night. A breeze lifted the curtains and cooled the kitchen air. The city roared distantly.

Persey looked both nervous and skeptical, but the knocking, thank God, stopped.

Nick had called Deirdre six weeks after his last visit. He said he'd been settling into his Bathurst Street apartment and had been too busy to get in touch, but it had been great seeing her and she ought to come for dinner sometime. And in the meantime he had a problem. He wasn't comfortable leaving Persey by herself all evening, but he had a date, and Persey had been keen to go back to the bookstore anyhow, and he just thought . . . would it be okay?

Deirdre had bitten back her disappointment, because after all what had she expected? That he would be asking *her* for a date? (God, she thought, please tell me that wasn't what I wanted.) Yeah, she said, sure, she'd be happy to see Persephone, and that at least was true enough.

Nick had dropped her off at seven. Persey had rummaged in the bookstore a bit, shared Kraft Dinner with Deirdre, watched a show on Deirdre's tiny portable TV set. Was dismayed that Deirdre didn't get Discovery or The Learning Channel. Deirdre played Boggle with her and won by a single point, but Persey was proud of finding SILICA and WASP (where Deirdre had found only WAS). Then they made tea and talked.

Nick had said he would be back by eleven to pick up his daughter. It was ten to midnight now.

"The oldest living things on Earth," Persey was saying, "are called archaebacteria—or at least people *thought* they were the oldest living things. But that's the interesting part. There might be something older. Scientists have dug up these ancient rocks, or the Martian meteorite is another example, with what look like tiny fossils. The problem is, they're *too* tiny. You need an electron microscope even to see them."

"Why is that a problem, Persey?"

"Because you need a certain size just to contain a long enough fragment of DNA to reproduce. And these things are too small, even smaller than viruses. So if they're a form of life, they're *weird* life. Nobody knows how they work. Maybe they're not even extinct. Some people think—"

Deirdre didn't find out what some people think, because the telephone rang, startling her. She jumped out of her chair, almost spilled her tea.

The phone call was Nick.

"I know I'm late," he said. "Things got a little complicated. I'm still out here in the fucking suburbs, Deirdre, and it occurred to me, even if I leave right now I'm still going to be an hour getting there, and by the time I get Persey home she'll be exhausted . . ."

This is not a guest house, Deirdre wanted to tell him. There are limits to our friendship, Nick. A few weeks of intimacy thirty years ago doesn't oblige me to take care of your daughter while you're out on some protracted pussy-chase.

But she couldn't say any of that because Persey was right here in the room with her, frowning at the phone like a disappointed infant.

"Not a problem," she said.

"Honest? Because if it's inconvenient—"

"No," she said, briefly hating him, "not at all. I can make the sofa into a bed. So when can we expect you?"

"After breakfast. Sleep late."

"Okay, Nick." She added, hoping the irony wasn't too thick, "Enjoy yourself."

"You're a goddamn saint, Deirdre."

A goddamn saint, she thought. What kind of saint is that?

She turned to Persephone. "It's your dad. He says—"

"I figured it out," Persey said flatly.

Deirdre fixed up the sofa with her best blankets and pillows in a slightly guilty effort to make Persey feel at home. Persey didn't have an overnight bag and she borrowed an old nightie of Deirdre's, ridiculously tentlike on her narrow frame. When Persey was propped up with a table lamp behind her and a book in her hand, Deirdre told her good night. "Sleep well."

"I'll try," the girl said. "But I really wish that sound would stop."

It had come again, the periodic distant knocking.

"I'll see what I can do," Deirdre promised.

When she was sure Persey was settled for the night Dierdre tiptoed down the stairs to the bookstore and through another bead curtain to the basement. She closed the basement door behind her, switched on the light and looked for the pearl baby.

There was no sign of it, and Deirdre began to feel afraid.

She wasn't afraid of the pearl baby itself. In the weeks since the pearl baby first opened its eyes, it had never seemed even remotely threatening. Most of the time it didn't even move, just sat in one place, turning its head like a radar dish, randomly looking. Its eyes were two black, glassy marbles. The eyes seemed never to move or focus, so it was hard to tell what the pearl baby was looking at or what it was seeing even when its head was aimed straight at her. Periodically the pearl baby would raise itself up on its stubby legs and walk from place to place, and its motion was surprisingly sure and smooth, its toeless flattened feet click-clacking on the floor. But mostly it was still. It didn't seem very energetic. It wasn't even hungry. The pearl baby didn't eat; it had no mouth.

It didn't frighten her, but neither did Deirdre feel maternal toward the pearl baby. She had birthed it, indisputably, but it wasn't a human child and she didn't treat it like one. That would have been wrong, self-indulgent, somehow gauche. Deirdre liked children well enough but had never been a mother and never missed it. The tick of the proverbial biological clock hadn't troubled her, and anyway that clock had run down a good fifteen years ago. Certainly the pearl baby would have made a poor substitute for a child. No, it was something much stranger. Something that had borrowed her creaking gynecological machinery for some purpose of its own.

What really frightened her was the possibility that the pearl baby might escape the basement (or the upstairs apartment where Deirdre kept it when she was alone). It would be seen, and there would have to be some kind of explanation, a reckoning, an inevitable pollution of the magic it represented.

She looked for the pearl baby behind the white-enameled washer and dryer, hunted for it between boxes of overflow stock from the bookstore. She began to imagine that it must have slipped out somehow—she pictured it lying in a back alley like a discarded china cat—when she saw that the door to the subcellar was ajar.

The pearl baby had knocked the door open: that was the sound that had alarmed Persey.

Deirdre followed the stairs downward.

The subcellar was brightly illuminated by the halide bulb and its enormous reflector. Her second crop of female cannabis plants had just begun to flower, the huge fan leaves yellowing at the tips. One of the containers had fallen over—no, had been *knocked* over, because here was the pearl baby crouched in a far corner of the room, groping with its stubby ivory arms through the floorboards.

It raised its head and looked in Deirdre's direction.

Deirdre ignored it for the moment and set about righting the fallen bucket. The stem of the plant had buckled, but not fatally; she set it right with a splint made of sticks and wire. When she raised the bucket she had to be careful, because the plant had grown a long central root through the perforated bucket-bottom and past the floorboards into the raw clay of the subcellar. The root was healthy and white and frankly enormous, thick as a beet.

Then she took the pearl baby in her arms and carried it up to the basement. It moved against her, not struggling, Deirdre thought, though she couldn't be sure, since the pearl baby's motions were generally slow. But she sensed no particular urgency from it. Was it her imagination, she wondered, this idea that she

could read the pearl baby's intentions? That some mute impossible communication had begun between them?

She braced a heavy box against the subcellar door so the pearl
baby wouldn't bother her plants again. Then she closed the upstairs door to keep the pearl baby confined, but this time she left
the light on; she thought it might prefer the light.

There were no further disruptive noises, and before morning
Deirdre was able to drift off to sleep in the comforting warmth
of her own bed. She dreamed about a family of bluejays made of
obsidian and turquoise; when they flew, their wings rattled
against their bodies like clinking china cups.

She woke to the sound of Persey rattling pans in the kitchen.

Deirdre stumbled out of her bedroom and found Nick's
daughter scrambling eggs in a Teflon pan. Persey's uncombed
hair was draped over the shoulders of the borrowed nightie, and
it was astonishing, Deirdre thought, how much younger she
looked when she wasn't dressed up in MTV drag. She made a
nice breakfast, too. Had probably made breakfast for Nick more
often than not.

Neither of them mentioned the noises of the night before.

Deirdre opened Finders at ten. A couple of University students
drifted in, eyed the shelves critically, purchased nothing. Persey
picked another book out of the science section, this one something about deep-sea geology. Nick—who showed up at eleven
looking shamefaced and wasted—had obviously underestimated
his daughter's intelligence. Or resented it.

Nick was fulsomely grateful for Deirdre's help and Persey
seemed actually unhappy to leave. Deirdre gave her a hug, which
Persey returned warmly.

At twelve Deirdre hung up the BACK AT sign with the clock
fingers pointing at twelve thirty. She rescued the pearl baby from
the basement and locked it in her bedroom upstairs. It seemed
to like the bed and it would stay there all day, sometimes, lolling
in a patch of sunlight like an upside-down bug.

Deirdre microwaved a Weight Watchers lunch and ate it without thinking of anything at all.

Persey had left behind her book about nanofossils, which was probably not a coincidence, Deirdre thought. One thing Deirdre had learned about Finders was that it fostered meaningful coincidence (*synchronicity*, the Jungians would say) the way a houseplant attracts gnats. It was part of the sour magic of the place.

She picked up the book idly, expecting to read a chapter or two, and found herself finishing it in bed that night. The world of deep life, hot life, and dark life was new to her, and she was fascinated by the idea of a parallel biology at work in granite and boiling water, a biology perhaps as old as the origin of the solar system. A biology operating in isolation from the gaudy chemistry of DNA-based life, intersecting it only rarely: the "prions" that caused so-called mad-cow disease, for instance. Another world, half-seen, barely discovered.

And she thought, of course, of the pearl baby, mineral-bright but born of a human womb, neither one thing nor another. To suggest that the pearl baby represented some hybrid of the human and the mineral kingdom was absurdly speculative, but it sounded right to Deirdre. Who was to say how much of the mysterious in human history might be the work of just such abortive cross-breeding, the failed effort of dark life to enter a new environment, like human beings launching themselves into the void of space?

But another question vexed her: Could mineral life be conscious, in the way human beings were conscious?

How much, exactly, did the pearl baby *understand*?

"Consciousness," according to current scientific thought, was something the higher mammals had evolved in order to help them reproduce, much the way a garden slug secretes slime. It had no special ontological status. The "self" was a genetically modulated and biologically useful illusion.

But if that was the case, could a different biology generate a different *kind* of consciousness?

The pearl baby didn't speak (couldn't speak, mouthless as it was) and showed no sign of understanding when Deirdre spoke to it. It had demonstrated no preferences or tropisms, except perhaps for the bright light in the subcellar. She could not comfort it or be comforted by it.

But it wanted something. Deirdre was sure of that. Often enough, at work in the store, Deirdre would hear it bumping against doors and windows upstairs. How strange this world must seem to it, Deirdre thought. Maybe that was its tropism: it was drawn to the strange. And she thought: Well, I know how that feels. She had been drawn to the strange all her life. She had pursued it relentlessly, knocked on its many doors, fucked it and married it. She had borne its child.

Nick continued to call on Deirdre for baby-sitting duties. Persey was old enough to spend a night by herself, and Deirdre suspected Nick's protectiveness was an expression of single-parent guilt. But that was okay. It got a little lonely in the store. So many of Deirdre's old circle of friends had drifted away or died or simply didn't call. Nick and Persey were a kind of surrogate family, and it wouldn't last, Deirdre knew; Nick would find some emotionally labile graduate student to play with, Persey would make new friends, Deirdre would see them less often and then never.

But in the meantime it was nice to have Persey over once in while. Deirdre didn't envy all the things Persephone was so plainly about to acquire—the interesting work, the husband (some earnest but affectionate young man with a parallel career, with whom she could discuss the reproductive cycle of the sea slug), the nice house (by the seaside, perhaps)—but there was an odd vicarious satisfaction in feeling these things in Persey's future, all the things Deirdre herself had refused or abandoned when she went chasing the wide world's end.

It can't last, though, she thought, at the end of another Friday evening with Persey and Boggle and bad television.

Deirdre had gone to bed early, sneaking a joint in the bathroom with the fan turned on to dispel the odor and protect Persey's putative innocence, though God knows there was enough ganja floating around the high schools to corrupt whole legions of saints and martyrs. The resinous cannabis from her subcellar tasted earthy and complex, and Deirdre wondered if this was how the submicroscopic particles of dark life had entered her, fertilized her womb by way of her lungs, used her body as a conduit into the human bios. And if so, then so be it. The ganja eased her toward acceptance, toward sleep.

She came awake to the ringing of the telephone.

Persey will get it, she thought, because Persey was closer to the phone, but the ringing went on until Deirdre was faintly alarmed, and she sat up and fumbled for her eyeglasses and stumbled down the hallway to the kitchen, past the room where Persey should have been sleeping.

The sofa was empty, the blankets tossed aside.

She grabbed the phone.

Nick. "Persey left her favorite sweater in the backseat of the car. Wanted to let you know in case she's looking for it, but I guess you guys already turned in, huh? What is it, eleven o'clock?"

"Ten to *one*, Nick."

"Jesus. I'm sorry. . . ."

"I hope you haven't been driving in this condition."

"No, I'm fine, but no, I haven't. Okay. Sorry, Deirdre. Back to bed with you. Everything all right there?"

"Why do you ask?"

"I don't know. Sometimes you just, you know, get a feeling."

"Everything's fine," Deirdre said, sweat beading on her forehead.

"Get away from it," Deirdre said.

Persey looked up from the corner of the basement between the dryer and the gas furnace, guilty and startled. "I'm not hurting it."

"It's not a doll. Stand up." Persey hesitated. "Stand UP!"

The girl jerked to her feet, eyes clouding, lip trembling. I'm just making it worse, Deirdre told herself, but it was too late to contain her anger. She thought the words *nosy little bitch* and bit her lip to keep the words inside. Persey demanded, "Well, if it's not a doll, what *is* it, then, and why is it locked up down here?"

The pearl baby paid no discernible attention. In its four months of life it hadn't changed much. Deirdre didn't think it was growing anymore. It was about the size of a lapdog. Round in all its dimensions, like the Michelin Tire Man, and shiny white, except for its eyes.

"That's really none of your business," Deirdre said.

"It's alive," Persey said. "You can't just keep it locked up in the basement."

"It *wouldn't* be locked up in the basement, except, except you—"

"You wanted to hide it from me."

"Protect it. Yes."

"I'm not hurting it."

"Persey, you don't think you're hurting it, but it's not—" Deirdre bit her lip. "It's *mine*."

"If it's yours, why don't you give it what it wants?"

"Do you have your house key on you? Because I'm calling a taxi. You need to go home while I sort this out."

"You can lock it up down here or you can keep it upstairs, but you're still keeping it away from what it wants."

"And how the holy fuck would *you* know what it wants?"

Persey didn't flinch. Her eyes grew distant in a way Deirdre didn't like at all. "I can hear it," she said. "You must be able to hear it too. If I can hear it, you can hear it. It wants what's down there. Not your stupid plants. Nobody cares about that. It wants what's under the floor."

And be damned, Deirdre thought, if the words didn't ring in her head like a bell: *true true true*. Which made it not better but worse. This rage she was feeling, was it jealousy? That the pearl baby's small voiceless appeals had been audible to someone not herself? She said, "You've been in the cellar?"

"Because it was knocking at the door. You put that box there to muffle the sound, right? But I heard it anyway. It *digs* down there. Digs the best it can with its little round fingers. It wants—"

"What?"

"The light."

"The lamp," Deirdre said. She had guessed as much.

"No," Persey said, "not the stupid lamp or anything to do with the pot plants. And I won't tell anyone about that anyway, if *that's* what you're worried about. The *other* light."

"What other light?"

"That comes up through the ground." Persey's expression went blank and distant. "Through the dirt."

Deirdre felt suddenly cold. "You're going home."

"You're not my mother."

"Of course I'm not your mother, but what do you imagine your mother would do if she was here right now? Or Nick, for that matter? Fuck it. I'm calling that cab."

Deirdre stalked up the stairs to the telephone in the shop. She thumbed through the old desktop Rolodex for a taxi company— she never took cabs herself—and punched a local number. The dispatcher told her she would have to wait twenty minutes. The bars were closing. Busy time. "Thank you," Deirdre said, "but hurry it up if you can." Her voice was unsteady.

Back downstairs, she discovered without suprise that Persey had pushed aside the box, opened the subcellar door and gone down there with the pearl baby.

Deirdre imagined herself telling the girl: This is not just because I'm envious. You can hear the pearl baby but it's not talking to *you*, not really. You live in that world with the good-looking husband and the nice clothes and the Woods Hole Oceanographic Institute, which is where you fucking *belong*. I could have had those things too, I really could, but I went after something else instead, and here it is, here it is, and you can't have it, you *shouldn't* have it. . . .

And I'm not your mother but I could have been somebody's mother and if I had been I would have said don't go in the cellar my daughter don't go in the cellar. . . .

Persey stood over the pearl baby, which was digging in the pebbled clay beyond the green extravagance of the marijuana plants. "The light," Persey said without looking at her. *"See?"*

Light came up between the rounded joints of the pearl baby's

fingers. The pearl baby wasn't an efficient digger but it was working very quickly. Specks of soil clung to the pearl baby's body.
The light that came up from under the ground was faint at first
and then brighter, the light of something rising, rising.

Deirdre grabbed Persey's hand. Persey's hand was slippery
with sweat and the girl pulled savagely. Deirdre pulled harder.
She got Persey in a kind of headlock and forced her up the narrow
steps into the basement and then up more steps to the bookstore,
where Persey's anger collapsed into fear and she began to shake
and cry. Deirdre felt the tears on her arm. She backed off a little
but kept her hands firmly on Persey's heaving shoulders.

"Come outside," Deirdre said, crisply but not angrily. "I'll wait
for the taxi with you."

"I don't have my sweater."

"Don't worry about it."

They stood on the sidewalk outside the door of Finders. Cars
came down Harbord Street in clusters whenever the stoplights
changed. It had started to drizzle.

Persey, still crying, sat down on the storefront steps. Deirdre
said, "You'll get all wet."

"I don't care."

Was there a sound from inside the building? A rumbling, an
upheaval under the foundation? But here was the cab, reflecting
the rain and the streetlights like a dark gem, sooner than promised. Deirdre opened the back door and helped Persey inside. She
gave the driver thirty dollars and the address of Nick's apartment
building.

Persey leaned out the window. "Deirdre? What'll you *do*?"

"Never you mind."

The cab disappeared down the rainy street.

Searching for volatiles in the kitchen and the bathroom, Deirdre
came up with a nearly full bottle of vodka, a can of lighter fluid,
and a plastic bottle of isopropyl rubbing alcohol. She took these
things down to the bookstore.

She sprinkled the fluids on the low shelves liberally, leaving a sort of corridor between the basement and the front door. Room, perhaps, for a final act of indecision.

Then she struck a match.

The thing that came up through the floor of the subcellar was brighter than the halide bulb (now flickering) and probably hotter. It made its own light, deep in the furnace of its body.

It held the pearl baby in its radiant arms.

It was a fountain of strangeness, as if mineral life had attempted to construct a multicellular organism from scanty blueprints and with the materials at hand: molten lava, coal, silica, random gems; a head like an immense half-geode; black pearls for eyes. Blood perhaps of thick murmurous oil. It bent into the small room like an enormous wasp.

And Deirdre didn't flee. She had waited for this all her life. Waited a little too long. But Persey was safe. That was important. She said, "I'm sorry about the girl. But she doesn't belong here."

The radiant beast said nothing, only reached for her with one of its shining appendages.

You can't live in two worlds at once. That's what she should have told Persey. You can love the human, or you can love . . . something else. But not both. Not both.

"I'm sorry it took so long," she said. She went to the mute beast willingly, like a child going home, and she smiled, even though the air had grown terribly hot.

AFTERWORD

The Diligent Reader will have noticed that the stories in *The Perseids* are interrelated. The same Diligent Reader might also have noticed that the connections between them are often obscure. That's because the stories were never intended to be a coherent common narrative or "fix-up" novel. The links are arbitrary and largely whimsical, borrowing a character here, a plot thread there. The significance of Finders, the imaginary second-hand bookshop that is the real connective tissue between these tales, emerged only after the earliest stories had been written. I've done minor retrofitting but made no effort to reconcile a number of inconsistencies. How can Rachel of "The Fields of Abraham" and William Keller of "Divided By Infinity" meet such different fates? The only explanation I can offer is Oscar Ziegler's: "There are as many afterlives as there are caverns in the earth, and each one is a unique ecology, godless and strange."

"The Fields of Abraham" is original to this collection, one of three previously unpublished stories. (The other two are "Ulysses Sees the Moon in the Bedroom Window" and "Pearl Baby"). All three were written specifically for this book, which gave me latitude to play with the common background and leave a few loose threads for other stories to pick up.

"The Fields of Abraham" (the title is borrowed from a song by Daniel Lanois) is the story to which the epigram from David Lindsay most closely applies. Groff Conklin once described Lindsay's antique novel *A Voyage to Arcturus* as a book "immensely worth reading, even though one is never really sure what it is all about." I hope "Fields of Abraham" is worth reading, but you may unwind the aboutness of it at your own risk. The story hovers around questions of sacrifice, duty, and love, but—

Sometimes a writer jumps into a narrative just to see what he can find there. This one, in retrospect, feels like a cold reservoir with something dark and spoiled adrift at the bottom. I've touched its carcass, but I don't really care to know what it *is*.

The setting—at least that part of it dealing with immigrant Toronto and "the Ward" at the beginning of the twentieth century—is as accurate as I am able to make it. Most of the stories herein have Canadian settings and several were written for nominally Canadian anthologies, but one of my ambitions was to write stories that reflected the urban Canadian experience, as opposed to extended meditations on ice, tundra, "the North," and so on. Margaret Atwood makes a good case for the brooding omnipresence of the wilderness in Canadian literature, but my own experience is necessarily more personal. I have lived almost exclusively in large, multiethnic cities. I can spell "muskeg" but I'm not sure I could define the word. I've visited the Canadian Arctic, and in my opinion it's a fabulous and daunting wild frontier about which someone else really ought to write.

Thanks are due to my thoroughly nonschizophrenic sister, Barbara, who suffers from migraine headaches. One night when I was five years old and just ready for bed—fumbling in the kitchen for a glass of water—Barbara wandered in with an expression of exquisite pain on her face and muttered, "There are people on the roof . . . I can hear them moving around. Tell them to stop."

She woke up the next morning feeling fine and to this day claims to have no memory of the incident. I, on the other hand, spent a long night under the blankets listening for "men on the roof."

Listen hard enough and *you* can hear them, too. They're up there, and they're up to no good.

———

"The Perseids" is the earliest of these tales. The story (and as a result virtually every story between these covers) owes its genesis to Don Hutchison, editor of the long-running Canadian dark-fantasy anthology series *Northern Frights*. I had not written a short story for many years when Don tapped me for a contribution to *Northern Frights 3* (Mosaic Press, 1995). He allowed me the latitude to cross some genre borders (i.e., to mount a science fiction engine in a horror-story chassis), and the result was this novelette, which met with a surprisingly positive reaction. (It won an Aurora Award for Canadian short fiction in English and was a finalist for the Nebula Award.) For which I thank Don profusely, and I recommend that the Diligent Reader seek out these anthologies as well as Don's other work, including the massively entertaining nonfiction *The Great Pulp Heroes*.

The bad guys in "The Perseids" are using the hallucinogen DMT to facilitate their (in the words of *Booklist*) "curious human evolutionary utility," but the story shouldn't be taken as an antidrug tract. The União Vegetale (technically, the Centro Espírita Beneficente União do Vegetal) is a real and perfectly legitimate Christian—essentially Catholic—religious movement. The UDV brought Ayahuasca, a traditional shamanic mixture of DMT-bearing *Psychotria viridis* and *Banisteriopsis caapi*, out of the Amazonian jungle and into urban Brazil. The church also has its North American adherents, who are obliged by our drug laws to be extremely circumspect about their spiritual behavior.

I don't do the church thing, but like many of my generation I have occasionally sipped from the mossy well of the hallucinogens. If there is a cautionary element in "The Perseids," it's a caution against those who step out from behind the Chrysanthemum Curtain with a dubious and apocalyptic historical agenda. The Mysteries are the Mysteries, and ultimately personal—maybe the most personal thing in the universe. Evangelism, in my opinion, is a failure of the imagination. Beware of prophets: the best visions are the ones they leave in the desert.

"The Inner Inner City" appeared first in *Northern Frights 4* (Mosaic Press, 1997). The long late-night walks were a feature of my younger days. The crowd I hung with was almost pathologically nocturnal and addicted to what my friend Phil Paine called "footfesting." I was very young and very naive and I learned a lot on those walks . . . how deliciously mysterious doughnut shop waitresses look at four A.M., for instance, or how much closer the stars are when the buses stop running, or why there are so many men in the park at midnight.

"The Observer" appeared in *The UFO Files* (DAW Books, 1998), an original anthology of UFO-related fiction edited by Ed Gorman and Martin Greenberg.

In Southern California, in the early to mid fifties, the distinct universes of astronomer Edwin Hubble, author/pacifist/mescaline-drinker Aldous Huxley, and famed saucer crank George Adamski did at least to some degree overlap. (Hubble and Huxley were close friends, and Adamski ran the burger joint on the road to Palomar.) This in the solstice years of California's prosperous and seemingly eternal summer.

I was born in that California. When my parents took me to Toronto in 1962 I was eight years old, exiled to an austere foreign town where the shops closed on Sunday and the weather actually *hurt*. Well, California ain't what it used to be, and I'm a patriotic Canadian now . . . even if I haven't taken out citizenship. Sandra makes the opposite journey, but she's invested with my childhood nostalgia for that lost world, that lofty plateau of eucalyptus and peacocks and winter sunlight.

Diligent Reader may harbor the suspicion that I don't actually believe in flying saucers or alien abduction. Diligent Reader is right.

(Did Sandra ever visit Finders, even though the shop isn't mentioned in the text? Yes. Because I say so.)

"Protocols of Consumption" first appeared in *Tesseracts 6* (Tesseract Books, 1997), edited by Robert Sawyer and Carolyn Clink. It was subsequently reprinted in the U.S. magazine *Realms of Fantasy*. *RoF* also reprinted "The Inner Inner City" and "The Perseids," and quite nicely, too, but for some reason I wasn't sent or didn't receive the proofs of "Protocols" and it appeared in *Realms* with transposed paragraphs and other typographical errors. Making it seem, perhaps, more an example of madness than a story *about* madness. It appears here intact.

I don't blame *Realms* editor Shawna McCarthy for any of this. Shawna was almost single-handedly responsible for jump-starting my career (another benefactor was Ed Ferman at *The Magazine of Fantasy and Science Fiction*), and she is my literary agent today. "Protocols" just happened to slip through a crack.

There really is a Sunnybrook Hospital in Toronto (now Sunnybrook & Women's College Health Sciences Centre after a series of disastrous health-care funding cuts by the Provincial government). F-wing is the mental-health department, and there really are no waiting rooms in F-wing. My psychiatrist used to practice in F-wing, and when I arrived early for an appointment I got to share the hallway with lots of folks who were (please, God) less functional than myself. "Protocols" and Mikey had their genesis when I eavesdropped on an outpatient therapy group waiting for their doc to show up. Pharmaceutical science has built only the flimsiest of bridges across the *mare tenebrarum*, it seems to me. But look: I made a short story out of it.

"Ulysses Sees the Moon in the Bedroom Window" was written expressly for this collection.

People love cats. Because we love them, we surgically alter their genitalia, keep them confined in our homes, and subject them to lethal injection when they become ill or inconvenient. At work in this story is the awful suspicion that something out there loves *people*.

(No, don't e-mail me. I know house cats have evolved into domesticity and need human care and attention for their well-being. But ask a panther or a kaffir cat his opinion.)

"Plato's Mirror" appeared in *Northern Frights 5* (Mosaic Press, 1999).

"Now I know in part," St. Paul says somewhere in Corinthians, "but then shall I know even as also I am known." For better or worse.

One of the pleasures of the first-person narrative is that you get to confess to sins you haven't committed. Which stand in for all the sins you *have* committed, but without the troublesome potential for embarrassment.

The narrator isn't me, but he's what I'm afraid of being, nights when I can't sleep and the rain ticks like a fast clock on the windowsill.

" 'It seems to me,' said she, 'that if we could have discovered a good while ago some sort of ray by which we could see into each other's souls, we should have gained a great many hours which are now lost.' " (Frank R. Stockton, *The Great Stone of Sardis*, 1891.)

"Divided by Infinity" appeared in *Starlight 2* (Tor, 1998), edited by Patrick Nielsen Hayden.

The story (and its denouement on the barren plains of an ir-radiated Earth) pays homage to all those book and magazine covers that lured me into science fiction at a tender age. I have always loved the written word above the visual arts, but there was something utterly compelling about closing an old Ballantine edition of, say, Arthur C. Clarke's *Expedition to Earth* and day-dreaming over the Powers cover, making up stories of my own to explain the yellow sky, the enigmatic lacquered statuary, the Dali harps and bedsprings. Or discovering Joe Mugnaini's stark, strange, sensuous drawings wrapped in Ray Bradbury's equally strange and sensuous prose. Check out an old copy of *The October Country*, find the Mugnaini illustrations for "Touched With Fire" or "The Crowd" and feel the eviscerating sunlight on those dry Victorian tenements. Humble magic.

"Divided by Infinity" was a Hugo Award finalist for its year, not, I suspect, because it's a particularly fresh or accomplished story, but because I was trying so hard to pluck the fundamental sf chord that it did in fact ring out for a moment.

"Pearl Baby" was written for this collection, about ten minutes before the deadline.

The idea here was to get a closer look at Deirdre Frank, who appears in a couple of the other stories as a minor character but who clamored for a story of her own. (I also wanted to turn the Demeter story inside out, like an old pocket, and see if I could find a shiny penny.)

Deirdre's love of the strange represents, I think, a real and legitimate esthetic impulse, though one not held in much esteem. Science fiction and fantasy cater to that urge the way "literary" fiction caters to the human need for intelligent gossip. The nineteenth century gave the impulse its due (that Pleasure Dome, that Raven), but the twentieth dropped it like a hot Freudian potato.

So the Strange put on its Appollonian suit and tie and went to live in the low-rent neighborhood of *Astounding Stories* and *Thrilling Wonder*.

You hear talk now and again of the death of science fiction, but I suspect the twenty-first century will be good for us—that the Strange will come leaping out of the closet with its ray gun in one hand and its bottle of laudanum in the other, delirious with possibility.

Thanks to those who were present at the creation: Jo, Jesse, and Devon; Taral (because I've been mining our conversations for story ideas for years); Phil (for being hard to impress); Janet and Paul; Alan Rosenthal (thanks, Alan) and Hope Leibowitz (thanks, Hope); Don Hutchison; and Sharry, who supplied research material, proofreading, and inspiration.